Displaced

Barbara Nadel

W F HOWES LTD

This large print edition published in 2018 by
W F Howes Ltd
Unit 5, St George's House, Rearsby Business Park,
Gaddesby Lane, Rearsby, Leicester LE7 4YH

1 3 5 7 9 10 8 6 4 2

First published in the United Kingdom in 2018
by Allison & Busby

A CIP catalogue record for this book is available
from the British Library

ISBN 978 1 52881 482 9

Typeset by Palimpsest Book Production Limited,
Falkirk, Stirlingshire

Printed and bound by
T J International in the UK

K

To my parents, who took me to Barking Park Fair

PROLOGUE

*T*he things people do for money . . .

There were four freaks, as they called them back then: the Ugliest Woman in the World, the Fattest Woman in the World, a Tattooed Man and the Ling Twins. The first three I could take or leave. Even as a seven-year-old child, I think I knew that there was nothing really that extraordinary about being ugly or fat. Not that the Ugliest Woman in the World was actually that ugly. She had a lot of warts on her face and she smelt, but so what?

It was the Ling Twins that held my attention. Siamese or conjoined twins, or so it seemed: a boy called Ping and a girl called Pong. Names that made me laugh at the time. Heavily made-up, no doubt so they'd look 'oriental', it's unlikely they'd ever seen Brighton, much less Bangkok. And yet at the time I believed they were real with a totality I've never experienced since. I think it was probably because Miriam had not long been born. I was finding it hard to adjust to no longer being an only child and so I resented her. Siblings present one with a dilemma. One feels one has to love them and indeed one will do all sorts of things to protect them. But no one can make you like them. Ping and Pong,

1

I believe, made me wonder what it would be like to have never been alone. It was a terrible thought and I clearly remember crying at the time. I also recall being comforted by the Tattooed Man who, by today's standards, was not very tattooed at all. But he was kind and I appreciated his attention. My mother wasn't there. She, as I remember it, was screaming outside the freak show tent.

'My baby! My baby! Someone's taken my baby!'

CHAPTER 1

Lee fucking hated modern Cockney rhyming slang. Things like 'Ronan Keating – central heating' and 'Jodie Marsh – harsh'. Daft rhymes bigging up stupid celebrities and other horrible modern obsessions like mobile phones and plastic surgery. But, that said, when he thought about his own current situation he could only say that it had all gone 'Pete Tong'. It had all gone wrong. Well not everything . . .

He had money, for once, and he hadn't had a dream about fighting in Iraq for over a week, so it wasn't all bad. But it had all gone Pete Tong with Mumtaz and that was the part of his life he cared about most. How could he have been so fucking stupid?

He looked at the small, pale man sitting in front of him and he forced a smile.

'So, Mr Levy,' he said, 'what can I do for you?'

Irving Levy, his potential client, was a small, pale man who could have been anything from fifty to seventy. An Orthodox Jew, he was dressed in a thick black coat and a Homburg hat, although he didn't have the side-locks characteristic of the

3

ultra-orthodox Haredi sect, which was a mercy. Once, long ago, Lee had been employed to find the errant daughter of one of those and it had been a nightmare. What he could and couldn't do and when had proved difficult to say the least. But he'd found the girl. Shacked up with a Rastafarian in Brighton. The parents had cried and then declared her dead. Interracial relationships weren't always easy even in the twenty-first century. He feared this man might have come to him with yet another one.

'Mr Levy?'

He cleared his throat. 'You won't remember this, Mr Arnold,' he said, 'I barely remember it myself . . .'

'Remember what?'

'It was 1962. I was seven,' he said. 'Which is why I say I barely remember it myself. As you may or may not know, every year there is a fair in Barking Park.'

'I've been a few times, yes,' Lee said.

The last time he'd gone he'd taken Mumtaz and her stepdaughter, Shazia. They'd all eaten too much candyfloss . . .

'My mother took me,' Levy said. 'And my sister, Miriam. She was only a baby, one year old. I went on little rides for small children. A carousel, a small railway, as I recall. Then I pestered to see the freak show. One doesn't find such things these days, they are distasteful. Even then, my mother didn't approve, but to a child the prospect of seeing

4

the world's ugliest woman is just too tempting. So she paid for me to go. And I saw the ugly woman, I saw a tattooed man and, to my horror, at the time, I saw Ping and Pong the Siamese Twins. Now of course they were not real – neither twins nor Thai – but they frightened me and I screamed. At almost the same moment my mother, who was outside the tent, screamed too. But for a different reason. She screamed because, having, as she said, turned away from Miriam for a moment, when she looked in her pram the next time, my sister had gone. And, in spite of an extensive police search at the time and in the months that followed, that was the last time anyone in my family saw Miriam. I have cuttings from local papers my parents collected at the time and I've written down what I recall about the incident myself.'

He pushed a brown folder across Lee's desk.

'Keep them. Look – at the time, the case of my sister's disappearance was famous. Now it's just history, but not for me. If Miriam is alive, Mr Arnold, then I want you to find her. And soon. Soon would be best.'

The woman was young and beautiful, but her eyes were ringed with dark circles and she had bitten her nails down to the quick.

'You will be safe here, Shirin,' Mumtaz said. 'I know it's a bit . . .'

Her voice trailed off. It had taken the group, known as the Asian Refuge Sisters, a couple of

5

years and a lot of heartache to get hold of this shabby house in Forest Gate. Keeping its location a secret from men who wished to harm the women who lived inside was even harder. But Mumtaz Hakim, private investigator, knew the group well and she trusted them. She'd directed several abused women to their door. But none of them had been from families like that of Shirin Shah.

She looked around the communal living room at the small, covered daughters of Bangladeshi bus drivers and battered Pakistani wives who spoke no English – Shirin stood out like a sore thumb. Tall, slim and wearing very fashionable Western clothes, Shirin came from Holland Park where she had lived with her Harley Street consultant husband in an apartment that was worth millions. Shirin had employed a housekeeper and a chauffeur, and had an account at Liberty in Regent Street. Unfortunately for her, what she didn't and couldn't have was children. This had upset her husband who had beaten her mercilessly because of her 'failure' to reproduce. Now he wanted to 'marry' a second wife who would and could have children. Shirin had refused to accede to this and so he had tried to kill her. But she wouldn't go to the police, and she wouldn't tell her parents, and so it was the refuge or nothing.

Mumtaz smiled. 'Everyone's very nice here,' she said.

Shirin looked down at the floor. 'I can't share a room. I can't!'

Mumtaz sat down beside her.

'Shirin,' she said, 'when Muna told me about you, she said you needed somewhere to stay and I've found you somewhere.'

Desperate and isolated, Shirin had finally opened up to her hairdresser, Muna, a woman from Manor Park. It had been Muna who had approached Mumtaz for help. The London Borough of Newham had its disadvantages, being one of the poorest districts of the capital was a big one, but it had a sense of community. And everyone in the borough, particularly its women, knew about Mumtaz Hakim, Newham's only Asian female private investigator.

'Being here will give you time to think about what you'd like to do next,' Mumtaz continued. 'Now you're no longer under threat from your husband, you can consider maybe who amongst your friends and relatives might help you.'

'None of them!'

'You think that now, but you may be surprised,' Mumtaz said. She held Shirin's hand. 'I kept the abuse I suffered at the hands of my husband a secret because I was both ashamed and frightened about what my family might think. But, actually, they were on my side and when my marriage did end, they were devastated that I hadn't told them.'

'You have nice parents.'

'I do. But I'm not alone. There are lots of wonderful parents.'

'Not mine.'

Mumtaz felt for her. Like her, Shirin was a Muslim and, also like her, her parents were devout. But if they were anything like Mumtaz's mother and father they were also kind, compassionate and loving. Mumtaz's husband, Ahmet, had died before she'd admitted his abuse to her father. The old man had cried. 'If only you had told me,' he'd said, 'I could have helped you.'

'We will see.'

Mumtaz stood.

'In the meantime, settle in here,' she said. 'And I will come and see you again tomorrow.'

'Thank you.'

The refuge was only minutes from her flat and so Mumtaz decided she'd go home and get a sandwich before returning to work. But then she saw a familiar figure let herself into the flat and she changed her mind. Shazia still wasn't speaking to her and so it was probably best to leave her alone. She was off to university in Manchester in less than a month, she'd obviously come back to gather more stuff.

Mumtaz wanted to cry, but she pulled herself together and got into her car.

'I was diagnosed back in January. But I'd not felt well for at least a year.'

'I'm sorry to hear that,' Lee said.

He shrugged. 'It is what it is,' he said. 'I've had one cycle of chemotherapy, which appears to have worked and so I'm now in what they call remission.

May last a few months, years, or the leukaemia may be back tomorrow – nobody knows. But time is a factor, Mr Arnold. Not that I've been idle. In amongst all the other tests I've had, which have been legion, I've also volunteered for a few, which is part of the reason why I'm here today.'

'Oh?'

'I got myself a DNA test,' Levy said. 'When you're about to die you wonder who you are. It's one of those cruel ironies life throws at us.'

Lee knew that one. Before he'd gone to the Middle East to fight Saddam Hussein's troops in the First Iraq War, he'd never thought about mortality. When he came back, he'd been unable to think about very much else.

'And what I discovered shocked me.'

'In what way, Mr Levy?'

'Irving, please.'

'Irving.'

'You look at me and you see an Orthodox Jewish man,' Levy said. 'But, unknown to me until I had the DNA test, was that my mother was a Gentile. I knew she was German. The story I grew up with was that she was the daughter of a wealthy pharmacist called Dieter Austerlitz and that she was the only survivor from that family after the Holocaust. But now, of course, I wonder.'

'Of course.'

'My father's family were British Jews,' he continued. 'Diamond cutters. That is my trade too. But my mother . . .' He shrugged. 'I do have cousins, on my father's side, but that is all the family I possess.'

'You want to know more.'

'If that is possible, yes,' he said. 'But my main aim is to find Miriam. I know I have left it and left it, but life carries one along, don't you think? Suddenly one finds oneself an old man with no time. Now my only wish, if it is indeed possible, is I would like to see her again before I die. I'd like that she inherit my estate, which is not inconsiderable. I live opposite Barking Park in a house that was recently valued at a million and a half pounds. Then there are my business interests. My cousins are people I barely know. They share only half my blood. Why should they get such a windfall?'

Lee leant back in his chair. 'Blimey.'

'A big ask?'

'I'll have to review any evidence about your sister's disappearance from over half a century ago,' Lee said. 'There may be leads and there may not be.'

'I accept that. I'm nothing if not a pragmatist. Dying does that to a person. But Mr . . .'

'Lee.'

'Lee, I have a notion that maybe Miriam's disappearance was connected to my mother's real identity. I have no evidence for this and, in fact, the only documents I have been able to find about my mother relate to a person called Rachel Austerlitz of Niederschönhausen district in what later became East Berlin. A Jewish woman and so

10

not my mother.' He swallowed. 'My sister Miriam disappeared a few months after her first birthday. We went to the fair as a treat. My mother rarely did such things. Maybe I pestered her?'

'Did your father go with you?'

'No, he was working. He always worked, all the time. In the end it killed him,' Levy said. 'He died of a heart attack in 1979. My mother died in 2001. To my regret, I never spoke about Miriam to her. I don't ever remember her speaking about Miriam. My recollection is of my sister disappearing, of my mother crying at the time, and then we had police in our house. But I've no idea for how long. I've no idea what conclusions, if any, they came to about her. If you're worried about the cost, then don't be. I've never married, I have no children and I work in a very lucrative trade. My fear is not about penury but about ending my life without making an effort to find my sister. That is what keeps me awake. I know time is short and I often feel unwell. I'm not up to doing this on my own.'

Lee nodded. 'Do you know how thoroughly the police searched the park?'

'No.'

'Because what occurs to me immediately, I'm sorry to say, is the possibility of your sister's body still being in the ground, in the boating lake or even in what was the old lido,' Lee said. 'Of course, I can try and get access to whatever details remain of the investigation, but that doesn't mean your sister's body isn't in that park somewhere.'

'I understand,' he said. 'Sugar-coat nothing. But also, you understand, my budget for this is without limit. I can transfer ten thousand pounds into your account today. This is just to start the investigation.'

'You don't—'

'And I want you to go to Berlin. Hopefully I will be well enough to go too. But that I don't know. My condition differs from day to day. I want you to find out who my mother was. Find the house where her family lived,' Levy said. 'It's a big job, Lee. You have to find two people: my sister and my mother. In that file I have given you, you will find the story of how my parents met. I have done everything that I can to bring some sense to all this, but now I can go no further without help. I may be in remission, but I'm tired. I just can't do all this myself. Will you please take my case?'

Crying wasn't something Shazia Hakim did easily. But looking around her old bedroom made her tear up. The One Direction posters on the walls, her old Blackberry on the bedside table, that stupid Chanel handbag her dad had bought her when she was fourteen . . .

She picked up the little framed picture Lee Arnold had taken of her and her mum at Barking Park Fair the previous year and she stroked it. What her stepmother had done was wrong, but could she really say she wouldn't have done the same?

Her dad had been a bad person. There was no getting around it. A gambler who risked his family consorting with gangsters, he'd been a drunk too, and then there had been the sex. When Shazia's mother had died, he'd turned to her to fulfil his 'needs'. Then when he'd married Mumtaz, he'd brutalised her. Of course, by that time it was all about money. In debt to a local crime family, the Sheikhs, he'd been out of his mind. Then they'd killed him. Stabbed, in front of Mumtaz, on Wanstead Flats in broad daylight. Only later had Shazia discovered that her beloved Mumtaz, her amma, had let her father bleed to death into the London clay before she even thought to call 999.

Even that she could forgive. But what had driven a wedge between the two women had been Mumtaz's failure to tell Shazia. This had led to her becoming a pawn in a game between her amma and the Sheikh family, which could have cost Shazia her life. How could Amma have done that? She'd said she'd had no choice and Lee, her amma's employer, had backed that story up. But Shazia couldn't and wouldn't accept it. She'd moved out and was now living with her amma's parents in Spitalfields. They still didn't know the truth, but they loved her and were good people. Her adopted grandfather, Baharat Huq, was even going to drive her to Manchester to take up her place there on her criminology degree course.

Shazia opened her wardrobe and took out her winter coat. She'd arrive in Manchester late September, but it was going to be colder up there than it was in London and so she'd need her coat. She put it on the bed together with a couple of shirts and her hair wand. She looked in her jewellery box, but decided she'd only take a couple of pairs of earrings and a big silver filigree ring her friend Grace had given her on her sixteenth birthday. Maybe moving to Manchester would cause her to review her style? Who knew how she would react? Maybe at the end of her course she'd have changed her mind about joining the police?

But then no, that would never happen. Not after what she'd been through and seen. There was more than just a career at stake for Shazia. There was getting even.

She picked up the photograph of herself and her amma, and put it in her bag before she changed her mind.

'Hi.'

'Wotcha.'

They shared little except greetings and work stuff, things private investigators needed to share. Lee found it stressful. But how could he even open a conversation about what had happened when she never looked at him? Was she ashamed? He assumed she was, but he didn't know.

'How was your . . .'

14

'Fine,' Mumtaz said. 'Settled in. She won't find sharing with others easy, but hopefully she'll have time to think.'

'Good.'

'And you?'

The only way forward was to disappear into the work.

'Bit of a windfall,' he said. 'One job, two cases and a man with some very serious money.'

He told her everything that Levy had told him and then he handed her the pages from the file he'd already examined.

'When we've both read everything he's given us – there's not much – we'll have a chat about where we go from there. It's not going to be easy,' Lee said. 'I'm just going out for a smoke.'

Mumtaz made herself a cup of tea. Lee would be outside smoking for at least twenty minutes, which would give her a good run at this Mr Levy's notes. But it wasn't easy for her to concentrate. She knew that Shazia still saw Lee from time to time because her parents had told her. They were friends and she wanted to tell him that it was okay, but she couldn't. It was ridiculous.

They'd made love. Once. She'd just told Shazia the truth about her father's death, the girl had stormed out and Lee had turned up to make sure she was alright. It had been passionate, tender and full of love. Only her subsequent guilt had ruined it. And it had – ruined it. He'd bared his soul, he'd told her he was in love with her, and what had she done in return?

She'd pushed him away. Because that was what decent Muslim widows did. Especially widows who had let their husbands die.

She opened Mr Levy's file.

Father met my mother in September 1945 in Berlin. He was with the British 131st Infantry Brigade and she was living in the cellar of her family's house in a district called Niederschönhausen. When I was old enough to know about the Holocaust, I asked her how she'd managed to survive when her family had not. All she would ever say was that it was because she was lucky. My father took her out of the ruins of her parents' house and her life began again. That was all I needed to know.

I have subsequently researched that period of German history a little and have found that actually Niederschönhausen was not in the British but the Russian sector of the city after 1945. How my father came to be in such a place is therefore a mystery to me, as my understanding is that, although the Russians and the other Allied Forces met, control of the various sectors of Berlin was strictly regulated. But I may be wrong.

Through the good offices of the Wiesenthal Centre, I managed to trace some of my

16

mother's family through both Sachsenhausen and Auschwitz concentration camps. Her mother, Miriam, for whom my sister was named, died in Auschwitz in 1943, along with her husband, Dieter, a pharmacist. My mother's brother, Kurt, died in Sachsenhausen in 1942. He was eleven years old. There are no records for Rachel Austerlitz, my mother. It seems to me that when her parents and her brother were taken by the Nazis, she disappeared. This fits in with her story such as it was. But how? By 1941 when the family were taken to Sachsenhausen, all Jews in Berlin had been rounded up. How did she evade that?

But here I am assuming that my mother was Jewish, which I now know she wasn't. Did my grandparents adopt her, maybe? She certainly took their name. The Nazis were nothing if not meticulous and her name is recorded with the other members of her family on a list of Jewish business people working in Berlin in 1937. So far I have been unable to find any other members of the Austerlitz family either living in Germany or Israel. Both my supposed grandfather's brothers and their families died in Auschwitz too. But my researches are far from extensive, mainly due to my illness. The furthest I have got is to establish that my grandmother Miriam's original surname was Suskind.

These were also business people, employed in the rag trade. The Suskinds in turn were related, through my grandmother's mother, to a family from Munich called Reichman and also to someone called Augustin Maria Baum. That isn't the most Gentile name I've ever heard, but it comes close. This means that the Suskinds could have had at least one Gentile relation.

A lot of people researched their ancestry via DNA testing. But in Mumtaz's experience, it often threw up mysteries people hadn't been expecting and didn't really want. She knew of two clients whose real fathers had turned out to be strangers from different communities. This had led to strained familial relationships, vicious accusations and bitter guilt.

She glanced at a few small newspaper cuttings about Miriam Levy from 1962, but the details contained in them were minimal. Not much more than a few fuzzy pictures of police officers searching Barking Park.

Lee came back into the office and sat down. He looked at her.

'Well?'

'I've only got as far as Mr Levy's own account of his researches and the newspaper cuttings,' she said. 'I've not looked at any of the documents.'

'They're mostly in German,' Lee said. 'Just go straight to his translations. But what do you think so far?'

She shrugged. 'I think it's a massive job. But, given that Mr Levy is so sick, I think we should maybe concentrate on finding his sister. I mean his family history is fascinating, but . . .'

'I agree. But Levy thinks that the disappearance of Miriam and his family history are connected.'

'Because one of his mother's ancestors may have been a Gentile?'

'No,' Lee said. 'When I talked to him he didn't bring that up. It's more to do with the idea that his mother was a Gentile. That her existence was some sort of deception either perpetrated by her or by her parents.'

'He mentions possible adoption . . .'

'Which may have happened.'

'But if so, then are there any documents to prove it?'

'Anything where the Holocaust is involved can potentially be a problem, particularly when it comes to finding documents and living witnesses,' Lee said. 'The Nazis kept records but, at the end of the war, they destroyed a lot of them. Also, if Rachel was adopted, it may have been unofficial. People just took unwanted kids in back then. My Auntie Margaret was taken in by me gran. I only found that out long after old Auntie Mags had died.'

'Yes, but this was a wealthy family, so I doubt whether that happened,' Mumtaz said.

She was right. Where a possible inheritance was involved, people were less inclined to just take unknown children in as their own. It didn't make sense. Unless . . .

'Unless the Austerlitzes took in both kids . . .'

'Because Miriam Austerlitz couldn't have children?' Mumtaz said. 'Maybe. But why Gentile children – if indeed Kurt Austerlitz was also a Gentile?'

He shrugged.

She looked him in the eye for the first time in ages and, for a moment, Lee wondered if she might smile at him too. But then she said, 'So where do we start?'

CHAPTER 2

'How fucking old do you think I am, Arnold?'

Lee hadn't really thought about it until now. Vi was just Vi. Fabulous in her own unique way, but . . .

'You were alive in 1962,' he said.

'Yes, I was,' Detective Inspector Violet Collins replied. 'But I'd only just started primary school.'

'Oh.'

'So unless you want me to talk to you about Janet and John or the relative merits of Black Jacks as opposed to Fruit Salads, I won't have too much to offer,' she said. 'Anyway, what do you want to know about 1962?'

Lee put his glass of Pepsi down on the scarred tabletop and watched Vi knock back her second gin and tonic of the evening with envy in his eyes. The Boleyn pub at the top of Green Street in Upton Park had been Lee Arnold's local, back when he was a soldier with a drinking problem, and then a copper with a drinking problem and a prescription drug issue. Now he was a sober, clean private investigator it was still his preferred boozer although, these days, it was more to do with the fact that the pub would for ever be connected to his favourite football team, West Ham United.

'A one-year-old baby went missing when the Barking Park Fair was on that year,' Lee said. 'Her name was Miriam Levy and she was never found.'

'Sorry to hear it,' Vi said. 'But I've never even heard of Miriam Levy. I was probably playing Cowboys and Indians with me brothers at the time. I went to the fair at Barking Park once or twice, but not until the seventies. This is a job . . .'

'Yeah,' he said. He went to the bar and got her another drink, then they both went outside.

Lee lit Vi's fag and then his own. He said, 'I know one bloke over at Barking nick, or rather what they call a Police Office over there now. Ronny Brown, but he's my age.'

'Can't help you,' Vi said. 'Old Barking nick was shut down. There's some custody suite down by the Creek and that office, but . . . Leastways I can't help you where Plod's concerned.'

'Does that mean you might know someone outside the Job?'

She thought for a moment. Then she said, 'Maybe.'

'Who?'

She paused again. 'Leave it with me,' she said.

Vi knew a lot of people and, although what Lee really needed was information about the police investigation at the time, he left it there for the time being.

22

When they finished their drinks, he took her home and they went to bed together – as they often did and had done for years, ever since they'd worked together at Forest Gate Police Station.

The Red Army of the Soviet Union captured Berlin from its German defenders in April 1945. They didn't take just that part of the city that would later become East Berlin, but the whole lot. Only later was Berlin divided up into sectors between the Soviets, the British, the French and the Americans. And so, until the British and other forces arrived in the city in July, the Soviets had the place to themselves. It was an aspect of European history that Mumtaz knew nothing about.

Mumtaz leant against the back of her chair and thanked the Almighty for the Internet. Of course, until she dug somewhat deeper she would only get a sketchy outline of what had occurred in Berlin in 1945. But it seemed that the district of Niederschönhausen, where the Austerlitz family had lived, had not only been taken by the Soviets when they entered the city, but had remained exclusively under their control until the fall of the Berlin Wall in 1989. So quite how Irving Levy's father had met his mother under those circumstances, Mumtaz couldn't fathom. Had Mr Levy senior met Rachel Austerlitz somewhere else in the city? Irving Levy was convinced his father had met his mother in her former home. But was that correct? Over time, the telling of stories altered and, whilst not actually lying, people misremembered and, unconsciously, filled in gaps with events that didn't happen. As a psychology graduate Mumtaz knew this, but she also wondered whether deliberate lying had taken place too.

Berlin in 1945, from the little she knew about it, had been a place ripe for the production of lies. A conservative estimate of the number of German women raped by the Soviets during the Battle of Berlin was two million. If that wasn't a motivation to lie, she didn't know what was. Because Mumtaz had been raped – by her husband – and that wasn't anything one could tell just anyone, mainly because a lot of people didn't believe that rape within marriage could exist. A man had his 'rights', just like the Soviet soldiers apparently had their 'reward' in the shape of German female bodies.

Mumtaz felt cold. Some believed that the Soviet leader, Josef Stalin, had promised his troops 'Nazi flesh' as reward for their loyalty and as payment for their own considerable suffering at the hands of Hitler's army. Some openly admitted that they just did it because they felt like it. But accounts written by German women were scant and, where they did exist, anonymous. Because who could or would own up to being raped by so many men one lost count? Who would own up to the subsequent disease, the abortions and the psychological agony?

No one and especially not, she felt, a woman who called herself Rachel Austerlitz.

Whoever she had been.

The garden was a nightmare. He'd not touched it all year and now bindweed was tapping at the stained-glass window of the downstairs lavvy. Not that the house and its considerable gardens had ever been exactly elegant – it hadn't. But until he'd got sick, Irving had managed it.

He'd not changed anything. He had maintained it and he had sorted out his parents' possessions when they died. Now it looked like one of those houses where hoarders lived with junk piled up at the windows and weeds creeping across the pathways. He'd seen programmes on TV about it. People who wasted their lives looking after dreck.

Had he wasted his life? He probably had, but what could you do? Like his father he'd spent every waking hour looking at, shaping and caressing some of the most magnificent stones the earth had ever produced. Stones worth millions. But he'd never had kids. He'd never even gone out with a woman.

If he were dishonest with himself, he'd blame his parents. Always shouting at each other, arguing over nothing, dragging him into their fights as each tried to get the upper hand. But what was that? A detail. If he'd really wanted to go out and find a life for himself, he could have done. The truth was that he was lazy. Better stick with the things he knew – warring parents, a house stuck in the 1950s and the blinding glitter of diamonds.

Right at the very back of his memory, he could just recall a time when his parents had behaved differently. Way before the fighting and the screaming – and Miriam. Was he wrong when he thought that all the really mad times came after she had been born? And disappeared?

Of course, the disappearance of a child was enough to send anyone round the bend and so that must have been the beginning of things going downhill. When his mother had got pregnant he must have been five, but he remembered nothing about it. All he really remembered about that time was the fair, the Ling Twins and his mother screaming as if she was being murdered.

Her dadu wanted her to make things up with her amma. Of course he did! Not that he knew anything about it. Both Shazia and her amma had told the old couple nothing. Shazia looked at the photograph Lee had taken of her and her amma at Barking Park Fair the previous year and she shook her head. Soon it would be fair time again, but she wouldn't go.

That evening had been such fun. Amma had gone on the dodgems where she'd proved herself to be quite the demon driver and had almost tipped Lee out of his car. They'd all got candyfloss round their mouths and she'd almost been sick when she went on the waltzer after eating the greasiest doughnut she'd ever had. Amma and Lee had kept on looking at each other the way her mate Grace used to look at her old boyfriend Mamba, and so she'd tried to give them some time to be alone together. She'd never been on so many rides on her own or gone to the toilet such a lot.

It had, however, been during one of these jaunts to the loo that she'd got scared. Making her way past the helter-skelter and through the maze of caravans at the back of the site, she'd found herself alone between two vast low-loaders. She'd obviously taken a wrong turn somewhere along the line and was about to choose which direction to take when a wizened figure approached her dressed in a silk dressing gown. At first, it had said nothing, but then as it, or as she later deduced she, got closer, the figure said, 'Are you lost?'

Shazia had smiled. A tiny old woman with a face like a brown leather pump was coming to help her.

'I'm looking for the toilet,' she'd said.

'Oh, I see,' the old lady had said. 'Is not far. Let me take you.'

'Thank you.'

The woman's voice was high-pitched and possessed an accent that Shazia couldn't place. Not that she spoke again. She simply took Shazia's arm in one tiny hand and began to guide her past the low-loaders and out into the tangle of caravans.

Threading an eccentric course between what were people's homes, Shazia couldn't help but look into windows where people were cooking, washing, having arguments and, in one case, kissing. She felt guilty. Why did people always feel they could look in through a lit window?

Shazia, ashamed, lowered her gaze, which was when she noticed the old woman's hand. Holding her elbow tight in what was a hard, sinewy grip, the hand was small, brown, withered and had the longest, most malformed fingernails Shazia had ever seen. Bright yellow and with the consistency of horn, these nails curled and twisted seemingly random courses away from her fingers, often resulting in vast circles as they came to sharp points at each tip.

Fascinated but also a little scared, Shazia let herself be led by the woman until, or so it seemed, the noises from the fairground had almost receded to nothing. When she looked up again she found herself standing outside a small shed. This, she surmised, was probably, if not the toilet, then a toilet. It certainly wasn't the one she'd been to before.

She'd thanked the woman before she noticed that she was no longer holding her elbow. Now she had the toilet door open and was smiling a toothless grin, ushering Shazia forward with one bizarre, horn-encrusted hand. Shazia, her heart hammering, thought about just running, but now she really did want to go to the toilet and so, slowly and cautiously, she went inside and locked the door. Only once she'd finished did she hear laughter outside. Some weird old fairground type had clearly had a right laugh freaking her out. Fairground people were notorious for playing tricks on their punters and the boys who operated the waltzer always got girls pregnant. Or so Grace said.

But when she left the cubicle, Shazia found that she was alone. She was also just steps away from the fairground where she could see Lee and her amma watching the brightly coloured carousel whirl round, carrying laughing children riding metal horses.

Shazia had looked back once to see whether the old woman was still around, but she only saw darkened caravans.

She'd said nothing to either her amma or to Lee, but the experience had stayed with her and, in a way, she felt glad that she wouldn't be going to the fair again this year. She'd be in Manchester, or at least preparing for her new life there, away from the East End, her past and the woman who had been both more cruel and more kind than anyone else she had ever known. Amma, who had lied to her. Amma, who she loved more than her life.

CHAPTER 3

'You want that, love? I got a lot of different sizes, colours . . .'

Mandy was tempted to ask the man who'd taken the lime green miniskirt she'd glanced at briefly off the dress rail what he thought an overweight woman in her forties might do with such a thing. Wear it as a belt? But she just smiled and said, 'No, thanks.'

Taking a trip round Barking Market was more a case of giving herself something to do than actually shopping, for Mandy Patterson. A chance to get out of her office on slow days. Several sizes too big for any of the ordinary clothes stalls, Mandy didn't fancy going to what she called the 'fat bird's shop' with all its 'freesize' stuff from Italy and trousers that could be seen from space. Occasionally she'd get something from one of the greengrocers, maybe a type of vegetable Ocado didn't have in stock.

She was looking at a load of dodgy pashminas when her phone rang. She shoved it underneath her chin and answered.

'Mandy Patterson.'

'Hiya, Mand.'

God, she knew that deep, dark-brown, common-as-shite voice.

'Lee,' she said. 'What's the problem?'

'No problem,' he said.

'So you're alright? You're not . . .'

'No, Mand,' Lee Arnold said. 'I haven't had a drink; I don't want a drink.'

'Good.'

Mandy had been Lee's AA sponsor when he'd given up the booze and, over the years, they'd become, albeit infrequent, mates.

'What I'm actually after is a meet up,' Lee said.

'Because?'

She knew he had an ulterior motive. Though her friend, Lee always did. But then maybe all PIs were like that?

'Something that may be of mutual interest has come up,' Lee said. 'How you fixed for dinner tonight?'

'Where?'

'New Moroccan place has opened up in Stratford, called Baba Ganoush. My shout.'

Oh, he knew her weak spots. She was a sucker for a tagine. He had her and he knew it. But still she had to make him work for it.

She said, 'What makes you think I'm free tonight?'

'Oh, well, if you're not . . . Well . . .'

'And yet sadly and tragically we both know that you know that I am,' Mandy said. 'Pick me up at eight and you have a date.'

She heard him laugh. 'Handsome.'

Mandy ended the call and went back to looking at the schmutter on display in the market. *Maybe,* she thought, *I should buy that lime green miniskirt. That'd frighten the bugger.*

Lee put his phone back in his coat pocket and then sat down on a bench overlooking the boating lake. He lit a cigarette.

'She could be in there,' he said, pointing at the water.

Mumtaz sat down beside him.

'Or anywhere in the park,' she said.

She hadn't been back to Barking Park since she and Lee had visited the funfair with Shazia almost a year ago.

'Do you think that your reporter friend will be able to put you in touch with ex-employees?'

'Mandy's a good girl and if there's a story in it for her, she'll pull out the stops.'

'Yes but, Lee, is there a story?' Mumtaz said. 'I mean, do you know whether Mr Levy will want his family history splashed across the local press?'

'I don't think he'll care if it gets results.'

'You must check it with him.'

He looked at her and said, 'Yes, Mum.'

She looked away. She hadn't slept after reading about the terrible events that had occurred in Berlin in 1945. Some of the German women had been raped thirty times, many of them had died. Then she'd gone first thing to see Shirin Shah at

32

the hostel. When she'd arrived the girl had been crying. She'd told Mumtaz that she couldn't stand the hostel, that she wanted to go home. It had taken all Mumtaz's powers of persuasion to make her stay. Her head was still not in the right place. She still saw her failure to conceive as her main problem.

'What about the police reports?' she said.

'I'm working on it.' He smoked. 'I never had much to do with Barking nick when I was in the Job, but Vi's looking into it. I doubt whether there's many blokes still alive from that time.'

'What about the fair?'

'Well that changed hands,' he said. 'Used to be run by a family called Mitchell, but they were bought out by a company called Lesters in the eighties. They're due to hit town on Monday 19th September.'

'I thought the fair didn't come until later in the month?'

'Not this year. Dunno why. Brexit?'

Mumtaz shook her head. Ever since the referendum on British membership of the European Union had produced a negative result, people who had wanted to remain, like Lee and Mumtaz, had started to blame everything on those who wanted to leave.

The park was quiet. Apart from a few joggers and a small group of dog walkers, they almost had the old Victorian park to themselves. A large green open space in the middle of a packed, still mainly poor, if changing, London borough, Barking Park's main attractions – the boating lake and a splash park – were aimed at kids who were clearly spending their summer holidays elsewhere.

'Whoever took Miriam could have buried her body anywhere here,' Mumtaz said as she looked at the vast areas of grass, trees and water around her. 'And when the fair left, its vehicles would have churned the ground up so much, how would anyone have even known where to dig?'

'Unless it was hot that year.' He threw his dog-end on the ground and stamped it out. He said, 'This is a big job and so I'm gonna get some of the casuals in to do the day to day so you and me can concentrate on this.'

Process serving and performing background checks, the bread and butter of PI work, carried on in spite of bigger, more lucrative investigations.

'Lee, do you think that Miriam Levy could still be alive?'

'Her brother thinks she could and so we have to assume it's possible.' He shook his head. 'I think, he thinks that because his mother wasn't who he thought she was, Miriam's disappearance is connected to that.'

'But if she was just taken . . .'

'We don't know that she was,' he said. 'That's what Irving Levy says, and what he says and the truth may be very different things.'

Mumtaz shook her head. They were due to meet Mr Levy at his house on Longbridge Road in an hour. Although, according to him, he'd shown them everything he'd managed to find regarding his sister, Irving Levy felt it was important for Lee and Mumtaz to see where she had lived.

After a pause, during which he considered changing the subject to something more personal, Lee said, 'I googled Irving's house. It's bloody massive.'

Croydon was one of only two venues the fair went to that was close to London. The other one was Barking. Back in the old days when Lesters Fair had been Mitchells they'd gone right in to Clapham Common. But old Mr Lester had been a country boy born and bred, and he'd changed the original routes to, largely, give the capital a wide berth. His son, Roman, hadn't altered things when he'd taken over in the noughties. So when first Croydon and then Barking came on the horizon, teenage fairground kids like Amber Sanders became excited.

'Lulu and Misty are going to go to Camden Market,' she told her mother, Gala, as they packed away and secured the crockery in the caravan's small kitchen. Just because Guildford was only thirty-four miles from Croydon, didn't mean they didn't have to carefully wrap up all their belong-ings and secure the fittings in their caravans.

'Are they.'

Amber knew from her mum's tone of voice that meant that she wouldn't be able to join her friends. Not unless she bunked off.

'Misty is twenty now,' Amber said. 'So she's not, like, a kid any more . . .'

'She isn't, no,' her mother said. 'But you are. You know the rules, Amber, no one goes off site until they're eighteen unless it's with their parents.'

'So you take me!'

She wrapped a Royal Wedding commemorative plate from 1981 in tissue paper and slid it carefully into its original box.

'And when am I going to do that, eh?'

'I dunno. In the daytime, when you're not working?'

'You mean when I'm working, or looking after you and your dad, or helping Mama take care of Nagyapa?'

Amber pulled a face. 'She can manage on her own for a few hours. If Nagyapa knows you need to take time off for me . . .'

'You think?' Her mother turned away. 'Just because you twist him around your little finger. I'm not talking about this any more.'

'Yeah, but—'

'Yeah, but nothing. Get on with the packing. We need to be on the road first thing tomorrow morning and I haven't even started putting the clothes away.'

Amber pulled a face, but she did as she was told. Her great-grandfather, Nagyapa, had been bedbound for years and now, at ninety-three, needed round-the-clock care. This was mostly done by her grandmother, Eva, or Mama as her mum called her. Nagyapa had been in circuses when he was young. He'd been a trapeze artist in a circus back in his native Hungary. When she was little he'd shown Amber lots of old photographs of himself and his little brothers and his sister flying in space across the great, grand circuses that had travelled across Europe in the 1930s and 40s. But then World War II happened and he'd ended up in England, a middle-aged man with arthritis who couldn't fly any more. Amber had only ever known Nagyapa as the crippled man who ran the duck shoot stall. But she knew that once upon a time he had flown, which was what she wanted to do. And, on the few occasions when Nanny Eva and her mother left Nagyapa on his own, Amber would go into his caravan and ask him what it took to be a flier. Over the years he told her much which, boiled down to basics, amounted to the fact that she had to be fit, flexible and she had to find a flying troupe who would take her. At sixteen, Amber was really getting on a bit to train from scratch. Her mother and grandmother had always discouraged her. But she was determined and she was very fit. She'd even taken some circus skills classes when a school she'd gone to in Kent had offered a short course during the summer two years ago. Her parents had disapproved and she'd had to lie and tell them she was only interested in clowning. But she'd told Nagyapa, who had smiled. He was much more capable of looking after himself than Nanny Eva or her mum liked to think. In fact, Amber had always thought that Nagyapa could do anything he wanted if he really put his mind to it. Apparently unable to walk for the last five years, Amber had nevertheless seen him get out of bed and even dance around his van when he thought no one was looking.

Amber loved her nagyapa probably more than any of her other relatives. He could and would do anything for her. But she knew he was no saint. Neither was she.

'What you have to understand about the Garden is that it was a closed world. Still is, at its core. But when my grandfather started working, well it was like something out of a Dickens novel.'

Irving Levy handed Lee a picture of a small man in a heavy coat and hat standing outside a very old building that looked as if it was just about to crumble to dust.

'Those houses were down the Clerkenwell end of Hatton Garden,' he said. 'Long gone after the war, of course. My grandfather, Isaac, must've been about twenty-five when that was taken. My dad was just a nipper. Like his father before him, Isaac was a diamond cutter, so was my dad, so am I. It's what we do. Dad joined up, in the army, in 1944, but he was back in London by '46 and he never left again until the day he died.'

As a kid, Lee Arnold had gone with his mother, Rose, to a similar house overlooking Barking Park. Like Irving Levy's, that had been a massive, dusty place filled with 'things'. He'd had nightmares about stuffed birds for months afterwards. At the time he hadn't known why his mum had to go to such a place. Later he'd learnt the house was owned by a gynaecology consultant to whom his mum had been referred for what she still called 'women's trouble'.

'Like priests your cutters keep the secrets of their clients and their stones,' Levy went on. 'I could tell you tales of jobs I've worked on that'd make your hair curl. Who I've worked for, what I've worked on and why. But it's not what we do. When you work in a world where a deal worth millions is sealed on the shake of a hand you have to be able to trust and be trusted.'

'Is there anyone still working who would remember your father?' Mumtaz asked.

Levy sat down. The chair he chose sagged even beneath his slight frame. Both the house and its owner were running out of oomph.

He sighed. Then he said, 'Working, not strictly, but about . . .' He shrugged. 'Most people look forward to retirement, or so I'm told. But in the Garden, things are different. Being there . . .' He shrugged again. 'Do you know the book *The Lion, the Witch and the Wardrobe*?'

Mumtaz said that she did.

'The Garden's a bit like an adult Narnia, the land the children go into through the wardrobe. There are nooks that look like cupboards that are actually workrooms that lead to tunnels underground.

39

Dark staircases take you to laboratories in the sky. The human mind is addicted to mystery and the Garden and its layout, how it works, what in fact it really is, remains one of the few genuine mysterious places in the world.'

'Yes, but . . .'

'I know of one person who knew my father,' Levy said. 'But he wouldn't know anything about my father's private life. The traditional men of the Garden didn't operate that way.'

'And yet you said they kept their clients' secrets,' Lee said.

'Clients', yes, but you didn't take your home to work, you still don't,' Levy said.

'And yet they would know about each other's families?'

'Oh yes, but there'd be no gossip. Not like these days where everyone, what do they call it, "shares" . . .'

Lee smiled. He didn't know much about Hatton Garden, but what he did know were East Enders and, through his maternal grandfather, East End Jews. And considering that most of the Jews in Hatton Garden originated in the East End, he couldn't quite believe they would be so different.

'Irving,' he said, 'let's be frank, shall we? The Jewish East End was always full of gossip. My mum's dad was one of 'em, I know. Maybe the darkest secrets weren't shared, but if you know someone who knew your dad I'd like to speak to him.'

'I'd have to be there with you,' Levy said. 'He'd never talk to an outsider on his own. The gentleman I'm thinking of is very frum. With respect, Mrs Hakim, you couldn't be there. People like this don't mix with women outside their own family.'

Mumtaz said, 'I understand.'

'Not that the Garden doesn't have its share of Muslim traders these days. We have several firms whose staff originate in the Indian subcontinent, and some of the ladies cover their heads. But that is a recent development and those people weren't part of my father's world, which was Orthodox Jewish, regimented by tradition and closed. And anyway, I don't even know whether Dad knew about Mum not being Jewish. I'm not even certain she did.' Then he changed the subject. 'You know the fair's on its way, don't you?'

Lee said that he did and that he and Mumtaz were going.

'You must talk to people,' Levy said. 'Go on every ride. Money no object.'

'We will,' Lee said, 'although whether that will help us to find your sister, I don't know. The company operating the fair has changed hands since Miriam's disappearance. Maybe all the previous staff went, maybe they didn't. I'm trying to get my hands on some police and press reports from the time, which may be more helpful, I don't know. But Irving, it was a long time ago.'

'I know! I know!'

'I mean, mate, we will do our best, but you have

41

to accept that if someone killed Miriam, her body could be anywhere in that park or even beyond.'

He shook his head and Mumtaz wanted to offer a reassuring hand to him, but she suspected he wouldn't appreciate it. Religious Jews like religious Muslims didn't do cross-gender affection unless they were related.

'I know I'm being a silly old schlemiel when I tell people I feel that Miriam is alive. How can anyone feel the presence of another after so many years? But if I die without at least trying to find her, I know I won't rest. Even finding out the real identity of my mother is only a way, possibly, of getting to Miriam. That's really a sideshow. That's not important to me, not now . . .'

But Mumtaz knew that it was. Irving Levy's entire identity was that of an Orthodox Jewish diamond cutter and so, because Jewish inheritance is carried on the mother's side of the family, discovering that Rachel was a Gentile must have hit him hard. Suddenly, close to death, he wasn't sure who he was any more and that had to hurt.

'If we find Miriam, then we give up on who my mother might have been,' he continued.

Although having already asked Lee whether he'd be willing to go to Berlin to follow up on his mother's story, this was clearly not going to happen. Irving Levy wanted to find both his sister and the shadow of his mother.

However, he had not, Lee thought, even considered how any potential 'Miriams' would try to prove their authenticity. It made him feel protective towards the man.

Irving Levy took his wallet out of his pocket and put a small black and white photograph down in front of Mumtaz. He said, 'This is the only photo I've got of Miriam. This house looks chaotic, but I've been through all my parents' things, except for the toot in the old garage, and this is all I've been able to find. I don't even know if there were any others. The woman holding her is my mother.'

Mumtaz looked at the battered little photo. A dark woman, probably in her thirties, unsmiling, her hair falling like a black lace curtain over her shoulders, held a laughing baby girl with white curls. The child was beautiful.

Lee picked it up. 'I'd like to take this if I may.'

'Oh no, I never let it out of my sight!'

Suddenly he looked like an old man, fearful and vulnerable.

'I need to make copies,' Lee said. 'You can have it straight back.'

'Oh, copies, yes. Why didn't I think of that?'

And yet he still looked scared.

'I was in the police and I know there are ways pictures of kids can be aged to see what that person might look like now,' Lee said. 'I'll also need recent photos of your mum and dad.'

'I can do that, yes,' he said. And then he shook his head. 'What an impossible task I've set you.'

'And I'd like to speak to your dad's old mate,' Lee

continued. 'People sometimes know things they're not even aware of. And if he liked your dad, I'm sure he'll want to help.'

Irving Levy just said, 'Maybe.'

They didn't speak to anyone except to each other and then only in whispers. Occasionally one or other of them would yell out if part of a rig was about to crush someone. John didn't understand why they were even with the fair. He understood they'd been with Lesters since dinosaurs roamed the earth, but why they had remained was a mystery.

He looked at the old fossils as he drove the truck off the site and onto the road. Apparently, donkey's years ago they'd performed in a freak show as Siamese twins. People still called them 'Ping' and 'Pong', although which was which was anyone's guess. Both of them wore black kimono-style dressing gowns and neither of them was ever seen without full 'Chinese' make-up. One of the blokes on the candyfloss had told him that they actually came from Newcastle. But who knew?

John Shaw had worked for the fair for the past five years. An electrician by trade, he was also part of the set-up team, positioning and testing the rides before they opened to the public. At nearly thirty, John knew he should have some sort of direction or ambition, but being on the fair was a laugh. He didn't have to worry about accommodation and there were plenty of excited girl punters gagging for a bit of wild fairground boy action wherever they performed. He'd heard that takings were down so far this year, but he didn't let that bother him. If Lesters packed up he'd find another fair to go and work in, or a theme park. They made loads of dosh.

In reality, driving old Ping and Pong from site to site wasn't really too much bother. They didn't exactly distract him from the road. But they did creep him out, especially when they took their hands out of the sleeves of their kimonos and revealed those bloody awful fingernails of theirs.

Mandy hadn't bought the lime green miniskirt from Barking Market. Instead, she wore the usual tent dress and sensible shoes. Also, as usual, she spilt half her dinner down her front. But then it had been a particularly sloppy tagine. Tasty but sloppy.

As soon as they'd finished their meal, Lee had taken her into the shed out the back of the restaurant, which acted as a 'shisha' pipe lounge. When they walked in, they were greeted by a fug of sweet apple-scented tobacco being exhaled by a small group of middle-eastern looking men. Pushing the shisha pipe to one side, Lee lit a fag and they both sat down on cushions that were really uncomfortably too near the ground for Mandy.

Once he'd settled himself, Lee said, 'So what do you reckon?'

Mandy shrugged. 'You can access the British Newspaper Archive online. An event like a child's disappearance won't be difficult to find.'

'Yeah, and thank you for that,' Lee said. 'I'll do that.'

'Yes, but you knew about that, anyway, didn't you?' Mandy said. 'What you really want is for me to spend every waking hour trying to dig up some old hacks who worked on the *Recorder* in the sixties.'

Lee said nothing. He'd started out asking Mandy about archive newspapers and then moved on to tap her about people who'd worked on the paper in the past. He could, of course, get names himself from the archive, but he knew that Mandy's dad had also worked on the *Ilford Recorder* and his tenure had begun in the late fifties. He also knew that, when he died, Mandy had taken all of his records, which she now kept in her small flat.

'Dad's been dead four years and he was one of the last to go, I think,' Mandy said. 'And anyway, why do you think I've got time to go through Dad's old contact book looking up blokes who are probably demented?'

'Because it's a good story?' Lee said.

'Oh, it will be if you find the woman,' Mandy said. 'But what if you don't?'

Lee shrugged. Failure was more possible than success in this case. Not that he'd thought about any sort of contingency. Eventually he said, 'Free tagines for six months?'

Mandy looked away.

46

He'd already bunged his ex-police artist/computer geek contact a grand of Irving's money to 'age' Miriam Levy's baby photograph. He didn't want to take the piss, but then he said, 'Alright, Mand, tagines for six months and a contribution to the charity of your choice.'

She turned her eyes on his and Lee felt a shiver run down his spine. She looked soft, but Mandy was as hard as nails.

'And if that turns out to be your rent, that's fine with me,' he said.

CHAPTER 4

He remembered everything. It was a curse. Sometimes he felt as if his head was a rubbish bin to which the dustmen never came. He wished they would. The Garden had been a different place when he was young and he'd preferred it. Back before the war there'd been no goyim, except for the few Italians that remained at the Clerkenwell end. But nobody minded them. They made suits and religious statues and he could even remember the last of the Italian barrel organ men. Their food, though not kosher, had been strange and delicious and, for yiddisher kids like Jackie Berman, always a guilty treat.

Since the war so much had changed and not just because of the bombing. New faces had appeared in the Garden, people from all over the country and beyond. Even shops, God help us, had opened where the public could go and buy a ring off the peg. Indians and Pakistanis many of them, buying jewellery fashioned to their tastes by other Indians and Pakistanis.

That, however, was only the Garden that the punters saw. Those in the 'trade' were open to the 'other' world, the subterranean labyrinths and jewel houses in the sky that were recorded in minute detail in Jackie Berman's never to be emptied head. There were rooms within tunnels within basements under the streets of Hatton Garden. Dead rivers and wells once used by alchemists, makers of guns and which had quenched the thirsts of resurrection men running for their lives from the peelers, their dead plunder slung over their shoulders.

There were places where nothing really went away. He'd heard people say things he could understand about manors like Spitalfields, Stepney and Limehouse. As in Hatton Garden, these were places where history lay thick and where those who knew where to look, like Jackie, could see things that passed others by.

Where dead men walked in daylight, where men with the faces of Old Testament patriarchs turned pebbles into gems, anything was possible. Jackie pushed himself further into the battered doorway behind him and watched as Irving Levy walked towards him with some tall goy in tow.

They wanted something.

The name Austerlitz had originated in Moravia. As far as Mumtaz could tell it was a name used only by Jews including, to her surprise, the father of the dancer Fred Astaire. But so far she hadn't been able to track down any Berliner chemist shop owners.

Irving Levy's mother, Rachel, had been the only member of her immediate family to survive the Holocaust. But there had to have been an extended Austerlitz family, if not in Berlin then somewhere else in Germany. Irving had concentrated on the family of his grandmother, Miriam Austerlitz, née Suskind, who was apparently related to a Munich family called Reichman. Through the Reichmans, although Irving didn't know exactly how, Miriam had a Gentile relative called Augustin Maria Baum.

Mumtaz sat back in her chair and put her pen to her lips. Irving Levy had by his own admission 'run out of steam' with his genealogical researches. He'd contacted the Wiesenthal Institute in Los Angeles, who had provided him with the Suskind/Reichman/Baum connection, but with no accompanying explanation. She could chase that up but, more significantly, she'd also discovered, via the Internet, that something called the Simon Wiesenthal Archive existed in Vienna. It was this, now less famous organisation, that kept the most extensive records of families affected by the Holocaust as well as those Nazis who had attempted to destroy them.

Mr Levy was keen for Lee or Mumtaz or both to go to Berlin to identify the Austerlitz family home in Niederschönhausen, if it still existed, and as he'd put it 'speak to people'. But who? Sick and possibly dying, Irving Levy hadn't thought about what he wanted to happen. Mumtaz sympathised.

She rarely thought things through in her personal life. Had she done so she would never have slept with Lee Arnold. Not that she regretted what had happened that night. It had been the first time she'd ever felt pleasure in sex. And he'd told her he'd loved her. Poor Lee. After that she hadn't known what to do and she felt that, tough old soldier that he was, she had, if not broken, bruised his heart.

She should never, never, never, never have taken him to her bed.

She looked back at her computer screen and typed in 'Niederschönhausen' and 'synagogues'. The Austerlitz family had probably been members of one of the local synagogues. The search came up with two and they were probably the biggest, most well-known synagogues in Germany.

Eva opened the caravan door and went inside. The old man sat in his bed, watching trash TV and eating caramels. The smell of him, though not strong, turned Eva's stomach. Piss and dust.

She stood at the bottom of the bed, blocking his view of the TV and said, 'I'm going.'

He said nothing, although he did register some irritation at not being able to see his programme.

Eva had expected no more. She shrugged and began to leave. Just as she got to the front door she heard him say, 'Send Gala, in case I need something.'

She took great delight in replying, 'Gala's busy.

And, before you say it yourself, so's your precious Amber.'

He frowned and Eva turned away. He had a glare like a gorgon.

'Then you come back quick and don't you go nowhere!' he said.

The desperation in his voice made her shudder.

Lee narrowed his eyes. It made his vision less distinct, almost smoky, which is what it would have been back in the nineteenth century. What remained of Hatton Garden's ancient rooftops had a random, flung-together feel to them. As if bricks, tiles and chimney pots had just been thrown together with no regard for symmetry or logic. It was also, Lee felt, a place that was out of time. His head began to swim.

'Vertigo can be a problem,' Irving Levy said as he put a mug of tea in one of Lee's hands. 'But rather that than being trapped in a basement.'

Lee, who was still getting his breath back from the long climb up four steep staircases said, 'Certainly gives you a workout.'

'Nearly kills him,' the old man who'd let them into the building said.

Irving Levy shook his head. 'Just come in, Jackie,' he said. 'And get Mr Arnold a stool, for God's sake.'

Jackie Berman went back out onto the landing while Lee looked around. Getting three of them in what wasn't much more than a cupboard was going to be a squeeze. And it was a cupboard that was full of stuff. Most of it lay on a bench underneath an arched Georgian window. A conglomeration of tools was how it was probably best described. But Lee recognised none of them apart from the six sets of old-fashioned balance scales, of decreasing size, that sat at the far end of the bench. Everything else had to be what Levy used to cut and polish diamonds as well as instruments through which to magnify stones and their facets. Bits of cloth and newspaper were attached to most of these articles. Levy sat down on the one high stool in front of the bench while the old man, when he returned, plonked down a pair of what looked like kids' stools on the remarkably clean floor. As Lee lowered himself down onto his stool, he noticed that the calendar on the wall dated from 2010. The old man kicked the door closed.

'This is where I work,' Levy said. 'Years ago I worked here alongside my father and he worked here with his father before that.'

'I done the sweeps,' the old man said. 'A big job when you've got two men cutting.'

'The sweeps?'

'When we cut diamonds there's residue or dust,' Levy said. 'This is valuable and so we collect it to sell on to manufacturers of grinding and sawing tools. Mixed with liquid it makes a keen cutting surface rock hard. Nothing is wasted.'

'Except your life,' the old man said.

Levy shook his head. 'You have to forgive Jackie,'

he said. 'Seventy years in the Garden which he loved, but won't say he loved . . .'

'I never graduated from sweeping!'

'You never wanted to!'

The old man waved a hand. 'Ach! And now me eyes have gone I'm useless. Rub it in!'

'Useless is relative, Jackie,' Levy said. 'Why do you think I've brought Mr Arnold here to speak to you if I think you're so bloody useless?'

'Him?'

'Yes, him,' Levy said. 'Mr Arnold is a private detective; he's going to try and find Miriam for me.'

'Your sister? She's dead.'

'She's missing, Jackie. No one knows whether she's alive or dead. But through Mr Arnold here, I'm having a go at finding out.'

The old man crossed his arms. 'Fool's errand,' he said. 'Why?'

Lee looked up at Levy. Had he told the old man, who clearly had been some sort of employee at one time?

'Because I want to know!' Lee interpreted this as he hadn't. 'She was my sister. Later this year I'm going to be sixty-one . . .'

'Last you saw of Miriam, you was seven,' Jackie said. 'If she is alive, where's she been all this time? Who's she been with? What's she been doing? Fifty-five years and not a word from you about your sister and now this? She's dead. Give it up! You'll drive yourself round the bend.'

54

'That's my choice.'

The old man shrugged his shoulders.

The Neue Synagogue was actually part of a cultural and educational complex known as the Centrum Judaicum. It contained archives relating to Berlin's Jewish community and at least one very enthusiastic archivist. According to Frau Metzler, the Austerlitz family had worshipped at the Neue Synagogue on Oranienburger Strasse. Close to their alleged home in Niederschönhausen, it had been a centre for the Liberal Judaism that had appealed to the pre-war Jewish elite. Mumtaz, on the phone from the more prosaic surroundings of Green Street, was fascinated.

She'd been completely upfront with Frau Metzler.

'So this is your client's mother's family,' she'd said when Mumtaz told her Irving Levy's story. 'He thinks.'

'Yes.'

'It's not a name I must say that I know,' Frau Metzler said. 'Austerlitz. But then if they all died . . .'

'Dieter Austerlitz, my client's grandfather, ran a pharmacy, although I'm not sure where.'

Not for the first time, the fact that Irving knew so little about his mother's family hit her. In spite of the trauma of Partition, she knew a lot about her mother's family. Significantly, she knew they had fled from their home in India to what was then East Pakistan. Even now older members of her amma's family mourned the loss of their home city of Faizabad. In India, so her mother had always said, her family had money. Whether that was just wishful thinking, Mumtaz didn't know. But at least she knew something.

'I will see what I can find out about the family Austerlitz,' Frau Metzler said. 'If you have any other names that might help, that could be useful.'

'They had family in Munich.'

'Put it all in an e-mail and I will get back to you as soon as I am able. I will need a little time.'

'Thank you.'

When she finished the call, Mumtaz sat back in her chair and looked up at the office ceiling. It needed a good swipe with a cobweb brush.

Then she thought how ridiculous even noticing something so trivial was. She really needed something else in her life besides her family and her work. Something, or someone, just for her.

Irenka Horvathy.

Eva touched the name, now fading as lichen ate into the gravestone, but not with affection. She'd died when Eva was seven and, apart from the manner of her death, all she could remember about her mother was the screaming.

Her father sometimes nagged her about not speaking Hungarian unless she had to, but she always told him the same thing, 'It reminds me of that old witch, Irenka.' Then he shut up.

And what a witch she'd been! Handy with her fists, spiteful, she'd made Eva's young life a nightmare. Teasing her dead straight hair into limp, lifeless curls with red-hot tongs, laid for minutes on end in the fire. One time she caught Eva's hair on fire, which had then prompted another fight between Irenka and Bela. That time he broke her nose. Worse had been to come, which was why she was here.

Rippleside Cemetery in Barking was one of the least restful places in which to spend eternity or even half an hour. Wedged between the A13 and one of the biggest council estates in the country it was always being vandalised. Last time Eva had visited she'd had to scrub a spray-painted swastika off Irenka's grave. If only they'd known her. She'd have loved that.

And yet Eva always made this pilgrimage. When the fair arrived in Croydon, she went to Barking to see Irenka. Bela knew and he hated it. But better that than wait until they arrived at Barking when, in his words, 'Someone might know who you are if you go to that grave.' Ridiculous old man. As if anyone would? As if anyone cared?

Eva picked at some moss on top of the stone in a half-hearted way and then sat down on the grass. The only reason she visited, apart from the fact that no one else did, was because, wicked old witch as she had been, not even Irenka had deserved to die like that. She had been wronged. Oh, she had been badly wronged!

The Twins, Ping and Pong, had first raised the alarm – in their own unique way. Screaming and waving their arms in the air. They didn't say what was the matter, they rarely did. But Tom, 'old Tom' even back in the late sixties, had seen the smoke and he'd run towards it. She'd been just about to get on the waltzer, a gratis ride before the punters arrived, but Tom, so he'd told her, he had stopped it, picked her up and run towards the smoke.

Irenka had still been alive when they found her. Bela always said that she wasn't, but Eva remembered it well. How could she not? Trussed up, her fat mother had rope around her feet, up her back and looped around her neck, she lay on her side in the middle of a cooking fire between their caravan and that of Mario the Tattooed Man. He, it was later established, had been in the freak show wagon at the time, but where had Bela been? He'd been around and he'd been drunk and he'd arrived before anyone – except the Twins. But they, as usual, had just melted out of sight.

Her hair had been on fire, Eva had recognised the smell from her experiences with her mother's hot tongs. And her face had blistered. When they took her out of the fire, Eva saw huge, fluid-filled bubbles on her cheeks and under her chin. Luckily, she'd lost consciousness by that time. She never regained it.

Why had she died like that and how? The story, which originated from who knew where, was that Irenka had been practising an escapologist act. And as a youngster Eva had believed it. After all, everyone said that had been the way it had happened. Nobody, clearly, saw the irony in the notion of an overweight, unfit woman attempting to emulate Houdini. As far as Eva had known, her mother did little except sit in their caravan and eat sweet dumplings.

It was obvious to Eva, now that she was an adult, that Bela her father had killed her mother. And life had been better once Irenka had died. Which was why she'd never said anything or tried to make her father visit her mother's grave. Because he never had. And, when they arrived in Barking, where Irenka had died, he wouldn't even say her name.

Irving Levy left to make the long journey through the tall Georgian house to the toilets in the basement. Once he'd gone, the old man said, 'He's sick, you know.'

'Yes,' Lee said. So he did know.

'And will make himself sicker with this stupidity. I reckon he goes to that park, you know. Like his father.'

As far as Lee knew, Irving's father had had little involvement in the search for his daughter. Although that could be because his son hadn't talked about it.

'He spent weeks, months in that park over the years,' Jackie said. 'He dug.'

'Dug?'

'All over. Got arrested once, although because of Miriam the coppers never pressed charges. And when that fair came once a year . . .' He shrugged. 'Wandering about through the dodgems and the sideshows like a lost soul, crying. She, his wife, she didn't care. It ate away at him.'

'How do you know this?' Lee asked.

'Because, son, this is the Garden,' the old man said. 'Men make deals so big here they could bring down countries. So you have to trust each other. This means you have to know about each other. I'm not talking about gossip here, just keeping on your toes. You understand?'

Lee didn't answer. He wanted the old man to elaborate.

Eventually, Jackie said, 'It's like this: if you work with a bloke you have to know he's a mensch. Old Isaac, that was Manny's father, he was so particular about sweeps, he'd have me washing me hands and sieving even when he wasn't cutting. Just as a matter of course!'

Lee knew what sweeps were, but sieving?

The old man explained. 'When you're cutting and you have to leave, say, for a call of nature, you wash your hands in running water over a bowl. This, you let settle. Then later you sieve the water through sacking to capture any dust as might have been on ya. Manny was religious about it, Isaac too. These were honest men. But Manny was also a troubled man. When that little girl went, I saw him fade. I watched his judgement cloud, his weight fall.' He leant in close to Lee's face. 'He made mistakes.'

'Cutting?'

'The Bourse wasn't happy. As his sweeps man I had an obligation – to Manny as well as the Bourse. I followed him. It was pitiful.'

The London Diamond Bourse, where men in heavy hats and coats, sporting traditional Hasidic side-locks, traded stones from across the world, was a powerful institution. If the traders lost confidence in a cutter, his whole business could collapse.

'He pulled himself together,' the old man said. 'But it wasn't down to me. I left that to her.'

'Who?'

'His wife,' he said. 'I couldn't confront Manny! He was my guv'nor! But I went to that posh house they had, and I told her that if he carried on the way he was going, they'd lose everything. She didn't like what I said or who I was, but she said she'd sort it and she must've.'

'What was she like?' Lee asked. He'd seen photographs, but he still had little idea about who Rachel Levy had been.

Although, as he himself usually put it, 'as old as God's pisspot', Jackie Berman's hearing was still sharp. He heard Irving panting his way up the stairs from the khazi and so he lowered his voice.

'She was as cold and as flat as a witch's tit,' he said. 'She didn't give a toss about Manny. She only perked up when I said they might lose money. Even thinking about her all these years on gives me the shudders.'

CHAPTER 5

'You coming Barking Fair this year?'

Grace swung backwards and forwards on the rusty old swing that had once belonged to her amma and her uncles.

Shazia said, 'I'll be at uni.'

'No, it's early this year. On the 19th. You'll still be here.'

'Dunno. Maybe.'

Grace was the closest friend Shazia had made at sixth-form college. A tall, lively, funny girl, she came from a very straight-laced Nigerian family with whom she had nothing in common.

'I'm going with Tom,' Grace said. 'But you can come too. Tom ain't got that stupid jealous of everyone thing that Mamba had.'

Benjamin 'Mamba' Nwogu had been Grace's previous boyfriend. A professional bad boy gangsta, Mamba had fascinated Grace for all of six months. Then the gang behaviour had started to grate. Interested in little beyond weed, he'd wanted Grace around, but didn't want to pay her any attention. She'd met Tom Campbell at Green Street Library of all places. That wasn't cool and neither was Tom, who was one of those super smart, super straight, and religious (shock horror!) boys whose parents came from Trinidad. But he was into her like no other boy Grace had ever met. She just had to say she wanted something for him to make sure she got it.

'I suppose it'd be a laugh,' Shazia said.

'Yeah.' Grace swung. 'Here, you know when you come home from uni for the holidays, yeah?'

'Yeah.'

'You gonna come back here or to your mum's?'

Shazia hadn't even thought about it. Since her falling-out with Mumtaz she'd stayed with her amma's parents, Sumita and Baharat Huq, and only visited the flat in Forest Gate when she needed something.

''Cause Brick Lane ain't round the corner,' Grace said. 'And if I see another hipster with a purple beard on a fixed wheelie I'm gonna lose my shit, innit.'

Shazia smiled. Although stiff with funky vintage and designer shops, Brick Lane and its environs wasn't a place for East Enders like Grace and herself. Those places were for incomers, be they the artists who lived in the Huguenot houses around Christ Church or the trust fund kids whose daddies had bought them warehouse conversions in Hoxton.

'I don't know yet,' Shazia said. She sat on the grass in front of the old swing, leaning back against a mossy stone birdbath.

'I dunno what shit you have with your mum, but make it up, yeah?' Grace said. 'You love each other, and also getting up here to see you uses up my Oyster.'

Clearly 'German efficiency' wasn't a myth. Mumtaz opened the e-mail and began to read it out loud to Lee.

He said, 'This is from . . .'

'Frau Metzler at the Neue Synagogue in Berlin,' she said. She read the effusive greetings to herself.

'So, here it says . . . "The family Austerlitz ran the Austerlitz Apotheke, which was on Rosenthaler Strasse in what is now Spandau district. The building survived World War II and was in the Russian sector of the city, which then became part of the German Democratic Republic. It is still an apothecary, but has no connection to the family. Dieter Austerlitz, his wife and children lived in Niederschönhausen at a large house on Grabbeallee which was number 67. Dieter and his wife died in Auschwitz in 1943 and their son, Kurt, in Sachsenhausen Concentration Camp in 1942. There is no record of anyone with the name Rachel Austerlitz dying in either Auschwitz or Sachsenhausen. This may mean that she died en route to Sachsenhausen, which is probable, as both Rachel and her brother suffered from tuberculosis."'

Mumtaz looked up.

Lee said, 'Nope. Irving's never mentioned it to me.'

'TB was a death sentence in those days,' Mumtaz said.

'Not always.'

'No, but still . . .' She read on, '"Dieter Austerlitz was one of two sons of Avram Austerlitz, also an apothecary, who died in 1920. He is buried with his wife, Izabella, in the Weissensee Jewish Cemetery here in Berlin. The brother of Dieter Austerlitz was called Wilhelm and he, his wife, Regina, and their three children all perished in Auschwitz in 1943. None of our members are old enough to remember this family, but if you do come to Berlin, I will be able to put you in contact with the wider Jewish community who may know more than I. I have yet to investigate Frau Austerlitz's family in Munich. But I must tell you that the name you gave as someone related to the Suskind family via a family called Reichman did make me nervous."'

'Nervous?' Lee said. 'That's a weird word to use.'

Mumtaz said, 'English isn't her first language. Give her a break. Neither of us can speak a foreign language with such fluency. My written Bengali is beyond awful. Anyway . . . "Augustin Maria Baum was a German nationalist. He was born in 1867 and died in 1938. He was a member of the National Socialist Party and a great admirer of Hitler. And so any connection to Jewish families has to be wrong."'

'Maybe it was a different Augustin Maria Baum,' Lee said.

Mumtaz looked back at her screen. Then she said, 'Frau Metzler says she will get in touch when she knows more.'

Lee shrugged. 'Irving may want us to prioritise his search for his sister, but I have to admit to a fascination with his mother.'

He told her what Jackie Berman had said about Rachel Levy.

'Makes me wonder whether old Irving's parents was the love match he likes to think,' Lee said. 'I mean, it's a romantic story, isn't it? Brave British squaddie finds hidden Jewish girl in great big ruined house in Berlin, saves her from the Russians and marries her.'

'Well, assuming that did happen, it is romantic,' Mumtaz said. 'Maybe by the 1960s, when this old man met her, Rachel was disillusioned. And she'd lost her daughter . . .'

She couldn't and wouldn't say any more and she knew Lee would know why. Shazia was off to university soon and Mumtaz desperately wanted to see her before she left.

Lee said, 'So it looks like we're off to the fair when it arrives.'

She was dreading it. They'd had such fun last year. But this time was different. This time it was work and she had to remember that.

'Jackie Berman reckons Irving's going to Barking Park,' Lee continued. 'I just hope he's not digging holes like his father. But I do want him to come with us so he can walk us through what he remembers.'

It made sense. And, although Levy claimed to be frail, he obviously had enough energy to go to work and do whatever he had been doing in Barking Park. If he was doing anything.

'I imagine he'll not want to,' Lee said, 'but it's important we try and walk him through what happened back in '62. He might remember nothing, but he might not.'

'Do you know if he's been to the fair since Miriam disappeared?'

Lee shook his head. 'I'm not sure. I do think we're not getting all the facts from Irving for some reason. I dunno why,' he said. 'He wants his sister back and I believe that's genuine. But there's something ain't right and I don't know what it is. As soon as you hear back from Germany we'll put all what you've found out to him and ask when he wants us to go to Berlin.'

'Before the fair?'

'Yeah,' he said. 'We've a few weeks and maybe if we can find out more about Irving's mother it'll help us in the search for Miriam.'

His phone rang and, when he looked at the screen, he smiled.

'If you're going to fly then you need to be lean.'

Amber finished her ice cream anyway and then said, 'I don't put on weight, Nagyapa.'

'You do. You mustn't,' the old man said. 'You're beautiful, but your tits are big. You must watch that.'

Luckily, Amber was used to her grandfather's 'Hungarian ways' – as her mother described his characteristic bluntness.

'Instead of going shopping with those girls with empty heads' – he meant Lulu and Misty – 'you should be practising. Practising, practising, practising. I know that where there is a horizontal you can throw a rope around – you should do that. The Twins know where they are. We have them all over the site. A fairground is a gift for a flier. But you must do this all the time!'

'And if Mum and Dad catch me, or Nanny Eva? They don't want me to fly, none of them! Only you want me to fly!'

'Because it is what you want, my little pigeon,' he said. 'I deny you nothing. But if you want me to say I am fine so that your mother or Eva can take you to Camden to just waste money, I can't.' He shook his head. 'I am not fine.'

'Yes, you are,' Amber said. 'I've seen you get up and make tea for yourself. And when we were outside Margate and Mum was sick, Ping and Pong looked after you.'

He shook his head. 'Only the freaks in the last resort,' he said. 'And that was. Your mother was sick and she needed her mother. How could I refuse? But you? You just want to go shopping. Why I should get those silent creeps to look after me again, I don't know.'

'I thought they were your friends,' Amber said.

He glared at her. 'No friends of mine.'

And yet it was only, apart from Nanny Eva, Ping and Pong that her grandfather spoke Hungarian with. They rarely answered, but they obviously understood him. And they had, according to her grandmother, lived around the old man most of his life.

'So I can't go shopping in Camden, then?' Amber said once the silence in that caravan got too much for her.

'Not yet,' he said. 'Tomorrow the fair will open and I do not want to be in this caravan on my own. I don't want these dirty London people looking in through my windows and seeing me. I know what they're like. They will rob you. And when we move on to Barking it will be even worse. Those East End people are the lowest of the low. I will give you money for Camden later, but only if you practise, you hear me?'

Gilda was getting on his nerves.

Remember Cousin Violet is coming and she's bringing people to speak to you, Dad, she'd yelled in his ear as if he was deaf or stupid. He was neither. Now his daughter was in the kitchen; as far as Bill was concerned, she could stay there.

His niece, Vi, was another matter. She was a right laugh, always had been.

Smoked like a trooper, drank like a fish and swore like a sailor. Pity she'd joined the coppers, but there it went. Bringing a couple of private detectives to

70

see him, so she couldn't be all bad. That lot were as dodgy as a wagon-load of monkeys.

The doorbell rang and Gilda made some weird nervous sorts of noises and then let them in. Since her and her husband had moved them all out to Gidea Park, Gilda had turned into Mrs Middle-Class, complete with that annoying put-on accent she'd developed. Soon she'd come out with the china cups and saucers and he'd end up slopping his tea on the laminate flooring.

Vi entered in a cloud of smoke followed by a tall bloke, who looked a bit foreign, and some very pretty Paki woman.

'Uncle Bill,' Vi said. 'How's it going?'

'I'm old, it's fucking shit.'

She kissed him. Gilda said she'd go and make tea.

'This is Lee Arnold, he runs the PI agency, and this is Mumtaz, who's his assistant.'

They all shook hands, and then Vi and the others sat down. Bill was tempted to ask Vi for a fag, but he knew that Gilda'd have a fit. So he looked at Lee Arnold and he said, 'Vi tells me you wanna know about the Levy baby.'

'The family want to try and find out what happened,' Arnold said.

He was a good-looking geezer, even if he did have black suitcases underneath his eyes. A bloke with a past if ever Bill had seen one.

'Left it a while, didn't they?' Bill said. 'But I don't

judge. How can I? Yeah, I was working Barking Funfair when it happened. I was muscle, back then, setting up the rigs. Lot of casual work on the fairs back in them days. When I wasn't on fairs, I done circuses and if I wasn't on circuses I worked with Vi's dad on the doors.'

Bill and his brother had worked the West End clubs as doormen sometimes back in the late fifties and early sixties. Mainly for Maltese mobsters, but they weren't frightened of them. Two hard Gypsy boys on the make could easily take a handful of 'Maltesers' as Bill liked to call them.

'It was the first day of the fair, called Mitchells back in them days,' Bill said. 'I was putting punters on the big wheel. Couples mainly, the girls pretending they was frightened to get their fellas to put their arms round them. Course, all the fellas wanted to do was grab their tits.' Then he said to the woman called Mumtaz, 'Sorry, love.'

But she smiled. 'It's fine.'

'Suddenly there's all this screaming,' he said. 'Up on the wheel all I could see was people running about like blue-arsed flies. I wanna go and have a look. But then I get told to stay where I am because a baby's gone missing and the coppers are coming. Geezers shouting about how they've closed the park. But I don't think they did. They did come quick, though. I dunno how. No mobile phones in them days, someone must've gone to the phone box up Faircross.'

'Faircross?' Mumtaz asked.

'It's a parade of shops on Longbridge Road,' Vi answered. 'So what did the coppers do, Bill?'

'Went all over,' he said. 'In caravans, through all the sideshows, in waggons, on the rides. But not just the coppers – we all looked. Little girl like that goes missing, you have to have a heart of granite not to want to help her. I saw the mother, poor thing.'

'What was she like?'

'When I saw her, it was like she'd turned to stone. When she first found the baby gone she screamed and screamed. But when I got to her she was just sat on the mud outside the helter-skelter, staring at nothing. Looked like she'd seen the dead. I tell you what occurred to me, shall I? What I thought was that by the look of her, that woman knew her kiddie had gone for good. I can't tell you how I knew it, but I knew it.'

'Gypsy magic,' Vi said.

Bill laughed. 'Cor blimey,' he said, 'don't let our Gilda hear you say that. She goes to the WI now and her Reg joined the golf club last year.' He shook his head. 'Story was the lady had left the kiddie in her pram when she had to go to the toilets. When she come out the little 'un had gone.'

'And nobody saw anything?' Arnold asked.

'I'm not the coppers so I don't know,' Bill said. 'But I never heard about no witnesses.' He shook his head. 'What I do remember is all the freaks running about all over the place.'

'Uncle Bill . . .'

'Nah! I don't mean what you think,' he said to Vi. Then he turned to Lee. 'Everyone's frightened to say anything these days, don't you find, boy? Political correctness?'

Lee said nothing. He'd heard the word 'freak' applied to all sorts over the years, including young people, Goths and foreigners.

'I mean, real freaks,' Bill said. 'Bearded ladies, lobster men, Siamese twins. Done a roaring trade, the old freak show. But the coppers going in frightened the poor sods rigid. I remember the Siamese twins particularly because they separated and ran in two different directions.' He laughed. 'That was a common con back in the day. Lot of 'em didn't even look the same. I remember one set was different heights . . .'

'Lee,' Mumtaz said, 'didn't our client write something about Siamese twins?'

'Yes,' Lee said. He looked at the old man. 'Our client, a relative who was a kid at the time, said he was at the freak show when the baby was taken.'

'Oh, it was always jammed with punters,' Bill said. 'People like to look at those less fortunate than themselves. Human nature, ain't it?' Then he frowned. 'You working for the Levy baby's brother?'

Neither Lee nor Mumtaz said anything.

'Thought you might be,' he said. 'Rich family of diamond dealers, I heard. Some copper told me. Said they had to take the little lad because his mother was off her head. That copper reckoned someone'd took the baby so he could get money off the father. Kidnapped.'

Mumtaz said, 'Miriam was never found.'

'That we know,' the old man said. 'Maybe if she was kidnapped, whoever had her killed her. Or p'raps the father did pay up, but never got her back. You wanna talk to the coppers.' He looked at Vi.

She said, 'Contacts over at Barking are few and far between. Mostly young lads who don't know where Barking Creek is these days.'

Bill laughed. 'Oh, fuck me, Barking Creek!' he said. 'We used to go down there when I was a nipper and we was still on the road. Good atching tan, the old creek. Nobody bothered you.'

Seeing the confusion on Lee and Mumtaz's faces, Vi translated. 'Atching tan is a Romany stopping place.' Then she said to Bill, 'Don't let Gilda hear you talk the old language, she'll have a fit!'

He laughed. 'Let her.' But then his face darkened and he said, 'Tell you what, though, one thing I do remember now is where that copper who spoke to me come from.'

'What kind of copper?' Vi asked. 'Uniform? Constable? Detective?'

'Young lad in a uniform,' Bill said. 'Never knew his name, nothing about his rank. Why would I? But we did share a fag and I did know his face. Lived down the Creek.'

CHAPTER 6

He looked at the e-mail and then at the certificate. Rachel Levy, his mother, had died of bone cancer. Slow and painful, it had taken a couple of years to eat her slight body. He remembered the way she'd borne the pain, her face pulled into agonised grimaces as she attempted not to show her distress.

There was nothing about tuberculosis. There never had been. It had been his father, Manny, who had coughed. But then most men smoked in those days, his old man being no exception. But not Rachel.

Irving put his mother's death certificate down and rubbed his face with his hands. The consultant could show him all the test results under the sun to demonstrate he was in remission, but he still felt rough. Too rough to go to Berlin; too rough to stand up to what might await him in Rachel's old house on Grabbeallee. Lee Arnold and Mumtaz Hakim had discovered more in one day than he'd found out in a year. But then Irving knew that he'd never really tried. Not properly. Even before the DNA test he'd known that something about his mother had been wrong, but he didn't know what. Then when he found out that she hadn't been Jewish his mind hadn't been able to take it. Or his body. It hadn't just been the chemotherapy that had made him so sick at that time.

Now, according to the Arnold Agency, he had a Nazi in the family too. Augustin Maria Baum. Irving had never heard of him. But then he'd died before World War II and so maybe he'd managed not to do very much harm. Irving knew that was probably a lie, but it made him feel better and so he went with it. No matter that when Arnold and Mrs Hakim went to Berlin they may well find out Baum had been a monster. That was all in the future.

Sara Metzler knew that anything was possible. Especially in her city, especially amongst the Jews. Survival in Berlin cellars and cupboards, sometimes for the entire duration of the war was just another of those Jewish miracle stories old people told to keep themselves alive. That it was incredible meant little to them. Only that they were true.

When the woman had phoned from London, Sara felt that she too, this Mrs Hakim, had been almost embarrassed by the story she told. A Jewish woman found by a British soldier in a house in Spandau. What was so amazing about that? Well, the fact that it had been a British soldier who had found her in that sector was odd. Surely by that time the woman would have been some Russian officer's property? And then there was the connection between the Austerlitz family and Augustin Maria Baum. Just thinking about his name made her skin crawl.

Baum hadn't been a major force in the National Socialist Party. In terms of anti-Semitic acts he'd done nothing. But he'd written much. His subject had been philosophy, which he'd taught at the prestigious Ludwig Maximilian University in Munich. He had used his position to publish papers with titles like 'Racial Purity – The Necessity of Segregation'. There were photographs of him shaking Hitler's hand. Sara hadn't managed to establish how he might have been related to a family called Reichman, but that was for later.

Her immediate problem was telling Mrs Hakim who now lived in the Austerlitz family's old house on Grabbeallee. The British woman had told her that she wanted to come to Berlin, see the house and, possibly, take photographs on behalf of her client. But given what Sara had just discovered from a colleague about the occupant of Grabbeallee 67, that may present a few problems.

One of them touched her arm and Eva cringed.

'What do you want?'

She spoke English. She knew they understood. Which one of them was it, anyway?

The twin hooked a long fingernail through the weave of her jumper and began to move. Eva followed. There was no point talking; they only spoke to her father.

Luckily, the journey was short although far from sweet. The twin left Eva in front of the unattended toffee apple stand. So her granddaughter had sodded off again.

Eva served the customers waiting for apples and then went to look for Amber. She found her beyond the Drop Tower, where some woman was screaming fit to wet herself, behind a defunct coconut shy. She'd rigged up a makeshift swing and attached it to the branch of a tree. It looked dodgy. But then even if it hadn't, Eva would have disapproved.

'Did Nagyapa put you up to this?' Eva said once Amber had reached the ground.

'No . . .' She looked away.

'You want to fly like he did, you have to start when you're a toddler,' Eva said. 'It's too late now. Give it up.'

'No,' her granddaughter said. 'Nagyapa says I can still fly and I can. You and Mum and Dad just don't want me to because you're scared.'

'Yes,' Eva said, 'and with good cause. You have no idea about the terrible things that happened when Nagyapa flew. He just tells you what he knows you want to hear. You've no idea about him!'

Amber picked up her shoes and slung them over her back by their laces. 'You're always so horrible to Nagyapa. You hate him because you have to look after him.'

79

'That isn't true.'

'Yes, it is.'

'I don't hate him,' Eva said. She didn't, in spite of everything. 'I just don't trust him and neither should you. You've no idea who he is.'

'Oh, and you have?'

'Oh, yes,' Eva said. 'I know who he is. And if I wasn't his daughter, I'd walk across the other side of the street to get away from him.'

Lee was glad to get out of the office. The silence around Mumtaz as she read about the Soviet occupation of Berlin was too much for him. She so obviously didn't want to talk. Vi's phone call had been a godsend.

It was lunchtime and so they met at Nathan's Pies and Eels on the Barking Road. They both had the works – pie, mash, liquor and hot eels.

Vi, whose treat this was, said, 'Thought I'd better have a word after Uncle Bill's performance yesterday.'

Lee smiled. 'I liked him.'

'Crooked as a fiddler's elbow.'

'So tell me something I don't know,' Lee said.

He knew she was in the middle of a massive London-wide investigation into the supply of so-called legal highs, like Spice and Mamba, to homeless people in the capital. So he was grateful she'd made time for him. But then maybe she'd wanted some time out from what had to be a difficult and depressing investigation? Those on

80

the streets, particularly people with mental health issues, were being deliberately targeted by dealers who liked the fact that the most vulnerable in society were also the most silent. Addiction had always been a wonderful gag.

'I never said nothing because I didn't want to have a row with the old scrote, but that copper Bill said he spoke to at the fair in '62 couldn't have lived down Barking Creek because there was no houses down there by then. All of them got destroyed by the floods in 1953. Whoever he was, he would've been moved out to the council estate at Thames View by that time,' Vi said.

'I spoke to a DS called Roy Wilkinson over at Barking on the phone this morning,' Lee said. 'I met him once back in the dark ages. He said he'd have a scout around when he's got a minute.'

Vi dug into a large piece of eel and closed her eyes for a moment as she chewed. Bliss. She said, 'Well, don't worry too much about it because our own Tony Bracci may be able to help you out.'

Why hadn't Lee thought of that? Vi's DS, Tony Bracci, came from a family of Italian ice sellers who'd started their business in Barking Creek.

'Only thought of it this morning,' Vi said. 'He's on leave today, but I'll get him to give you a shout tomorrow.'

He thanked her. Then she said, 'Had a phone call from young Shazia the other day. She's doing criminology at Manchester.'

'Yeah.'

'Did you know she's living with the Huqs?'

Of course he did and Vi would know that, but what she didn't realise was why. Which was the reason she was asking.

Lee kept his head down. 'Yeah. Dunno why.'

He saw Vi shake her head.

'What?'

'I know you know,' Vi said. 'So share.'

'It's between Mumtaz and Shazia,' he said.

'Yeah, but . . .'

Lee suspected Vi knew what he'd done with Mumtaz and he could see she was jealous. She always had been, in spite of the fact, as far as he was concerned, that she and he were just 'fuck buddies'.

'If you want to know, ask Mumtaz or Shazia,' Lee said.

Vi put another piece of eel into her mouth and said, 'You're no fun.'

'The name of the man who now owns the Austerlitz family house is Gunther Beltz,' the woman Mumtaz had come to know as 'Sara' said. 'He is fifty-five, retired and he was an East Berliner until 1989, like me. I didn't know him in those days, I should say, although a colleague of mine did. But of course, he was a member of the Party – we all were.'

'The communist party?'

'Of course. There was no other party in the German Democratic Republic, what we call the DDR. It

82

was not permitted. All were members of the Party, which took care of people's needs for education, healthcare, housing. Provided you always kept to the Party line.'

Mumtaz had been a child when the Berlin Wall had come down, when people from the East had demonstrated their hunger for the freedom to choose a system that wasn't controlled by the Party.

'What is unusual about Herr Beltz is that he inherited the Austerlitz house from his father.'

Mumtaz frowned. 'Unusual?' she said. 'How?'

'Mumtaz, the DDR was a communist state,' Sara said. 'No one owned property. Only those at the very top of the Party could do such a thing, but they were very careful to keep that from the people. Only when the Wall came down did we realise how much they had lied to us.'

'So this Herr Beltz was an MP or something?'

'No,' Sara said. 'But there are a group of people we don't know all the names of even now. Although this man's name was known. Many have been put in prison since Unification. But not all. Not him. There are still, we know, members of the security force known as the Staatssicherheitsdienst, who tortured and killed for the Party, loose on our streets.'

Mumtaz was shocked. She said, 'This man may be one of them?'

'He was one of them.'

'And this Staat . . . I'm sorry I can't say it. Who . . .'

'Oh, they were also known as the Stasi,' Sara said. 'One in four East Germans belonged. I expect you have heard of that name. Gunther Beltz was a member of the Stasi.'

It was one of those days. Firstly, the carrots she was going to use for that evening's soup had boiled over onto the kitchen floor, then her bra had collapsed. Not that what Lesley Jones called her 'norks' were so big they'd burst free. It was just that the bra itself had given up the ghost. Henry the Jack Russell was younger than that bra. So was Techno.

At sixty-two, Lesley wasn't old enough to get a pension, but she wasn't working either. After art school she'd been an art teacher and then, more latterly, a police forensic artist for the Met. But she'd fallen out badly with the police, mainly because of the way she treated witnesses to crime. Which was, were one to be generous, more 'direct' than was strictly necessary. Had Lesley not bought a large, semi-derelict house in Tufnell Park back in the late seventies, she would be what Lee Arnold would call 'skint'. But she had bought that vast house, which she now lived in together with a shifting population of young tenants who paid her a fortune to exist in a place without central heating.

Lesley looked at her computer screen and frowned. Age progressing from a picture of an infant was always a challenge. But this one had been especially tough – hence the lack of attention she'd paid to the carrots. The bra was just age.

A knock at the front door meant that either one of the tenants had lost his or her keys on the Tube or Lee Arnold had arrived. Either way, Henry barked and jumped up and down wetting himself. Just in case it was Arnold, Lesley put the dog in the garden. Henry didn't like men.

She had to squeeze past two pushbikes, her own beloved motorbike and a Victorian painting of Gladstone to get to the front door where she found the only copper she'd managed to get in with when she'd once, briefly, worked for Newham CID. In fact, Lesley had fancied her chances of a romance with him.

When she thought about it, Sara Metzler had heard the name 'Austerlitz' before, in connection with the Hollywood musical star, Fred Astaire. But the family of the pharmacist Dieter Austerlitz and his wife, Miriam, had been unknown to her. This happened. New victims of the Nazis were still coming to light and probably would continue to do so for the foreseeable future.

Of course, the fact that Dieter, his wife and son had all died in the camps was a tragedy. But the idea that the daughter, Rachel, seemed to have just disappeared was intriguing. According to the British woman, someone who had called herself Rachel Austerlitz had arrived in Britain in 1946 with her English husband. But she hadn't been

Jewish. She'd married a Jew and lived as a Jew, but she'd been a Gentile. Was it possible that the Austerlitz family had adopted a Gentile child? Sara didn't think so. Not back in the twenties or thirties when Hitler was on the rise. Jews were already beginning to bear the brunt of German anger even before the Nazis came to power. After all, someone had to be to blame for the Great War and the subsequent humiliation of the German defeat.

Sara wondered whether Rachel had been an imposter. Someone who passed herself off as a Jew in order to try and escape the orgy of rape and pillage that had accompanied the Soviet occupation of Berlin in 1945. There was some anecdotal evidence that may have happened, although it had made no difference to the Russians. They'd taken all and any women they had wanted. But then, in Rachel's case, the soldier who had taken her had been British. And that in itself had been unusual in that sector of the city. Spandau had been captured by the Red Army in 1945 and remained under Soviet tutelage until 1989. Back in the early days there had been some movement between the Western and the Eastern Sectors, but not a lot. Once the Soviets arrived, they tended not to leave.

What was indisputable to Sara was that Rachel Austerlitz was still unaccounted for. And, as a Jewish Berliner, as well as a human being, Sara felt it was her duty to help this British woman

86

find her. When Mumtaz and her business partner came to Berlin she would do all she could to help them. Even if that did mean having to meet a former member of the Stasi.

Sara had seen the file that hated organisation had kept on her once. Afterwards, she'd not stopped shaking for twenty-four hours.

The face on the computer screen wasn't what he'd been expecting. Not that Lee had possessed a particular look in his head. He just hadn't anticipated this one.

'You sure she'd be blonde?' he said as he peered at the image.

'That's grey,' Lesley said. 'She'd be fifty-six now.'

As usual Lesley was standing behind him, far too close. Whether she just had no concept of personal space or she fancied him, Lee didn't know. But he suspected the latter. Which was troubling because, according to Lesley, they were in that massive house all alone.

'Miriam, the kid, had blonde hair,' Lee said.

'Babies often do,' Lesley said. 'Most of them darken. It's why blonde hair is so prized. Associated with youth.'

She was as grey as pewter and had been for as long as Lee had known her.

He could see she'd done well. Although the only photograph that Irving Levy had possessed of his sister had been a mother and baby shot, he could still tell that the projected adult Miriam had evolved from the small child. Lesley, as was her practice, had aged the child in ten-year sections, providing a projected likeness of Miriam at ten, twenty, thirty etc., up to the age of fifty-six.

'Of course, this person's image may have altered due to accident or illness, but this is what I estimate she'd look like now provided she's kept reasonably well,' Lesley said.

In spite of the grey hair, Lesley herself had a face that was almost completely unlined. This she attributed to a vegan diet and a lifetime of cod liver oil.

Miriam Levy didn't look a lot like either of her parents. She was small-boned, but her face was wider than her mother's, her skin darker. Lesley said, 'Her hair would probably have been brown when she was younger.'

'How'd'ya work that out?' Lee said.

'Well, the father had black hair . . .' Lesley began.

'And the mother.' Lee pointed at the photograph of Rachel holding Miriam.

'No,' Lesley said.

He looked up at her. She almost had her hands on his shoulders, which was alarming. Christ!

'The woman's hair is dyed,' Lesley said.

'How do you work that out?'

'The colour's too harsh for her face. It looks matt, unnatural. Trust me.'

'If you say so,' Lee said. He turned back to the screen. 'What about weight?'

'Not easy to estimate because, again, shit can

happen to people,' Lesley said. 'But both parents were slim so it's likely that the daughter wouldn't be big. Although I always adjust things upwards a bit when subjects arrive at middle-age. Most of us stack it on a bit post-fifty.'

She hadn't and nor, Lee observed, had Miriam Levy to any great extent. He moved in closer to the screen and stared into the aged eyes of the woman he was seeking. There was still a sort of vestigial childish joy in them. Was that real or was that just something only Lesley had seen. But then if Lesley had seen it then so could others . . .

Lee felt what he feared was the slap of an unfettered breast against the back of his jacket and he froze. Had Lesley's affections for him turned desperate over time? But then, mercifully he heard the front door open. A young man's voice yelled into the kitchen.

'Les! Can I pay you this month's rent in sex, please?'

CHAPTER 7

The old man didn't take his eyes off the television screen.

'The girl is young; one must let the young make their own choices.'

Eva said, 'You didn't let me.'

'That was different.'

Bela laughed at some nonsense on the screen.

'Gala doesn't want Amber to fly and neither do I,' Eva said. 'I want things to stay as they are. Specifically, I don't want you to meddle. If you didn't encourage the girl, she wouldn't have these ambitions. When you try to change things, nothing good happens.'

He looked at her. 'Haven't you had a good life, Eva?' he said. 'Haven't you always had enough to eat? Somewhere to stay? Work? The love of a man, for a time?'

She shook her head. 'Don't make me say something I don't want to say.'

'In case my poor old heart can't take it?' he said.

'No. In case I can't take it,' she replied. 'In case I say something we both know I shouldn't.'

He turned back to the television screen.

★   ★   ★

He'd forgotten how far the Arnold Agency's office was from Upton Park Tube Station. Almost in Forest Gate, for God's sake! And then there were the stairs. By the time he arrived at the private investigator's office, Irving Levy was exhausted. Just as well Lee Arnold had bottled water and made a very good strong cup of tea.

'I would've come to you,' the PI said as he put the drinks down in front of him.

'Ach, I have to come this way to get home,' Irving said. 'I may get a taxi from here.'

It was eight o'clock in the evening, which wasn't late for an experienced diamond man. Some of them worked well into the night. But he could tell that Lee Arnold was eager to be elsewhere. Mrs Hakim was nowhere to be seen.

'I wanted you to see what the forensic artist came up with using your family photograph,' Lee said. He laid an A4 sheet of paper down in front of him. 'This is Miriam now.'

His mother had never allowed her hair to turn grey. Even as an old woman she'd kept it black and, in latter years, it had looked dreadful. Falling over her shoulders like limp, black strings. But he could see her in this stranger's eyes. That look she always gave a person whereby they would feel she knew things that strictly she couldn't. Or shouldn't.

'She doesn't look like me,' he said. 'She was, as I recall, darker-skinned than me.'

'This ageing technique is thought to be pretty accurate. But obviously not a hundred per cent.

So what do you think? Is the impression what you expected?'

'I have no way of knowing,' he said. God, that face was making him sad! He'd hoped for maybe some recognition, but that only existed in the eyes and that made him want to weep. In his dreams Miriam was beautiful, like his mother. But this woman wasn't beautiful. Her nose was squat, like a pig's, and her eyes slanted downwards, the opposite direction from his own. 'I don't know.'

Maybe sensing that the image had unnerved him, Lee Arnold said, 'It just gives us something to go on. That's all.'

'It's good . . .'

'Ex-police artist,' he said.

Irving handed the A4 sheet back.

Lee Arnold said, 'Oh, that's for you. I've got me own copy.'

'Ah, yes.'

He took it reluctantly. He didn't really want it.

Lee Arnold said, 'We've also found out some more about your mother's old house in Berlin.'

He was glad of the change of subject. He put the photograph in his pocket. 'Oh?'

'Yes, we have the current owner's name, a Herr Gunther Beltz.'

He looked at Irving as if he maybe thought that name should be familiar to him, but it wasn't.

'Inherited it from his father, apparently,' the PI continued. 'But because Spandau was East Berlin in those days, of course that must've been dodgy.'

Made sense. In the communist world where all property was theft . . .

'Turns out Herr Beltz was a member of the East German Security Forces.'

Irving wasn't a political animal, but he did remember that the East German security forces were greatly feared. He also remembered what they had been called. He said, 'The Stasi.'

'Yes,' Lee said. 'I thought they'd all been tucked away donkey's years ago. But apparently not. This is all Mumtaz's work. She contacted a local synagogue and they've been very helpful. But, given who the current owner of your mother's house is, there may be some problems gaining access.'

'I have no issues with East Germany,' Irving said. 'My only desire is to see what it looks like now.'

'Which is why I think that you should come to Berlin,' Lee said.

Irving shook his head. 'Even though I am in remission, the drugs I must take to keep things this way, as well as the ones I must then use to counteract the side effects of my medication, mean that if I travel I must get documentation from my consultant. It's a major operation and I'm not sure that I'm up to it.'

'I understand that,' Lee said, 'but I'm worried that someone who belonged to an organisation like the Stasi may be guarded and secretive, and I believe that you as a relative of the previous owner . . .'

'I have nothing to prove that. My mother came here empty-handed.'

And yet to see that house . . . When he'd originally discovered that his mother wasn't the person she had claimed to be, Irving had wondered whether the key to who she actually was remained somewhere in that house. Logically, after a devastating war and years of Soviet rule, that was unlikely. Also, he had no way of knowing, now that his father was dead, whether his parents had actually met in that house. Maybe his mother had been a prostitute his father had met and fallen in love with somewhere else in Berlin? Such things had happened. And yet if the house had remained in the hands of just one family ever since the war, there was a possibility that they had retained some of the original contents . . .

'I just think that it would be more compelling, for this Herr Beltz, if you came too,' Lee Arnold said. 'Also, I think you want to come, don't you?'

Irving smiled. 'To see Berlin and maybe find some clue to this mystery? Of course I do,' he said. 'But I also don't want to burden yourself and Mrs Hakim should I become ill.'

'So speak to your doctor,' the PI said. 'And when we get back the fair will almost be upon us. As you said yourself, Irving, this is a big job. And we're all on an uncertain timescale.'

That was a nice, tactful way of putting it. But then Lee Arnold and Mrs Hakim were nice people. In fact, they were probably the nicest people he'd met for a long time. Irving said, 'I'll make an appointment with my doctor as soon as I can.'

She'd expected him to call or even turn up in person, but hearing his voice still came as a shock.

'Good evening, Wahid-ji,' she said.

Her hand shook as it held the phone up to her ear. This was the man who had planned to marry her Shazia. Wahid Sheikh was the brother of local gangster Rizwan Sheikh, a scumbag, now disabled by a stroke, to whom her late husband had been in debt when he died. In reality, she had paid her husband Ahmet's debt some years ago, but then blackmail had come into the equation. Mumtaz had seen the man who had stabbed her abusive husband one evening on Wanstead Flats. Naz Sheikh, favourite son of Rizwan, had been almost like her saviour at the time. As she'd watched Ahmet bleed out into dry grass, she'd given silent thanks to Naz for ending her misery. Only later had she discovered just who her 'saviour' was and why he had killed her husband. She'd fought to save Shazia from the pain of knowing that she, her stepmother, had effectively killed her father and the Sheikh family had exploited that. This had resulted in seventy-year-old Wahid demanding Shazia's hand in marriage. And so Mumtaz had told the girl the truth herself. Shazia had left her that very day.

'I'm still paying you. What do you want?' Mumtaz said.

95

She knew that the wedding the old man had planned had been organised through the Sheikhs' various companies and associates and that, in reality, Wahid Sheik had laid out no money of his own at all. But she was a pragmatist, she'd known all along there would be a price for his 'disappointment'.

'Now my doctor tells me I have a problem with my prostate,' the old man said. 'I cannot but think that, had I a wife to care for me, my life would be both pleasanter and cheaper. I will need an operation and then I must buy in care . . .'

'So buy it in,' Mumtaz said. 'Use the money I still pay you to keep away.'

'I fear it will have to increase,' he said.

There had been a time when she'd almost been free. When she'd finally got her courage up to tell Lee. It hadn't been easy. In spite of the terrible things the Sheikhs did to everyone around them, she'd felt like a traitor to her community. Lee had said he'd gather evidence on the family and when he had enough, he'd make sure he got them put away. But then they'd slept together, which had ruined everything. Now he didn't seem to care any more . . .

'I give you what I can whilst not putting myself on the street,' Mumtaz said. 'You have many successful businesses, Wahid-ji. You are a wealthy man.'

'I manage,' he said. She imagined him smiling, like the harmless old man he wasn't. 'But my health has broken down since your daughter disappointed me so badly.'

'She's—'

'Oh, I know where she is, Mrs Hakim,' he said. 'With your parents.'

Of course he knew!

'Now if she would change her mind . . .'

'That's not happening,' Mumtaz said. 'Leave her—'

'Oh, I will. But it will be contingent upon an increased fee,' he said. 'No one is as sorry as I.'

And then he ended the call. Mumtaz allowed herself a flash of anger as she threw her handset across the room and shouted, 'Fuck you!'

She'd already lost her house, all her valuables and her beloved stepdaughter due to these bastards! Her breath became short and laboured. She attempted to calm herself. At least Naz was dead, she had that to be grateful for. Murdered by a Pole he was pressuring to commit violent acts for him. He'd deserved to die. It was just a pity the Pole hadn't taken a few more Sheikhs out too. Because those that remained were still blighting her life and, so far, she couldn't see an end in sight.

Walking was good. Walking worked. At least it had always done so for Sara Metzler. And, even at night, her walking very often led her to this place, the Soviet War Memorial in Treptower Park. Not that the memorial was just a statue or even a group of structures. It was a vast complex of immense red granite sculptures, heroic statues and sixteen huge sarcophagi representing the five thousand Soviet soldiers who had died during the Battle of Berlin in 1945. As a child of East Berlin, Sara had visited the park with the school many times. Her teachers had, she clearly remembered, been at particular pains to show them the figure of a heroic Soviet soldier standing over the remains of a broken swastika.

'That,' her history teacher Frau Mueller had told them all, 'is what happens to fascism.'

The subtext to that being, of course, that 'if you Germans ever give Russians any problems ever again, we will kill you.' It was fair enough and, as a Jew, Sara understood and was, for many years, grateful to the Soviets for saving her family from certain death. That was until she found out the truth.

When her mother was taken ill for the last time in the 1980s, Sara had already become disillusioned with the DDR. Not being allowed to have your own opinions, listening to endless bombastic nonsense dressed up as fact was galling, while being followed and having your every move recorded by the hated Stasi was terrifying. When Mrs Hakim had contacted her from London about the Austerlitz family and she'd found that their old house had been settled by an ex-Stasi operative, she hadn't been surprised. Stasi officers always got what they wanted.

Before her mother, just prior to her death, had

told Sara about her father, she had fantasised that maybe he was in the Stasi. But it was worse than that. He had been a Soviet officer, maybe even one of those who had raped her mother in 1945. After all, a lot of them never went home. That Gerda Metzler had been a Jew who had suffered at the hands of the Nazis had meant nothing to them. But it had meant a lot to Sara because she suddenly didn't know who she was. Or rather, she realised that she had never known.

Of course, the English woman hadn't told her a huge amount about her client. A member of the Austerlitz family, apparently, or so he had thought. Too sick to leave the UK himself, he was sending Mrs Hakim and her business partner instead. Although what they might find was anyone's guess. Foreigners came to the city all the time looking for answers. The children of Nazis, grandchildren of Holocaust victims, the mad, the sad, the lost. Few found anything that improved their lives or even provided some enlightenment about their past. Where so much death and destruction had happened, was it too much to expect revelation? Probably.

A sound of laughter caught her attention and Sara watched as a group of black-clad young people ran past her and disappeared into a tangle of bushes. Probably, she thought, on their way to Spreepark, the old abandoned fairground on the banks of the River Spree. Once an East German pleasure park, it was now abandoned, providing entertainment only to young urban explorers.

But then Sara didn't miss it. Such places, which dealt in organised fun, had always struck her as sinister. Mainly because those who ran them were merely playing a part. Nothing in such places was real. If anything, Spreepark was a metaphor for the whole entity that had once been the DDR.

'Do they ever sleep?'

Amber's father looked up from his paperwork and said, 'Ask your grandfather. Far as I know, he's the only one who actually talks to them.'

Amber continued to look out of the caravan window at the 'Siamese' twins, Ping and Pong. They were standing quite still in front of her great-grandfather's caravan.

'Some people say they can speak English and others say they can't,' Amber said. 'I was thinking the other day, I've never actually heard them say anything more than single words.'

'I'm surprised,' her father said.

She frowned.

David Sanders looked up from his figures again and said, 'Because of all the time you spend with them. And yes, your mother's told me.'

Amber felt her face turn red.

'It's those two who rig up the dodgy flying equipment you try to use. Don't deny it, Amber. Your mum told me all about it. I know you love your nagyapa, but he's old, he lives in the past and he's got no concept of health and safety. Ditto the

Twins. Old Bela may well have been the best flier in the world back in the year dot . . .'

'He was,' Amber said. 'He's shown me photos. He performed all over Europe. He was presented to the King of Greece and Adolf Hitler.'

'Adolf isn't someone you boast about, Amber.'

'I know, but—'

'You're a fairground kid,' David said. 'Like me and your mum. This isn't a circus. If it had been you'd have trained for that, but it isn't. Nagyapa was flying from the moment he was born back in Nowhere, Hungary. Now he's as old as God, he's reliving his past. Forget it and don't hang about with the Twins. You know they cause trouble. Now let me get on with this paperwork, will you? Enough to drive me mad.'

What he didn't add was that they also always did whatever Bela Horvathy wanted and that was usually a bad thing. Old Bela, he thought now, probably liked being introduced to Adolf Hitler. He had been, David reckoned, a man after the old bastard's own black heart. A lot of Hungarians had capitulated with the Nazis when they'd invaded the country in 1944 and, although Bela had always maintained he had been in the Resistance, David had always doubted that. The old man, in his experience, was sly. Dodgier even, he sometimes thought, than those vile Twins. God alone knew who and what they were.

CHAPTER 8

Lee Arnold had expected sod all from Barking nick regarding a copper from Barking Creek – and he'd got it. But, nudged by Vi Collins, Tony Bracci had come up with enough to ask Lee to meet him at what had once been Barking Creek's pub, the Crooked Billet.

Needing to get to Forest Gate nick for nine, Tony had asked Lee to meet him at seven, which meant that the PI was even more red-eyed than usual. This wasn't helped by the early morning mist that, so locals had it, tended in reality to hang over the Creek for most of the time. As he watched Bracci walk towards him, Lee sucked hard on the fag he hoped would keep the mist at bay.

'Morning, mate.'

Tony Bracci, blonde of hair and fair of skin, was the most unlikely Italian Lee had ever met. And yet the family were well-known, both as ice merchants years back and as staunch members of the local Catholic community. Lee remembered Tony's dad, Carlo, well. Unlike his son, he'd had black hair and skin the colour of tanned hide.

'Tone.'

Lee held his hand out, which Tony shook.

'Old Billet looks a bit sad these days, don't it?'

Both men looked up at a nondescript building covered in 'Keep Out' signs and partially hidden by chain-link fencing. It seemed to bear no relation to the tatty 1930s boozer they'd both once known. A truck carrying concrete blocks, bounced along the pot-holed surface of River Road in the direction of the massive Barking Creek Barrier and then turned off into a yard full of shipping containers. The area still retained its old connections to the river and seafaring even though it was difficult these days to catch sight of either the Creek or the Thames.

'So . . .' Tony rubbed his hands together. 'I was born on Thames View, as you know. But the grandparents and me dad, until he was twenty-five, lived here. Back in those days it was called Creekmouth Village, but it was completely destroyed in the flood of 1953. The whole lot of us were moved to the Thames View Estate. But, according to my Aunt Cissy, we all kept in touch. Very tight-knit it was here and, although most of the old inhabitants of the village worked at the Lawes Chemical Factory back in the old days, some of them, like my family, did other things. Sadly for some of the more lively oiks, one family was all coppers.'

'Did you know them?' Lee asked.

'No. But Auntie Cissy – she weren't Italian, but married me Uncle Mario – she did. Name of Askew.'

Lee said, 'She still alive, your aunt?'

'No,' Tony said, 'but me cousin, Chiara, her daughter is like the historian of the family, goes on websites what tell you who your great-uncle twice removed was. So when the guv told me what you was up to last night, I give Chiara a bell. She told me the Askews still live on Thames View on Stanley Avenue, across the road from me Uncle Mario. He's got dementia now, poor sod, so he don't know what time of day it is. But Chiara and her brother used to play with the Askew kids from time to time and she still knows a woman called Brenda who's got an old uncle who may be who you're looking for.'

'Great. So why . . .'

'Did I want you to meet me here?' He smiled. 'Because Chiara is going to meet us here. Should be along to open up the caff across the road any minute.'

That was the first time that Lee had realised there was anything as civilised as a caff in the area. Although what Tony was looking at looked like nothing more than a garden shed.

He'd got up at the crack of dawn to telephone the doctor's surgery, but even so he hadn't been able to get an appointment that morning. So many booked online now, it just wasn't right. But the receptionist with the posh voice had given him a really early slot the next day and so Irving knew he should be grateful. Advance appointments very rarely happened these days.

The park was already open and so, although it was in the opposite direction to Barking Tube Station, he went in. All the usual early morning crew were in evidence: dog walkers, joggers, alcoholics, kids smoking with their mates in the bushes before school. Digging was impossible this time of day and besides he had no energy. Also, although he couldn't stop himself doing it sometimes, he knew really that even if Miriam had been buried in the park, her body was going to be deeper down than he could manage. Maybe he'd come back after work?

In two weeks' time the fair would come. He'd been several times over the years, but it still frightened him. Those Siamese twins were long gone, or at least he'd never seen them since that terrible day when Miriam had been taken. Freak shows like that were a thing of the past. But the fair still made his blood run cold. Such shifting bands of people always had to be suspect. He could still remember his father talking about 'Gypsies and vagabonds' whenever the fair arrived. Understandable in light of what had happened to Miriam, even though his father never spoke her name. Also, Irving had the feeling his father had taken a dim view of travelling folk a long time before his daughter went missing. Strange in one whose race was considered a 'wandering' nation. Maybe it was because the Levys had been in England for many generations?

Irving decided to walk once around the lake and

then head for the station. A woman was being dragged along by a Rottweiler whilst trying to talk to a man with a pug. It was impossible. People were ridiculous. The things they did very often didn't make any sense. His father had hated the fair and yet he'd let his wife and children go to mix with the 'Gypsies and vagabonds' without a murmur. Or had he? Maybe Rachel had taken them in spite of him. He was, after all, mostly at work in those days. Irving couldn't remember. But what he did know was that it was only after Miriam's disappearance that his parents' rows began. Had they been caused, at least in part, by the fact that his mother had taken the children to the fair without her husband's consent? In those days, particularly amongst religious Jews, women did very little without telling their husbands. But then, of course, his mother hadn't been Jewish, had she? And so maybe her visit to the fair had been by way of a statement about who she really was?

Irving hoped that he found at least some trace of her if or when he went to Berlin with Lee Arnold. Whoever she had been.

'He's not gone in the head like Dad. He just can't get about because of his hips.'

Tony Bracci's cousin, Chiara, was a plump woman in her mid sixties. She had short, fat legs, a bosom the size of a bookshelf and masses of dyed red hair, which sprouted from her head in every possible direction. She also made a brilliant fry-up for which she'd take no payment from either her cousin or Lee Arnold.

Once she'd fed all her regulars – blokes working on local building sites, truckers, a cab driver who may or may not have been her boyfriend – she joined Tony and Lee at their table outside the caff and lit a cigarette. She'd begun talking about a bloke called Tommy Askew, her friend Brenda's uncle, immediately. Apparently he was the youngest of three brothers who'd all been in the Job. The other two were long dead.

'I'm sure he'd be happy to talk to you about the old days, love,' Chiara told Lee.

'I'd be grateful if he could,' Lee said.

'He has a carer go in twice a day now, but only to do jobs for him. Me and Brenda take him a dinner a couple of times a week. He likes a plate of pasta. Still got all his marbles.'

'Do you know if he was ever called to the fair at Barking Park?'

Chiara shrugged. 'I dunno, love. Possibly. I know his brother Ray done the carnival a couple of times. In fact, I think he married a carnival princess, although you'd never have known it to look at her.'

Tony smiled.

'You can laugh all you like, Tone,' she said. 'But you must remember old Rita Askew, face like a smacked arse.'

Lee used to be taken to Barking Carnival by his mum when he was a kid. He remembered it as a fun evening out where he and his brother, Roy, were allowed to stay up late and look at lots of pretty girls dressed like bridesmaids. But it had nothing to do with the fair.

'Can you ask Tommy if he'll see me?' Lee said.

'Yeah.'

He picked up his phone. 'If I text you my mobile number, can you let me know?'

'You can give me your number any time, love,' Chiara said and then told him her number.

Once he'd sent her the text, Lee said, 'I don't want to put pressure on the old bloke, but if he can see me soon . . .'

'He ain't going nowhere,' Chiara said.

They all knew that wasn't necessarily the case, but no one said anything.

When they finally left the caff, Lee said to Tony, 'Nice breakfast. I'll probably come back.'

Tony smiled. 'Just be careful of Chiara,' he said. 'She's been single for years. Them extra-thick rashers of bacon may come at a price.'

In common with most of the Arnold Agency's 'casual' operatives, Jasvinder Patel and Mike Craig were both ex-coppers. And while Mike had only done ten years in the job, Jas had worked fifteen years, three of those in CID. It was therefore to Jas that Mumtaz gave the more complicated case. It involved discreet surveillance of a woman suspected by her husband of having an affair. It needed to be handled carefully as the suspected 'other man' had strong links with organised crime. Mike, on the other hand, had a full day's worth of process serving from Dagenham to Shepherd's Bush.

Once she'd allocated jobs, Mumtaz sat down at her desk to look at her e-mails. But then her phone rang.

'Arnold Agency. How can I help you?'

'Oh.' It was a woman's voice. 'Oh, is Lee in?'

'No, not yet,' Mumtaz said. 'Can I help you?'

'I've tried his mobile, but all I get is voicemail,' the woman said.

'He's with a client, I understand.'

Mumtaz didn't know that. All Lee had told her was that he was going to be late.

'Oh.'

'Is there anything I can help you with?' Mumtaz asked.

There was a pause.

'I am his business partner.'

'Mrs Hakim?'

'That's it,' Mumtaz said.

The woman sounded pleasant enough. Probably middle-aged, slight estuary accent . . .

'My name's Amanda Patterson,' the woman said. 'I work for the *Ilford Recorder*.'

Mumtaz knew the name. Mandy was Lee's AA sponsor. He'd also contacted her about Barking Park Fair.

'Oh, yes.'

'My late dad was, like me, a reporter on the

Recorder and Lee asked me to look something up for him in my old man's archive.'

'About Barking Fair, yes, I remember him saying.'

'Well, I've got something,' Mandy said. 'But I'm not sure whether it's what he wanted. I can't find anything about the little girl who went missing in the early sixties, but Dad did cover a story about an accident at the fair in sixty-eight.'

'I see.'

Probably irrelevant by the sound of it and so Mumtaz said, 'Shall I ask him to give you a call when he gets in?'

'Probably best,' Mandy said. 'He's got my number.'

And then she hung up.

Mumtaz turned to her computer and opened her e-mail. It was heaving with messages, most of which were spam and other rubbish. She decided to make herself a cup of tea. The call she'd had from Wahid Sheikh last night had left her unable to sleep properly and so she was tired. But then what had she expected? Denying that family anything wasn't something one just 'got away' with. When she'd told the old man he wasn't marrying her daughter, had she really expected him to just go away? Time had passed and so maybe she had.

But that had been a mistake. Now back in the real world again, she'd have to find some more money from somewhere.

★ ★ ★

'Can I help you with anything?'

Ever since she had retired from her job as a cleaner, Sara Metzler had filled her life with reading, walking and volunteering as an archivist at the synagogue. She had never dwelt on the fact that back in the old days of the DDR she'd been a respected translator of, very carefully vetted, English textbooks. She had deliberately filled her life. However, maybe, in the case of this Austerlitz business, she was filling it a little too much.

'Ah . . .'

The man who stood in front of her was tall, dark and didn't look happy. But then why would he be when she, a stranger, had been staring at his house for fifteen minutes?

What she said was lame.

'You have a beautiful house . . .'

'Yes, it is, but . . .'

He was actually quite good-looking. But then, contrary to popular belief, a lot of them had been. Honeytraps could not be set using any old rubbish.

Suddenly, he smiled. 'I apologise for my tone, Frau,' he said. 'But I'm not accustomed to having people stare at my house. Do you, possibly, have a connection to it?'

One always had to be careful what one said to the Stasi and, so Sara had been reading, that applied particularly in the case of what had then been young, eager operatives like Gunther Beltz. The photograph she'd googled of him didn't do him justice. Like the house at number 67 Grabbeallee,

Herr Beltz was much larger and more attractive than his picture.

Sara said, 'No. I am simply just a person who appreciates architecture.'

She wasn't lying. She did. And the four-storey house was impressive. Though constructed of grey stone, which gave it a rather dour appearance, it had a charm that Sara associated with venerable houses from the nineteenth century. Such places exhibited attention to detail in their finely proportioned windows, mature gardens and ornate entrances. Many buildings like this had been destroyed in World War II – too many.

'I like it,' the man said. But he didn't elaborate upon the subject or give his name. But then he wouldn't.

'Do you know—'

'I'm afraid I can't tell you anything about it,' he interrupted. 'And even if I could, I have to work.'

'Oh . . .'

'I am a writer,' he said. 'I saw you from the window of my office. And now I must go.'

He turned on his heel and walked away in a very stiff, what some might interpret as a Prussian manner.

He didn't and hadn't told Sara to go, but she knew that was what he wanted.

And once she had gone, Gunther Beltz switched his camera back on and looked at the photograph he'd taken of the woman through his French windows.

★　　★　　★

Lee waited for Mumtaz to go on her lunch break before he phoned Mandy back. He knew that was petty and stupid – he did need to share information about the Levy case with her. But this morning she had been even more monosyllabic than usual and it had pissed him off. How long was this guilt she carried about their one night of passion going to continue? And when was he going to be able to stop obsessing about it?

'Hi, Mand,' he said when she picked up the call. 'Mumtaz said you had some info about Barking Fair?'

'Probably not what you were after,' Mandy said. 'But looking through Dad's old toot I did come across one story he covered that happened in the park. Not the missing baby, I'm afraid.'

'Oh.'

'The story Dad covered happened in 1968,' she said. 'September . . .'

'Fair season.'

'Right.' She read, "Police were called to an incident at Barking Park Fair on Saturday 21st September 1968 at approximately 7 p.m. A fairground employee, a woman, had fallen onto a cooking fire and sustained extensive burns. Thought to be a Hungarian national, it is said that the woman's name is Mrs Horvathy. She was taken to the London Hospital at Whitechapel where she remains in a critical condition."'

'Blimey, why couldn't she get out of the fire? What was she, ninety?'

113

'I don't know,' Mandy said. 'Maybe she was pissed. But she died. Two days later. Again, Dad only wrote what in effect was a note. He didn't say anything about her age, her family – nothing. I suppose such people just pass through, don't they. And what with her not being English . . . Apparently no suspicion of foul play.'

'Seems the fair's had its share of tragedy,' Lee said.

'Those things give me the creeps,' Mandy said. 'They've always got dodgy blokes working on the rides who take unnecessary risks and pinch your bum.'

'They've never pinched mine,' Lee said.

'Oh, you know what I mean – girls' bums.'

'Does your dad's report say where she's buried?'

'No,' Mandy said. 'Just another dead foreigner. People didn't give too much of a shit back in those days.'

'No,' Lee said. 'No, they didn't.'

Then, when he'd put the phone down, he began thinking about Miriam Levy again. Had the search for her been less thorough than it should have been because the kid had been Jewish?

Another night of no sleep wasn't going to do her any good at all. Sara Metzler got up and went into her kitchen. She opened the drawer where she kept her medicines and took out a packet of sleeping tablets. She took two.

She shouldn't have gone to the Austerlitz house; it had unnerved her. She didn't really know why.

114

She had no connection to the family and Gunther Beltz, in spite of his past, had been perfectly pleasant to her. No, it was the house itself that had upset her and she didn't know why.

Was it just simply due to the connection it had to the lost Jew, Rachel Austerlitz? Sara went back to bed and closed her eyes. She would feel better when the woman from England and her partner came. At present she felt very alone with this, even though she knew that if she wanted she could talk to any of her colleagues at the synagogue. But somehow she didn't want to. She knew it was irrational, but that most of them were West Germans put her off. When the Wall came down in 1989, loads of them had moved east in order to take advantage of lower property prices and that still rankled. Very few easterners lived in big houses even now. Only those, like Gunther Beltz, who had clearly played the game on both sides of the old divide.

What secrets, she wondered, did he hold in the darkest recesses of his heart? And what evidence of those secrets existed in his house?

CHAPTER 9

Irving Levy didn't mind when they went to Berlin, as long as it was soon. Where they stayed was up to Mumtaz and so she booked them all onto a British Airways flight from City Airport in three days' time, and chose a hotel that was central and, from the photographs online, looked comfortable. They would stay for four nights, which meant that they would arrive on the Monday and leave on Friday morning. There was little point being in the city at the weekend when so many businesses and services would be closed.

She was, however, nervous about Mr Levy's state of health.

'I hope he's going to be up to this trip,' she told Lee when he came back into the office with a bag of doughnuts for what he considered his breakfast. It was 11 a.m.

'His doctor reckons he can go, so who are we to argue?' he said. He sat down. 'We're more likely to get into that house with him in tow.'

'I know you think that . . .'

'Yes, I do,' he said and fixed her with a look that said he wasn't open to contradiction.

His phone rang. Mumtaz went to the small bathroom at the back of the office and splashed cold water on her face. She hated this awkwardness between her and Lee, but she didn't know what to do to put it right. She knew that she was as much, if not more, to blame than he was. But she also knew that she had a lot on her plate. Even though Shazia wasn't talking to her, the girl was starting university at the end of the month, and then there was the issue of an extra £150 a month for Wahid Sheikh. Lee would go mad if he knew she was hiding that from him, but she didn't even know how to begin a conversation about it.

When she returned to the office, Lee had just put his phone down.

'I'm going out,' he said.

'Oh?'

'That old ex-copper I had a lead on from Tony Bracci wants me to pop round,' he said. 'Turns out he was on the Levy investigation back in '62. Probably be a good idea for you to come with me.'

And it was a good idea. This elderly policeman could possibly provide some more information about Miriam Levy's disappearance. But being in a car alone with Lee wasn't something she looked forward to. Enclosed and alone, awkward subjects could arise. Would they either just sit in silence or would he interrogate her about why she was behaving as if she was ashamed of him? It was a fair question. Even if it was one she didn't want to hear.

She heard him say, 'Well? Coming?'
And so she said, 'Yes.'

The little bitch was off doing her own thing again. Amber knew it was half-price day and so the site would be heaving. Even those slutty mates of hers, Lulu Lee and Misty Dobos, were on the booths taking money. Where was she?

Gala Sanders had never felt that her daughter had given her much respect. David, her husband, was an easy-going man who came from a laid-back family of old-fashioned English showmen. All the kids in that family ran wild. The only person Amber ever really listened to was her nagyapa – a man who had largely ignored Gala for most of her life. Or so she felt. The reason her mother had given her for this was that Bela was a very moral man who couldn't cope with the idea that Gala had been born out of wedlock. It was nonsense. The old man just didn't care. Gala had always felt his ambivalence, which was one of the reasons why she'd refused to learn his language, or teach her daughter.

A big gaggle of kids in school uniform poked fivers for their half-price wristbands through the hatch at her and one of them said, 'Eight.'

'What, eight of you bunking off school, is it?' Gala said.

One boy said, 'We got teacher training day, innit.'

'So why you wearing your uniforms?' Gala said.

The kids drifted away leaving only abuse in their wake.

'Old slag!'

'Fuck you, man!'

'Cunt!'

She'd heard it all before as had the people who came after the kids.

'Two please,' a bloke in a tracksuit standing next to a pregnant woman said.

'Ten quid.'

The bloke handed over the money. Gala gave him his wristbands and then served a small group of pensioners.

Nagyapa and even her mother would have just taken the school kids' money and let the buggers in. Their attitude was always 'it's their responsibility, not ours.' It excused anything and Gala hated it. The only place it didn't work was amongst family, and there you did as Nagyapa said whatever the outcome. Gala knew he was encouraging Amber to fly. That was probably where she was now, rigging up a temporary trapeze somewhere on the site, no doubt with the Twins in tow. Too scary to be exposed to the punters, Ping and Pong lurked amongst the caravans, always ready to do Nagyapa's bidding. All Gala's life they'd given her the creeps. The way they only spoke in whispers and then in ways only Nagyapa could understand. And what her mother had said about them, years ago, when Gala was a child, still resonated in her head now.

'Don't ever make Nagyapa choose between you and those two,' Eva had said, 'because he will choose them, every time.'

'Cor blimey, I think everyone from Ripple Road to Faircross come out looking for that kiddie. I can still remember the mother screaming. As if she was being burned alive.'

Tommy Askew was in his early eighties. He had bright, intelligent blue eyes, a face that smiled easily and the twisted, shrunken body of the severe arthritic. Lee Arnold thought that life was a bitch.

'Course, we was trying to conduct an organised search, and so when every Tom, Dick and Harry turned up, it made our job harder than it should've been.'

Lee said, 'Did you interview anyone?'

'No, that was CID's job. But I nattered with people. I was just a constable at the time and so I was there to show the uniform and provide muscle in case the situation turned rough. But it never. I never had a problem with the travelling people, myself. I know they ain't welcome everywhere, but on the two occasions I come across them, I never had no bother.'

'Two occasions?'

'The Levy baby was one and then a few years later we got called out to an accident involving one of the travelling ladies.'

'Was that the woman who fell on the fire in 1968?' Lee asked.

'That's it,' Tommy said. He took a couple of tablets from a bottle on the table next to his elbow and took them with water. 'Sorry about that – painkillers.' Then he continued, 'That was an eye-opener.'

Mumtaz, who had up until that time been silent, said, 'In what way, Mr Askew?'

Tommy shifted in his chair and grimaced as he moved. He said, 'They still had freak shows back in them days. When we was called in on the Miriam Levy job, the brother of the baby had been inside with all the tattooed men and bearded ladies. To be fair, they was taking care of the little fella. Just normal folk, really. But then at the back of the tent were these – what they called? – 'Siamese twins'. Joined all down one side they was, so one had the left arm and the other the right, if you see what I mean. Every time the Levy kid looked at them, he screamed harder, and I don't blame him. They give me the right willies. Cold, dead eyes and strange fingers like twigs. I could shudder now just thinking about it. But anyway, when the lady died in the fire in '68, I saw them again. But this time they weren't joined. Most of them Siamese twins shows was a scam, but I was still shocked to see it.'

Mumtaz remembered what Irving Levy had said about the Siamese twins, how they had frightened him, and wondered whether he knew they had been a con.

'Them two, the Twins, they found the woman

in the fire,' Tommy said. 'Weeping like their mother had died. Turned out the woman weren't nothing to do with them, although they was all Hungarian.'

Lee took his phone out and looked at his note-book. 'Called Mrs Horvathy,' he said.

'That's it,' Tommy said. 'Big woman. Had a husband and a little girl.'

'So the Siamese twins were Hungarian?' Mumtaz said.

'That's what they spoke,' Tommy said. 'The dead woman's husband had to translate. But then it weren't, according to old Sergeant Riches, who was my guv'nor at the time, suspicious. The poor woman had been practising some sort of act and had fallen in the fire and that was it. Stan Riches had no time for foreigners.'

He looked sad.

Mumtaz said, 'What did you think, Mr Askew?'

The old man shifted painfully in his chair once again. 'Me?' he said. 'I thought someone pushed her in the fire. I never looked closely at the poor lady. Last I saw of her was when she was being took to the London Hospital screaming her head off. But I did see that she had a rope round her neck.'

'Like she'd been hung?'

'Or something,' he said. 'Story was she'd been trying out some sort of escapology trick when she had her accident. But, not being funny, the woman had to be forty if she was a day and she was a good twenty stone. That, to me, was more than foreigners being odd. That was impossible. But then it was declared an accident, so what could I do? The fair moved on; the woman's buried in Rippleside Cemetery. Catholic funeral. I was one of the few people who went.'

'What about her family?' Lee asked.

'I never saw the husband or no one,' Tommy said. 'Just me, the undertaker, the priest and some woman done up like a Victorian widow. Probably one of them ghoulish types who like to go to strangers' funerals.'

Luckily, neither her dadu nor her didima were at home when she got in. Shazia ran up the four flights of stairs to her bedroom, closed the door behind her and then stood panting against it. She hadn't seen the man who had thought he was to be her husband for months. But then suddenly and strangely far away from his native manor of Newham, he'd turned up on Brick Lane. And he'd smiled at her.

Shazia had nearly screamed. Surrounded by posh girls in vintage dresses and Dr Martens boots, she hadn't felt able to say anything to him. So she'd just run away. Wahid Sheikh, God damn him! She'd hoped never to see him again! And there was no reason why she should, unless . . .

Since she'd stopped speaking to Mumtaz, over *him*, she had no idea what might be going on with her amma and that accursed family. She had assumed, maybe because it was easier to do so, that now they had no hold over Amma in terms of what they could tell Shazia, that they had no leverage with Mumtaz at all. But then maybe she was wrong? The old man had looked so pleased with himself, she couldn't help thinking that he had sought her out deliberately.

As she began to calm down, Shazia went and sat on her bed. She was going to university at the end of the month. What could the old bastard do to her now? She knew the truth about her father's death. In spite of the fact that he had been her father, she understood why Mumtaz had let him die. She wasn't sure she wouldn't have done the same herself. It was the fact that her amma had used her as part of a battle she hoped would eventually undermine the Sheikhs' hold over them that had caused their rift. Seemingly it had worked, and Shazia had wondered whether she should contact Mumtaz again and make things up with her before she went to uni. But seeing the old man again had changed her mind. By the expression on his face, he hadn't given up his pursuit of the Hakim women – quite the reverse.

'We had that park apart searching for the Levy baby,' Tommy said. 'Scoured every bush and flower bed. We even had blokes in the boating lake and what was, then, the lido. Went through all them poor buggers' vans – they didn't have much, poor sods. We found nothing. Not even the toy the kiddie was supposed to have taken with her. Course the locals blamed the fairground folk and they blamed the locals. Wasn't much fun at the fair for several years after. Fights between travellers and locals, that sort of thing.'

'Do you have any sort of theory about what happened to Miriam?' Lee asked.

'I think she was took,' he said.

'Did you dig?'

'We did, but how deep down would a body have been at that stage? No, I think she was took and, for what it's worth, I think she was took by someone outside the fair.'

'Why?'

He smiled. 'People like to think that because most of my family was in the police that that's how we've always been. But we have a past. Me great-grandfather was a traveller. Dad remembered seeing members of his family when they stopped down at the old Creekmouth Village years ago. Wouldn't talk, but then travelling types are tight-knit. It's how they stay safe. Folk blame 'em for everything. But for me, that's lazy. And it's dangerous. Look at what Hitler done and you can see where that goes.'

When Lee and Mumtaz emerged into the litter-strewn streets of Thames View, they both felt sad. Lee lit a fag, and looking around at the bleak early sixties architecture, he said, 'Christ, this place is a shithole.'

Mumtaz said, 'Must've been nice when it was

built, especially for the people who had experienced the flooding back in '53.'

'Yeah, but look at it now,' Lee said.

Admittedly, it was a dull day, but the small, down-at-heel shopping centre at the heart of the estate looked like the sort of place where people got mugged.

As they walked back to Lee's car, Mumtaz changed the subject. 'Do you think the way the police searched the park back then was thorough?' she said.

'Probably not by the forensic standards forces who can afford to use such technology apply today,' he said. 'Plus great gangs of locals would have confounded things. All those sorts ranging about doing their own things. Anyone could have taken the kid and I think Tommy knows that. I think that's why he thinks it was a local rather than a traveller.' He shook his head. 'And then there's that toy the kiddie had, which I don't think Irving remembers . . .'

CHAPTER 10

Germany. It wasn't that Irving had avoided it, he'd avoided almost everywhere. Except Amsterdam and Jerusalem. His father had taken him to the Dutch capital back in the seventies, mainly to meet his diamond contacts in what was, arguably, the city of diamonds. Jerusalem had come later, when he decided to go just after his mother died. It had been a trial. Too hot, too loud, too violent, and the food disagreed with him. He'd felt nothing when he'd visited the Western Wall. But then maybe that was because he wasn't a Jew?

Lee Arnold offered him a mint, more to pass the time and probably to help with the PI's cigarette craving, but Irving declined. City Airport's departure lounge contained all the usual retail outlets that airports tended to offer – Smith's, Costa, Boots. What was different about it was that it overlooked what had once been the Royal Albert Dock. When Irving was a child, some relative – he couldn't remember who – had brought him down to the docks to see what was, then, a hub of British industry. In reality it had been declining even then.

All long gone now, the airport had been built opposite the new steel and glass Newham Council offices. And that was strange. To fly somewhere from an airport in the East End, for God's sake. Who would ever have thought it?

'Are you OK?' Mumtaz asked.

'Yes, thank you,' he said.

'They should call the flight soon,' she said and smiled. She was a nice woman.

'Yes.'

He'd been up all night. Nerves. The taxi had picked him up at eleven-thirty for the one-fifteen flight. He'd met Lee and Mumtaz ten minutes later, which had been a mercy as it had stopped his stomach churning. Just the thought that they might stand him up for some unknown reason had meant he'd had to run to the toilet as soon as he'd arrived. But of course they'd come and of course he'd felt ridiculous.

Now all he wanted to do was sleep.

The Austerlitz family hadn't been rich. But they must have made a decent living. Apothecaries were educated people, part of the solid base of Jewish business people who had made up a large proportion of the Berliner middle classes in the city, pre-World War II. Their gravestones reflected this. Unostentatious, but well-made granite memorials, only distinguished from their Gentile counterparts of the same vintage by the addition of a Star of David carved at the bottom of each stone. Of course, neither Dieter Austerlitz, his wife, Miriam, or any of that generation were represented. But Sara had tracked down Dieter's parents, Avram and Izabella, both of whom had died in the 1920s. Avram's two brothers and their wives were also buried in the same vicinity. Interred with others of similar social standing, Sara also recognised the names of prominent pre-war jewellers, furriers and owners of once famous cafes.

The English woman, Mumtaz Hakim, was flying in with the man who claimed to be a relative of the Austerlitz family later on that day. Called Irving Levy, he was dying, apparently. How apt that Sara was now pushing branches of un-pollarded trees aside to look at the memorials to his ancestors. To be able to find such graves so easily was a privilege not given to so many of Europe's Jews. Sara was glad she would be able to show this place to the Englishman, even if the thought of also showing him the Austerlitz house gave her the shudders. Was it just the fact that an ex-member of the Stasi lived there that made her skin crawl? It was cold and she was alone in a deserted cemetery and so of course her skin creeped a little. Every so often she looked over her shoulder. That was to be expected.

Of itself, the house was a reasonably attractive nineteenth-century building. A little ornate for Sara's tastes, but typical of that time. It was somewhat grey in colour, but now that it was autumn the whole city had a slightly grey tinge. She'd lived in Berlin all her life and so Sara had got used to that. She cleared a space in front of Izabella's gravestone and found a small collection of pebbles.

Had they been put there or had they simply ended up in front of Izabella's stone? It was a Jewish tradition to put stones on gravestones; Sara still put them on her mother's grave whenever she visited. It showed the dead they were not forgotten and it told the living that someone cared.

It was as she was looking at the pebbles that Sara noticed another gravestone, just behind Izabella's. It was small and looked as if it had been carved by an amateur.

During his lifetime, Lee Arnold's father had talked about World War II incessantly. Referred to simply as 'the War' the old man had bored the pants off both his sons about his exploits in post-war Germany fighting the remnants of the once powerful German war machine. He both hated them as 'bloody foreigners', but also admired them as people who 'stood up for themselves'. One of the things he'd really admired was the regime's monumental airport at Tempelhof, to which he'd given his highest accolade of 'handsome'.

Compared with Tempelhof, Tegel Airport was a bit of a let-down. Small when compared to Heathrow and boring, Lee felt that it wasn't unlike a more efficient version of Manchester Airport. Even the people looked much the same as they did back home.

Lee carried both his own and Irving's cabin bags. The diamond cutter had slept for the entire flight and, when he'd woken, he'd been groggy. All in all the one-hour-fifty-minute flight had been a pain in the arse. Food and drink had been basic, the overhead lockers had been rammed and the same set of kids seemed to have been in the bogs for the whole duration. With Irving between him and Mumtaz, Lee knew that he should have slept or read. But he'd tried to talk to her, which had gone down badly and now she was looking at him like he'd just farted in church.

Once they'd cleared immigration and customs, Irving said, 'To hell with public transport, let's get a taxi.'

It was a Mercedes – of course it was – driven by an English-speaking Turk who continually pointed out one grey, rain-dappled building after another. Lee didn't listen. Here he was in the city his father had been sent to in the 1940s and which he had banged on about until his death. His dad had only been sixty when his liver had finally given up the unequal struggle with booze. Lee was only just over ten years younger and, although he'd given up drink, he felt old age creeping into his bones, especially when the weather was wet and cold. Christ, Berlin was going to be a joy if it was going to be nothing but rain and massive 1960s Soviet-style architecture.

When they finally reached their hotel, yet another grey 1960s lump on a road called Neue Rossstrasse, it wasn't only Irving who needed a lie-down. Lee, too, found himself unable to move from his minimalist little hotel room, which, though spare, had a very luxurious bed and a great view over a huge internal atrium. It was only Mumtaz who went out. She was going, she said, to meet her contact Frau Metzler at a Starbucks in the central Alexanderplatz plaza.

Mumtaz had her teeth into the Levy case in a way Lee knew that he didn't. And he didn't because his mind was absorbed in his love for her. And he knew that was wrong. And it wore him out.

'I don't know why you want to do it,' Misty said. 'People do that when they're, like, kids. Just because your grandpa flew . . .'

'Nagyapa,' Amber corrected.

'Whatever.' She waved a limp hand in the air. 'I don't do the Hungarian thing, I mean who does?'

Misty's parents, Milos and Amalia, did and, in fact, neither of them could really speak English. But Misty liked to gloss over that. It was no secret, at least from her friends, that as soon as she could, Misty wanted to leave the fair.

The third girl sitting on Amber's bed was Lulu, a tiny dark-haired Gypsy girl. She said, 'But we're a fair not a circus. You should join a circus.'

Amber shook her head. 'I have to have something to offer them, don't I?'

'You can work on the sideshow, like you do here until . . .'

'Ah, but I don't want to!' Amber said. 'I want to go in as a flier!'

'But you're shit.'

Misty sniggered. Amber, furious, tried to cuff Lulu round the head, but she missed. Then they all laughed.

'I'm sorry, Amber, but I've seen you and you need to practise more,' Lulu said.

Suddenly subdued, Amber sighed. 'I know,' she said. 'I'm so bored here.'

'Aren't we all.'

'So get out,' Misty said to her friends. 'As soon as we get to Barking, I'm going up Camden . . .'

'Buying loads of clothes won't help!'

'No, it won't,' she said. 'And in fact, I will wear my best, most revealing clothes when I go there because the best way of getting out of here is to marry your way out.'

Lulu's eyes almost popped out of her head. 'Are you serious?' she said. 'Marry?'

'Or live with,' Misty said. 'I'm not bothered.'

'"Not bothered"?' Lulu said. 'Christ, I don't believe you! My old man's already got me lined up to marry some cousin who lives in Liverpool. But I ain't doing it. Fuck that!'

This was the first Amber had heard of this and she said, 'What are you going to do?'

Lulu shrugged. 'I dunno. But I'm not marrying no knuckle-fighter from Birkenhead. I'll run away.'

'To what?'

'I dunno.'

All three girls stopped talking and then Amber said, 'I don't want to leave . . .'

'I thought you was bored . . .'

'I am, but if I could fly, get my own act, maybe have it as a show on its own . . .'

'We ain't a circus,' Lulu said.

'No, but Nagyapa said that in the old days fairs and circuses were all the same, really. There were sideshows around the rides, freaks and . . .'

'Ah, we've enough freaks as it is, what with your grandpa's mates,' Lulu said. 'Me mum, you know, she reckons they're demons.'

'Demons!'

'They're Hungarian, so they're mad,' Misty said.

'You're Hungarian,' Amber said.

'Not for long.' She took a small mirror out of her handbag and examined her make-up. 'Once I'm with the man of my dreams, I'll be someone else. I'll be one of those women who get their hair done and go to spas and drink champagne.'

Lulu pulled a face. 'Oh, and so some bloke'll just do this for you because you're pretty?'

'Yup.'

'What'll you do if he's an old bloke?'

'He won't be,' Misty said. 'He'll be young and handsome and rich.'

'Are you mad?' Lulu looked to Amber for some sort of support for her view that Misty was living in a fantasy world. But she found none.

'When I've learnt to fly and got my own show, I'll get married too,' Amber said.

'So who's the lucky man?' Misty said.

'Oh, no one here!' Amber shook her head. 'There's no one here!'

'But there'll have to be if you want to stay,' Lulu said. 'God Almighty, all this talk about marriage is making me need some fresh air!'

She got off the bed and left Amber's caravan. A travelling fair kid all her life, Lulu nonetheless couldn't believe quite how unrealistic other travelling children could be. Especially about things like marriage. All hearts and flowers and love – and yet they had to know, as she did, that marriage on the road was tough. Her parents rowed all the time. Most people's did.

Although she loved them both, Lulu thought that Amber and Misty were as daft as brushes. Especially Amber. It was all romance with her. The flying, the listening to her grandfather's mad old stories about circuses in the old days, the weird stuff her mum and her grandma sometimes said. Lulu's father had seen Gala Sanders and her mother, Eva, fight once, years ago. He'd said it was the most vicious conflict he'd ever witnessed. It was, he'd said, as if that family was at war with itself.

It was called a Pumpkin Spice Latte and it was tooth-rottingly sweet. It was also massive. Whenever Mumtaz looked down at the drink, she wondered whether she would survive it. Just the whipped cream on top was enough to harden the most pliable arteries.

Sara Metzler, who had paid for their drinks, had gone for something rather more modest: a regular cappuccino. But then she didn't look like the sort of woman who was a slave to calories. Probably just under six feet tall, she was an angular woman in her sixties. She was retired, so she said, her work at the synagogue being of a voluntary nature.

'My mother survived the Holocaust here in Berlin,' she said once introductions had been made. 'My father I never knew. All I know about him is he was Russian.'

Starbucks in Alexanderplatz was just like Starbucks in London with the exception of the location, which was close to the futuristic Berlin Television Tower. Mumtaz thought it looked like something out of a 1970s kids' TV series. But at least it had been easy to find.

'My mother hid for the entire war,' Sara continued. 'Many people never owned up to being Jewish ever again. There are people walking around this city who don't know they're Jewish. Maybe they even hate Jews.' She smiled. 'The year your Mr Levy's parents met was a time when a lot of lies were told. No one was innocent. When the Red Army invaded Berlin my mother was pulled out of the rubble and raped. The Soviets passed her round like a bag of cookies. Then, in

136

later years, she found a protector and saviour in my father who was a Soviet commander. Or so she said. Some women simply gave themselves to the invaders. I do not judge. People do what they must to survive.'

She drank her coffee.

Mumtaz stared. It wasn't every day, even in a job like hers, that someone told you such intimate details about themselves and their family with no preamble.

'I don't know what to say,' she blurted.

Sara smiled. 'I suggested we meet here at Starbucks because I knew it would be familiar to you,' she said. 'That was one reason. Easy to find. Also, Alexanderplatz was very central to what was East Berlin. And East Berlin is, I think, crucial to the story of your client and his house here.'

'If it is his house . . .'

'As you say. But one thing you must understand and not forget is that, divided, now together, we are a city here in Berlin that nevertheless does not heal,' she said. 'I am and remain an East Berliner. I can speak Russian, like most of my fellows, although unlike most of them I can speak English too.'

'Very well,' Mumtaz said.

'I learnt from the BBC Radio,' she said. 'Which was forbidden in the DDR, but one does what one must to survive. I think all East Germans, if they are honest, would say that even in the darkest days of the DDR, none of us expected the regime

137

to survive for ever. Well, maybe some did. Your Mr Levy's story of a family that does not really know itself is not unusual here. But I am anxious to meet him. All this must be hard for him if he is ill.'

'He's resting at the moment,' Mumtaz said. 'My business partner, well he's really my boss, is resting too.'

'Men.' She shrugged, then leant across the table. 'However, I must say that I wonder why exactly your Mr Levy is here. It is easy, I think, to find out about this family Austerlitz.'

'For you, yes,' Mumtaz said. 'But he's ill.'

'But for you . . .'

Sara Metzler knew Irving Levy was in town to try and solve a mystery. Now Mumtaz told her about the abduction of his sister, Miriam.

The German woman didn't talk for a long time. Then she said, 'I think we must now wake your Mr Levy. There is something he needs to see before he goes any further with this matter. It will, I think, determine whether he wishes to continue with this.'

'You going to Barking Park Fair this year, guv?' Tony Bracci said.

Vi Collins looked up from her computer and said, 'Wasn't going to. Why? You offering to take me?'

He shrugged.

'Lee Arnold got you thinking about it,' Vi said.

Tony drank from his coffee cup. 'Them missing

kids cases get inside your head,' he said. 'I never heard of it until now.'

'You're too young.'

'The one I do remember is that young girl who went missing in Devon in the seventies.'

'Genette Tate,' Vi said. 'Yeah, I was working down at the old nick at Plaistow back then. Still open, that one.'

'I thought she was found?' Tony said.

'No. The late Robert Black was in the frame, but nothing was proved, then he died.'

'Christ.'

Vi turned her chair round to face him. 'Body'd be heavily degraded now, even if it did come to light. Although I think I read a few years back that some of Genette's DNA had been gathered from an item of her clothing. No chance of that with the Levy baby and it was a fuck of a long time ago.'

'Could be she was abducted and doesn't know even now.'

'Anything's possible,' Vi said, 'although how you bring a small kid into a community and say it's yours without arousing suspicion, I don't know. Everyone'd have to collude and we know that even the tightest families and friends have their weakest links.'

'True.'

'If she was alive then there would've been a whisper.'

'Provided someone heard it.'

She nodded. Then she said, 'I think someone would.'

'So you think Lee Arnold's on a bit of a wild goose chase with this thing then, guv?'

'Yes, I do, Tone,' Vi said. Then she added, a little bitterly, Tony felt, 'He's always been one for chasing unicorns and rainbows.'

Lee held Irving's left arm, Mumtaz his right.

The leaf litter underfoot was slimy and smelt of rot, which, given they were in a cemetery, wasn't something to be dwelt upon.

'You see?' the German woman said. She pointed to a name on a small gravestone. Pointless really; Irving had cancer, he wasn't blind. She read, '*Rachel Austerlitz, died 1944*. In an air raid, possibly.'

Did Irving sag a little? Maybe for a moment. Then he said, 'I have to say that to see my mother's name on a grave that isn't hers is an unsettling experience. But then how do we know that this grave is that of Rachel Austerlitz from Niederschönhausen?'

'Her grandparents, the parents of Dieter Austerlitz, are buried here too,' Sara said. She showed him.

'You know,' he said, 'my mother's grave is in East Ham Jewish Cemetery. It gives her name as Rachel Levy. This Rachel and my mother . . .' He shook his head. 'And yet my mother was a Gentile. What can I say? If this is the real Rachel Austerlitz, then who was my mother?'

Sara put a hand on his arm. 'And who is this Rachel Austerlitz?' she said. 'There is no record of this grave in the inventory of Weissensee. We know that in the war people were buried here in secret, but generally they had no stone. To me, this makes little sense. It makes me wonder even whether there is anyone at all in this grave.'

'I do too, for their family,' Irving said. 'My mother was not an Austerlitz. But I would still like to see the house where they lived. My father and mother may not have met there, but it is the nearest place I can get to them now. If it's a lie then it's a lie.'

Sara smiled. 'Of course,' she said. 'But before we go there, you must, I think, go to another place first. Without that place you will never understand the house in Niederschönhausen, or rather its resident now. And believe me it is important that you know who he is.'

CHAPTER 11

As a child, one of the few cultural icons that had affected the rather moody kid Lee Arnold had been was James Bond. The actor who played Bond during his youth was the urbane and slightly wooden Roger Moore. Back then, Bond films had been larky – full of gadgets, girls and exotic locations. Lee clearly remembered truly believing that if he worked for MI5 he would automatically get laid. And now here he was in the office of someone who had once been a real spymaster.

Wood-panelled, the vague sunlight outside filtering through thick, dusty net curtains into what looked to Lee like a TV office from the 1970s, Erich Mielke's lair was anodyne. The man himself, head of the Stasi from 1957 until the fall of the Berlin Wall, had been anything but. Spymaster, murderer, blackmailer, Erich Mielke had held power of life and death over East Germany for over thirty years. A literal reign of terror, all orchestrated from an office that looked as if it belonged on the old television comedy show 'The Fall and Rise of Reginald Perrin' about a middle-aged middle-manager having a nervous breakdown. It was so ordinary.

Sara Metzler, their attentive guide, was outside the building drinking coffee and smoking. Lee would have preferred to be doing the same, but he had to admit that this stroll he was taking with Mumtaz and Irving Levy through a place that had once seen men with unimaginable power sign away the lives of the helpless was thought-provoking. He could feel it too. The malevolence was in the walls.

Irving, who had been silent for a long time, said, 'This Herr Beltz worked here.'

'I don't know about here,' Mumtaz said. 'This was Mielke's office. He may have come here. I don't think he was very high up in the Stasi.'

He shook his head. 'We have no idea in Britain,' he said. 'To spy on your fellow citizens! Didn't anyone learn anything from the Nazis?'

'This form of communism was imposed by the Soviets.'

He waved a dismissive hand. 'It's all the same.'

'Of course.'

A group of Germans were ushered into the office by a guide who told them a lot of facts and figures that Lee and the others couldn't understand. When he'd finished, they stayed for a minute at the most and then left.

Lee noticed there were two grey telephones on what had been Mielke's desk. They looked exactly the same as the phone his parents had in his house when he was a kid.

'Frau Metzler wants me, I think, to reconsider going to the home of the Austerlitz family,' Irving said. He'd brought a stick to help him walk, which he now leant on.

'The current owner was in the Stasi and so he might not be open to visitors. He may even now fear reprisals,' Mumtaz said. 'And even if he doesn't, I can't believe that someone who was once involved in denouncing and imprisoning people is going to be the most welcoming host.'

'But if his father owned the house before him then he may know something,' Irving said. 'You are right, Mumtaz, he may not be welcoming or pleasant, but this is an opportunity to maybe find a clue to my mother's real identity. It may not be, but if I don't try, I will never know.'

He left the room. Alone with Mumtaz, Lee said, 'Even if we manage to get in, this is going to be tough on him.'

'I know,' she said. 'But if you don't take risks in life, how can you ever achieve anything?'

He couldn't help himself. He said, 'Maybe you should think about that too.'

But she looked away.

The woman was called Sara Metzler, a volunteer at the Centrum Judaicum. The daughter of a single mother, Rolfe had been right inasmuch as she'd had a file. Only those from the old East ever sought him out. Sometimes it was to reminisce, but sometimes they had other purposes. As a Jew,

Metzler was probably in the latter camp. Or so Rolfe said, but then his father had also been a ghastly anti-Semite.

Gunther Beltz despaired. How many people had he come across who held such views? Of course, their old Soviet masters had a whole folklore of evil that revolved around Jews, rather in emulation of their old enemy Hitler. Didn't these idiots know it was the Jews who had invented Socialism?

The DDR would have been like paradise if it hadn't been for its ignorant people who didn't know what was good for them. Gunther had done his bit, but what did that matter when you were surrounded by idiots?

Had the Metzler woman come to see the house? Was she a relative? Her surname wasn't Austerlitz, but what did that show? Maybe she'd married or changed her name for some other reason? People did. In the new, unified Berlin you could be anyone you wanted to be – provided you could forget your past. Or ignore it, or get therapy, or kill yourself . . .

Had the woman, assuming she was connected to the family in some way, been to the cemetery at Weissensee? Even if she had, what of it? And if she came back, he'd just send her away. It was hardly fair and, considering what the Austerlitz family had been, could be construed as dis-respectful. But what could he do?

Gunther Beltz didn't want to be disturbed. Not

by anyone. It was too frightening. Or was it? Could it not also be illuminating?

Everything was new, which was a good thing. An old chemist's shop could be filled with old medicines that could damage people. But what the Rosen Apotheke made up for in hygiene, it lost in character. There was nothing, as far as Mumtaz could see, that gave even the slightest hint about a history.

'This area was very Jewish before World War II,' Sara said. 'My place of work is not far. But not all buildings have yet been acknowledged as having a place in Berlin Jewish history. This, what was the Austerlitz Apotheke, is one of them. Had the family been more prominent, this would be different, but I imagine it's the same as everywhere, it is only the rich and the famous who make history.'

Mumtaz saw Lee shake his head.

'Christ!'

It was true. The hovels his ancestors had lived in hadn't survived, but Buckingham Palace was probably still good for another hundred years.

Mumtaz watched Irving Levy watch customers come and go. Taking things down from shelves and paying for them at the counter, handing over prescriptions, empty medicine bottles and names of things scribbled down on bits of paper. The sick seeking relief. Today from a man who looked as if he came from Pakistan, in the past from local Jewish gentleman Dieter Austerlitz. Then as now, did the sick really care where their medication came from? Or from whom?

In the Rosen Apotheke, people smiled or grimaced, talked with their hands or remained impassive, just as they had always done. And yet there was not a shadow of the Austerlitz family and, after Sara made some enquiries, which came to nothing, they left.

Out in the early autumn chill of Rosenstrasse, Irving Levy came to a decision.

He said, 'I think I want to see the Austerlitz house now and, if possible, meet its owner.'

'He may not let us in,' Sara said.

'No. But what is the purpose of my being here unless I find that out?' he said. 'You told us this man's family have lived in the house a long time. If that's the case then he may know something.'

Mumtaz hoped that he did, while fearing what would happen if he didn't.

The child would ask questions!

'The Dobos family are liars and thieves,' Bela said. 'Don't listen to them.'

'But Misty's my friend,' Amber said. 'I just want to know why she doesn't want to be Hungarian.'

'Because people in this country look down on you,' Bela said.

'Why?'

'Why?'

Where did she want him to start? The snobbery of the English? The fact that all Eastern Europeans were looked on with suspicion? He could talk for hours about what Misty's grandfather Ferenc Dobos had done and why a very talented wire-walker had left his country in 1945 to hide himself in a wretched British fairground, but he wouldn't.

'If you don't like what she says then stop talking to her,' he said.

Amber pouted. But Bela didn't care. Let the child wonder. That stupid little bitch Misty didn't know anything. He doubted even her father did. Bela himself had warned Ferenc that if he ever broke his silence, he would kill him. He'd worked too hard to put his own family beyond reproach to let some wire-walker ruin what was already a most imperfect life.

And family came first. Always.

It wasn't the size of the house that struck Irving first. It was large, but what really stuck out for him was a small curved alcove between two windows at the very top of the building containing a statue. It looked like a man, but he could be wrong about that; whoever it was wore long, flowing robes. To have a house with its own statue was something, wasn't it? Like the really great Jewish families – the Rothschilds and the Montefiores.

But Grabbeallee No. 67 wasn't a palace. It was a big house, which stood in the middle of a small garden, a large nineteenth-century villa with tall sash windows, stucco-encrusted balconies and a strange wooden entrance that looked a little like a detail from an Alpine hotel. It was clearly middle European. It was the house of people who had done well, who were accepted and, more importantly, were entitled. That didn't, in Irving's experience, often apply to Jews.

'Looks empty to me,' Lee Arnold said.

'Maybe he is out,' Sara said. 'Stay here, I will go and ring the bell.'

She walked up the stone steps to the 'Alpine' entrance and pulled a large bell chord. They all heard it clang and reverberate. In fact, as its sound died away, Irving imagined he could hear it chiming softly and endlessly in every last room. But no one came.

'He must be out,' Mumtaz said.

She was probably right; the trusting, practical voice of Mrs Hakim frequently was. But Irving had his doubts. What would he do if strangers came to call and he'd once belonged to a hated organisation like the Stasi?

Sara Metzler called out. A stream of German he didn't understand, although he did manage to recognise some words. 'Austerlitz', 'haus', 'England'. Then she wrote a note and put it through the door.

When she joined them in the street, she said,

'I have to admit to you that I may have upset Herr Beltz when I found this place some days ago. He didn't like me standing outside. I've just told him that some relatives of the previous owners would like to come and see the house if that is possible. He may or may not allow it.'

They moved away. But Irving stayed. Silent and dark the house looked dead to him now and he had the sudden notion that what he was looking at wasn't anything to do with him at all. It made him shudder.

It was like looking at the corpse of someone he didn't know.

And so the 'new' Germany where everything went was trying to open up another sore. What good did such things do?

Gunther had stood well back from the drawing room window. He knew he hadn't been spotted. He also knew that Sara Metzler had lied about why she had come to see the house that first time. She'd come for those English people. The tall man, the Jew and the Muslim woman. The Jew had to be the relative. He wanted to see the house and where was the harm in that? If that was the real reason.

But then how could the Jew be a relative? The entire family had died. That was what his father had told him. That he knew himself for a fact.

Gunther turned away from the window. *They've come because of me,* he thought, *because of things I have done.*

I will not let them in.

CHAPTER 12

'Your brothers and sisters are the only people you can trust when I am gone. Blood is all that matters. It is only blood that will guard your honour and catch you when you fall.'

The words of his late mother always came into Wahid Sheikh's mind whenever he had to go and visit his brother Rizwan. Since his stroke, Rizwan Sheikh lived with his daughter, Saadia, and her husband and children in Dalston. Like her father, Saadia was mean and ill-tempered and her house, even in winter, was like a vast empty chest freezer. Wahid went there reluctantly, usually only, like now, when Rizwan summoned him.

It hadn't been much fun for Wahid being one of only two brothers in a family of ten daughters. The women, including his mother, had all idolised the favoured elder boy, Rizwan. Wahid they'd used as a servant, fetching and carrying for all of them, especially the sainted little rajah, the eldest son. Stupid and cruel, Rizwan had led his brother a dog's life. He still did. Wahid had never wanted to join his brother's admittedly considerable organisation in London but, when Rizwan could no longer take care of business, he had come. Now he was summoned again, for an 'update'.

What was he supposed to say?

Yes, Rizwan-ji, your thuggish sons and stupid henchmen are still trafficking women, collecting protection money and taking care of your illegal gambling clubs where people lose their shirts every day. Your enemies are still being tormented – oh, and by the way, I may have prostate cancer . . .

Saadia let him in and took him up the stairs to her father's bedroom. Fat and pasty, Rizwan Sheikh lay on a chaotic bed covered in DVDs, pens and paper, empty teacups and crumbs. By way of explanation, Saadia said, 'Won't let me tidy up, will you, Daddy-ji?'

Rizwan made a growling noise and then motioned for his brother to sit down. Although his brother was unable to speak, Wahid knew what he wanted and so he gave him his report, omitting any sort of criticism or allusion to his own health issues. However, when he got to the place where he was required to speak about the Hakim family, his brother stopped him and wrote something down on one of his pieces of paper. When he looked at it, Wahid said, 'Of course I've not forgotten. How could I?'

He watched his brother try to smile and was slightly hurt by the fact that he had made him happy. But then that was what blood did . . .

⋆　⋆　⋆

The hotel bar was in the vast atrium in the middle of the building. And although it wasn't particularly inviting – the decor was rather sterile – it did have comfortable chairs.

Lee bought the drinks, none of which were alcoholic. He felt the barman viewed him with suspicion. But then what else can a recovering alcoholic, a Muslim and man on medication drink but lemonade or Coca-Cola?

Irving looked pale and gaunt and Lee was in two minds as to whether to bring up 'business', but he did.

'Have you had a chance to think about Miriam's toys?' he asked.

Mumtaz and Irving took their drinks, and then he said, 'You mean the special toy you told me the police had looked for?'

'Yeah.'

Tommy Askew hadn't been able to remember what the toy was and so Lee had asked Irving if he could remember.

'Still nothing comes to mind, I'm afraid,' he said. 'In fact, I don't remember her having toys. She must have done, but nothing I remember. She slept in my parents' room, I think, and so I suppose she must've had her toys in there. Back in the sixties children didn't have many toys. Not like now.'

'Seventies weren't much better,' Lee said.

Mumtaz smiled. 'I was very privileged,' she said. 'I had a Cabbage Patch Doll before anyone else.'

Lee remembered seeing those dolls. Every girl

wanted one in the early nineties and yet, as he recalled, they were ugly-looking things.

'You know,' Irving said, 'I think that maybe never having had children of my own, the subject of toys may have passed me by. I struggle to remember even my own toys. I know I had a train set and Meccano, but I don't remember anything else. I wouldn't have had – what do they call them? – action figures.'

'Why not? I had Action Man,' Lee said.

'Dad only approved of educational toys, where you build or make. Even as a young child I spent much of my time in the Garden with Dad's colleagues. It was and remains a very masculine world.' Then he changed the subject. 'Frau Metzler seemed to think that Herr Beltz was in.'

Lee had felt that too.

'He's ex-Stasi,' he said. 'God knows what he did in the old days of the DDR. Maybe he killed people?'

'Surely if that were the case he would be in prison?'

'The way I understand it, there's a lot still not known about the Stasi,' Lee said. 'You saw that museum. It was part of a whole complex of buildings that used to belong to the Stasi. Stuffed with files that are still unread.'

'And the Stasi themselves destroyed many of them when the Wall came down,' Mumtaz said. 'Maybe Herr Beltz's was one of those.'

'And yet he must still live in fear, because if

people like Frau Metzler can find out he was an agent so can others,' Lee said. 'The Wall came down in living memory and so if he did, at the very least, snoop on his neighbours there are going to be people out there who have it in for him.'

Irving put a hand to his head. 'So what do we do?'

The night air was cold and the street largely deserted. Irving had gone to bed after he'd finished his drink and, not wanting to be alone with Mumtaz, Lee had left the hotel to have a smoke.

Sara Metzler, God love her, had gone back to her office at the Judaicum to see what else she could unearth about the Austerlitz family. Finding that unrecorded grave of Rachel Austerlitz had hit all of them hard, even though, given the evidence from Irving's DNA test, it was to be expected. Was the house on Grabbeallee a red herring? There was no real evidence that Irving's dad had ever been there, and in view of the fact that it had been in the Soviet sector, that seemed unlikely. But also there had to be a reason why Irving's parents had told him they had met in Niederschönhausen in the house of a family called Austerlitz. Was the clue in what Manny Levy had done in the war? Had he, in spite of being a mere private, had some sort of job that meant he had a connection with or to the Russian forces? Had he spoken Russian?

Lee lit another fag and took his phone out of his pocket.

★   ★   ★

'I do not pry, as you know,' her father said, 'but I think you should maybe be the bigger person and make this thing, whatever it is, up with Shazia. The girl looks so miserable and she should be happy. She is about to go to university! You must do something!'

Mumtaz flopped back on her bed, her phone jammed against her ear. She'd just got off the line to Shirin Shah, who expected her to do something about the fact she still didn't like the refuge. Why did people always want her to have an answer for everything?

'What can I do if she won't take my calls?' she said.

'She won't?'

'No. I've rung her four times since I got to Berlin and she just cuts me dead.'

'So try again. I will tell her she must speak to you.'

'Oh, don't do that, Abba!'

'Why not?'

'You can't interfere in this,' she said.

'I've no idea what it's about! All I know is that your mother and I suddenly find ourselves parents again!'

Of course they did. Guilt made Mumtaz end the call and then she closed her eyes. It was great that Shazia had felt confident enough in her parents' love to go to them after 'that' talk, but it had to be a strain for the old couple. And they hadn't asked for a penny towards Shazia's keep, which was just as well. Skint, yet again, she didn't dare ask Lee for a pay increase, not because he couldn't afford it, but just because she was afraid to talk to him about anything personal.

'Mumtaz.'

And now here he was, knocking on her door! How could she both want and not want him to come in?

She fixed her hijab and then said, 'I'm coming.'

'Frau Metzler?'

Sara had thought the building was empty. She looked up from her computer screen. Like her, Horst Klein was a volunteer archivist at the Centrum Judaicum. Older than her, he'd been born in 1934 in the Berlin district of Scheunenviertel, an old Jewish enclave near the centre of the city. When the war began, his family went into hiding. Miraculously, they had all survived. Herr Klein was like a beacon for Berlin Jewry, Sara always felt. Intelligent, kind, knowledgeable and tough.

'Herr Klein.'

'What are you doing burning the midnight oil?' he said.

She told him about the Austerlitz family, their house, and about the people who had come from London to find them. He shook his head.

'One of those families where everyone died. I didn't know them.'

'You were a child.'

'I was.' He looked down at the floor. Then he

158

said, 'But I do recall that house on Grabbeallee. It was pointed out on one of those endless educational trips they used to put us on.'

Like Sara, Horst was an East Berliner. He'd worked as an engineer at the Klingenberg Power Station until the Wall came down.

'Do you remember anything about it?'

'Oh, only that it was one of those places where one of their "Heroes of the Revolution" was born.'

'Do you know who?'

He shrugged. 'I didn't listen. The Stasi dragged me in once. I tried to "mend my ways", but in reality I just got better at hiding my boredom.'

Sara smiled. They'd all done that to a greater or lesser extent. But then she thought about what he'd just said.

'Do you know who brought you in?' she said.

He shrugged again. 'Some Stasi officer. I don't know. Who were those people? Well, they were people we now see walking the streets and we do not know. They were our neighbours, our friends even . . .'

'Do you know the name Beltz, Herr Klein?' she interrupted.

'Beltz? Was there a Beltz in the Politburo?'

'Joachim Beltz, yes,' she said. 'A very minor member. Later it was discovered that he owned that house on Grabbeallee. His son still lives there. He was a Stasi officer.'

Herr Klein leant back in his chair. 'So many were,' he said.

'That "Hero of the Revolution" you were told

about was born in that house. It wasn't Beltz, was it?' she said.

He thought for a moment and then he said, 'I'm sorry, Frau Metzler, I really don't know. This was back in the fifties and I was day-dreaming. For all I know the devil could have been born in that house.'

He found a chair as far away from her as he could and sat down. Mumtaz looked at his face and felt her heart ache. Doing the 'right' thing made him frown.

He said, 'I've been looking at Irving's old man's military service. He was in the 131st Infantry Brigade during the war. It was a territorial unit, apparently, which must mean that Manny Levy had been too old for regular service or he'd been in Reserved Occupation for some reason. Now that lot were amongst some of the first British units to enter Berlin in 1945. Course the Soviets were already there; they'd staked their claim to what they wanted.'

It wasn't easy sitting upright on the bed and so Mumtaz sat slightly nearer to Lee on a chair over by the wardrobe.

'Then on 7th September 1945, once all the Allies were in the city, the Soviets suggested a victory parade,' he continued. 'The US, France and the UK weren't keen, but they went along with it to please Stalin. So all the top-notch Russians were in town as well as General Patton from the US. But the British and the French sent small-time

160

generals. It was lip service and the Russians knew it. They call it the "Forgotten Parade", apparently. And, by us of course, it has been largely forgotten.'

Mumtaz said, 'OK. How is this relevant?'

He'd bustled into her room like someone who'd just found the Holy Grail.

'Because,' he said, 'it was during and around the time of the Forgotten Parade that the Western Allies and the Soviets got to meet and greet and go where they wanted.'

'And so?'

'And so Manny Levy could have entertained himself or been entertained by Soviets in their sector,' he said. 'He could have met a pretty girl in a house on a street called Grabbeallee.'

'But that doesn't automatically place him there.'

'No, but it opens up the possibility that he was there,' Lee said. 'It doesn't mean that he actually was, but he could have been.'

'And yet the girl could have been anyone,' Mumtaz said.

'She could. But she must've known the name Rachel Austerlitz, at the very least.'

'Because she used that name.'

'Yes.' He paused for a moment, a hand at his lips and then he said, 'The girl was a Gentile, as we know now, but she gave the name of a Jew to a soldier she may or may not have known was Jewish and . . .'

'And so she must have either known of or known

161

Rachel Austerlitz,' Mumtaz said. 'And Lee, she lived as a Jew and so she must've had some knowledge about their customs . . .'

'Maybe she was a friend?'

'Maybe.'

They sat in silence for a moment and then Lee suddenly blurted, 'Mumtaz, I'd like things to be . . . between us . . .' He shook his head. 'I'd like things to be back the way they were, before . . .'

'Me too,' she said.

'I mean it's not ideal . . .'

'Please don't say any more.' She turned away. Then she said, 'It's how it must be.'

'I know that's how you see it.'

'It's not something that can happen,' she said. 'Whatever we may feel.'

She felt his hand on her arm and she pulled it away. Then she looked at him and saw that he was in pain. It made her want to cry.

'Mumtaz . . .'

She stood up and moved away from him. 'No,' she said. 'Please go now, Lee, for God's sake.'

She heard him stand and walk across the room. He stood, just for a moment, at the foot of her bed – it was unbearable – and then she heard the door open and close behind him.

Mumtaz threw herself onto her bed, burying her face in her pillows, and howled without even a thought about what Irving, whose room was next door, might think.

★   ★   ★

162

They were outside his van; he could hear them, sniggering. What were they up to now? In the old days they'd gone out at night to gather wood and try to find a rabbit or someone's chicken for the pot. Later it had been rats. He'd eaten more rat than he cared to remember. They all had.

Bela Horvathy opened his bedroom window and saw that they were lighting a fire.

'What are you doing?' he hissed. 'Fires are forbidden on the site these days!'

They both looked at him. The made-up faux oriental eyes had become part of them and he now found it hard to see past them or even tell them one from another. They didn't speak. Even Hungarian seemed to be beyond them now. He wondered sometimes whether they were dementing.

He tried again. 'Put the fire out,' he said. 'Go back to your van and go to bed!'

Neither of them moved. The bastards were like statues.

'We break camp tomorrow,' he said. 'Go to sleep. You'll need energy to pack up.'

But they just carried on staring at him, unmoving.

Eventually, he said, 'There is a limit to my patience, you know.'

And then they both laughed at him until he shut the window.

CHAPTER 13

Frau Metzler and her English people would go away. Gunther Beltz threw the note, and her mobile phone number, into the fire. Over the years, a few people had come to the house looking for something – never this – but something. That was why he occasionally employed Rolfe. Young, he may be, but he knew everyone and had many, many interests in the city. Armed with Rolfe's information he was usually able to make such people leave.

Why would they stay? In 1989 he'd seen the writing on the wall – literally – and he'd made arrangements to expunge himself. Of course, people could still recognise him, make accusations, but there was nothing to back them up. Let the occasional lunatic yell at the house. Every fourth East Berliner had been in the Stasi. Some of those who accused him probably among them. The issue was not what he had done, but that he had this house. They were jealous.

What none of them knew was that he had this house for a reason. But then maybe, if Frau Metzler had her way, that was about to change. Maybe, he thought, he should give her her way. But it was too late now. Her number was on the fire. Gunther Beltz put her from his mind.

The taxi driver understood his weird German pronunciation, thank God! Maybe it was because he was a Turk and so accustomed to non-standard German voices. He took him straight there.

Now standing outside number 67 Grabbeallee, Irving didn't really know what to do. He'd come to see the house again, on his own, mainly because he wanted to know whether the feeling of dread he had felt coming from it that first time had been real. Frau Metzler was a wonderful guide and an enthusiastic advocate of Berliner Jewry, but she was also an East German and so she had, naturally, reacted to the house of a former member of the Stasi with fear.

Irving knew that, compared to her, he was fortunate. Born in the 1950s, he'd been raised in a Britain that had been poor and shabby but free. His father had been well-off and had owned his considerable home long before home-owning became the norm in the UK. No one had spied on anyone, as far as he knew, and there had certainly not been any ominous knocks on the front door in the early hours of the morning. He'd lived in a Britain that had been an essentially good place, and he was grateful. With luck, the country would survive the recent upswing in mindless nationalism, but then he probably wouldn't be around to see that much of it.

He pulled his coat closely round his body and shivered. It wasn't yet 6 a.m. and the grey streets of Berlin had yet to warm up. He told himself he hadn't been able to sleep, but it wasn't true. He didn't want Lee or Mumtaz to know where he was. He was paying them, yes, but he felt they were kind people as well. Both of them wanted to help and because they had their own troubles too – he'd heard them arguing and then Mumtaz crying in the night – he was especially grateful. Now, at sixty, he realised what huge amounts of time people wasted denying themselves what they really wanted and needed. He'd seen the way they looked at each other, and how, sometimes, they didn't. Was it religion that kept them apart? If it was, he'd tell them what he thought about that. Religion was why he was standing here now, torturing himself by looking at a house that made his blood freeze. A proper Jew. What was that even, anyway? What did being one matter?

He began to feel tears sting his eyes and it made him feel stupid, old and alone. This house was just a house. Bricks and mortar with a dash of stucco and wood. What did it have to do with him?

But as Irving looked at it, he saw that the front door had opened. Just a crack.

*   *   *

166

Lee watched him go in. He hadn't slept and so, when Irving left the hotel, he was already out in the street lurking by the ashtray. He'd heard him tell the taxi driver where he wanted to go and had jumped in a cab himself. Although the Stasi no longer had any power, he'd not felt that his client was entirely safe. But now Irving was inside and so Lee would just have to wait. Fortunately, if Herr Beltz was anything like the operatives he'd read about at the Stasi Museum, he'd know he was there. Also, in terms of harming Irving, that was unlikely. Why call attention to himself by having an 'incident' with a foreigner? It didn't make sense.

But then he had been in the house when they'd called the previous day and so it was likely he had something to hide. That or he was afraid. That was possible. How did one live in a democratic nation like Germany when one had worked for a previous, repressive regime? Where had old Stasi men and women gone? Unlike Russia, where the former KGB had simply morphed into instruments of repression on behalf of Putin, ex-Stasi operatives were, as far as he could tell, looked upon with distaste if not outright hostility. Christ, you could even get access to the files they'd once held on you. The new Germany aspired to transparency.

He looked at the house and saw the two men framed in a window on the first floor. Sara Metzler had told them that few East Germans spoke

English even now and so he wondered how they were communicating.

'Your friend outside,' Herr Beltz said, 'would you like him to join us?'

'What friend?'

Irving looked out of the window into the street, but saw no one.

'The tall, dark man who followed you here,' Gunther Beltz said. 'I will admit he is well hidden, but I can see him. Behind the tree.'

He looked again and then he saw something. A movement, the edge of what could be a coat. Had Lee Arnold followed him? Irving said nothing. In one way he hoped that Lee had tailed him but, in another way, would that make a difference to what was going to happen with this very ordinary, if slightly unnerving, man?

'I was trained by an agency that taught people to be very aware of their surroundings,' he continued. 'But then I imagine Frau Metzler has told you that.'

Irving realised that this man would know Sara's name, after all she had written it next to her phone number and posted it through his door. But he seemed to be suggesting that she knew he had been in the Stasi. How did he know that?

'So, you are here to see this house,' Beltz said. 'You have a family connection?'

'My mother, yes,' he said. 'She was German. She met my father, who was a British soldier, in this house in 1945. Or rather, that was what she always said. I've since discovered she wasn't, or rather couldn't, have been who she said she was.'

'Why is that?'

He couldn't go into all that with this stranger. The more time he spent in his company the more uncomfortable Gunther Beltz made him feel. Or was that just his imagination? Number 67 Grabbeallee was a dark, old-fashioned house; it was cold and Herr Beltz had not so much as offered Irving a seat.

'You think you are related to the family Austerlitz?' Beltz said. 'If you are . . .'

'I'm not. I thought I was, but I've discovered that I'm not,' Irving said. And then, unable to stand any longer, he plonked himself down into a large armchair and sat. 'I'm sorry, I'm not well . . .'

Beltz ignored him.

'If you are,' he said, 'as I was saying, then you would be related to one of the minor heroes of the DDR.'

Irving didn't care. 'My mother called herself Rachel Austerlitz,' he said. 'I now know she was no such thing. Herr Beltz, I don't care that you were in the Stasi; it's not my business what you may have done in your past. But I am dying and I need to find out who my mother was. For all my life I thought she was Rachel Austerlitz. But she wasn't. I saw her grave when I got here. My mother was a Gentile and if you know of any way such a person could have come from this house, then I ask that you take mercy upon me and tell me.'

Mumtaz picked up her phone and, when she saw who was calling, she answered immediately.

'Shazia!'

'When do you get back from Berlin?' the girl said.

She sounded shaky. And, although Mumtaz was overjoyed to hear from her, she wondered what was wrong. 'Shazia . . .'

'We need to talk,' she said. 'I need to see you before I go to uni.'

'Well, yes. Yes, that's what I've always wanted. I—'

'Don't think everything's all forgiven because it isn't, but we have to get back to normal and . . . and I do love you.'

Mumtaz leant back in her chair. The breakfast on the table in front of her untouched and entirely forgotten. She said, 'And I love you too. All I've ever done has been—'

'No, Amma, don't talk now,' Shazia said. 'Just come home safely on Friday.'

When the girl rang off, it was as if a great weight had fallen away and Mumtaz began to actually feel hungry for once. Shazia hadn't forgiven her, but at least they were in some sort of dialogue, even if Mumtaz believed that the girl had sounded more anxious than she would have liked. She poured herself some tea and then began to tuck into the small bowl of muesli she had taken from the breakfast buffet. Maybe, later, she'd even have a roll and jam. She hadn't slept for much of the night and so she knew she could do with the energy a good breakfast might provide.

Had Lee's need to see her about the Forgotten Parade been just a pretext to get into her room? The night before was now filtered through a blur of tiredness, upset and, latterly, elation. She knew that in reality Lee's appearance in her room had probably been a bit of both. It was quite a breakthrough to discover an actual date when Irving's father could have met his mother. It meant that the story he'd been told as a child could at least be partially true. And Irving himself had told them that he'd felt there was something about that house . . .

'Mumtaz.'

She looked up, her thoughts interrupted by a foreign, female voice.

'Sara.'

'I've just had a phone call from Lee,' Sara said. 'Come. I have a taxi waiting outside.'

'A taxi, to where?'

'To Grabbeallee 67. Lee and Mr Levy are there already, with Herr Beltz.'

She knew she shouldn't be there. She should be packing up her van. But Eva was mesmerised. The way the Twins hitched up a rig using nothing but washing line and the high sides of the Wall of

Death machine was little short of amazing. What her granddaughter did once the rig was stable was less impressive. She wobbled on the makeshift trapeze like a drunk.

But she let Amber swing from one side to the other and didn't yell at her until she turned.

'Get down here, young lady!' she said. 'You're supposed to be helping your mum pack up the van!'

Amber pulled a face, but she sat down on the trapeze in preparation for coming down. The Twins sniggered.

Eva, sick of them, switched to Hungarian. 'And you two can shut up and go and prepare to move too!' she said.

They looked at her. She was used to that.

'So go,' she said.

And then something strange happened. One of them spoke.

'Don't tell us what to do.'

Amber, climbing down the rope, almost lost her grasp. The Twin's voice, even though she didn't know what it was saying, sounded like a cough from a sepulchre. Eva helped her down and sent her on her way. Then she turned to the Twins.

She looked at them. 'So,' she said, 'we make our way to Barking and you find a voice.'

They said nothing.

'Not that it bothers me,' she said. 'Say what you like. No one can understand you.'

The other one spoke. 'Everyone understands death. It's a universal language.'

172

Eva felt a jolt in her chest. 'Is that a threat?'

Again they said nothing.

'Because if it is then you'd better think about yourselves before you start pointing your fingers at others,' she said. Then suddenly she was furious. Nothing that had happened in her life had happened without being affected by them! She looked at their wrinkled made-up faces, their vile, filthy fingernails and she wanted to be sick.

Eva screamed, 'Put my granddaughter in danger again and I will snap every bone in your sick, dry bodies. If it wasn't for you . . .' She dared herself to say what she always wanted to say to them, but couldn't.

'Well?' one of them said.

'If it wasn't—'

Eva caught herself. To say it made it unbearable.

If it wasn't for you, my father would have cared for me!

As she walked away from them, Ping and Pong began to snigger again.

CHAPTER 14

He made coffee.

'I never learnt to make tea, far too English,' Gunther Beltz said as he placed the coffee pot, cups, milk and sugar on the dining table in front of the window. 'I only learnt the language so that I could recognise it when I heard people like you, Frau Metzler, listening to the BBC.'

Sara didn't react. She saw the Brits smile, thinking he was joking, but he wasn't. She knew that. She also knew that he hadn't changed in all the years since the fall of the DDR. She knew the type, those who would go back to the 'old' days in a heartbeat, because back then they'd had power. Sara wanted to know what he'd done, wanted to dig into what counted for his soul and see the dark and dirty things he'd taken part in to keep himself safe.

But that was not why they were there. As Beltz had said once they were all assembled, he would tell them what he knew about the Austerlitz family provided they did not record his voice, write down his words or ask him about anything else.

How many people had Gunther Beltz killed? Enough to still be afraid.

He spoke.

'The Austerlitz family had an apothecary in Berlin since the middle of the nineteenth century. Good people, they tried to care for the sick even if they sometimes couldn't pay. Of course to many, especially in the bourgeoisie, they were just Jews.' He shrugged. 'My grandfather began working for the family just after this house was built in 1910. There used to be a coach house, which was where the family kept their carriages and horses. My grandfather drove for them, then my father – by which time horses had given way to cars.'

'My family lived above the coach house. My grandfather the driver, his wife the housekeeper and the children, my father and his sister. Joachim, my father, later drove, but he also worked in the garden; his sister was a maid. My father was fifteen when the Nazis came to power; his sister, Adeline, one year younger. What you have to understand now is that Herr Dieter Austerlitz, as well as being a Jew and an intellectual, was also a communist. Many Jews were. And some Gentiles. My father was one. He went to meetings – with the blessing of his employer – but not his father. When Kristallnacht took place in 1938, my grandfather was one of those who took to the streets to break the windows of Jewish businesses in Berlin. But by then, my father was in Moscow.'

'How?'

'Although Jewish businesses were heavily curtailed by 1938, Dieter Austerlitz still had friends. He knew it was only a question of time before my father was arrested. He put him on a train to Hungary. By the end of the year he was in Moscow. That was why Dieter Austerlitz was a Hero of the DDR. Because as Frau Metzler will know, my father went on to become part of the Politburo of the DDR, and so to save such a person's life . . .' He shrugged. 'It was important. As for the Austerlitz family . . . The parents and the young son went first to Sachsenhausen and then to Auschwitz. My grandfather had died by then. My grandmother and Adeline remained in the coach house. What is significant for your story, Herr Levy, is what happened to the Austerlitzes' daughter, Rachel.'

'If you and those freaks keep on encouraging her, my granddaughter will have an accident,' Eva said.

Gala, her daughter, was tying down the crockery in the kitchen of the old man's van, but she couldn't understand as she couldn't speak Hungarian.

Bela said, 'They hanker for the old days. They're old!'

'Oh, and you let them because . . .' Eva said. 'Some relics from Budapest you choose to have with you—'

'They came to this country with me. In the Magyar Circus—'

'Yes, played in front of Adolf Hitler; I've heard

it. I don't care. By the time you got here none of you were still flying – or so you told me.'

'That is true,' he said. 'They were as they are now and I worked the sideshows. But we had to find somewhere to be, Eva. You don't know what it was like.'

'I know you were part of the Resistance to the Nazis, or so you say.'

'I was!'

'So you would have had no trouble coming here! Unless you lied . . .'

'You don't know what it was like,' he reiterated. 'It wasn't easy, and with them . . .'

'Who you owe nothing, as far as I can see!' she said. 'Who are they, anyway?'

Her father said nothing.

'Were they partisans or did they perhaps work for the Nazis? Was that why it "wasn't easy"? If I even understood your relationship with—'

'We worked together,' he said. 'We were fliers. One gets close to people. All my family died in that war, I had only them!'

'Yes, well now you do have a family,' Eva said, 'and we've looked after them enough. They're old and they're mental. I don't want them in my life any more.'

She looked at him, noticing how small he'd got and she shook her head. 'Awful things we have never spoken about have been done. We both know it. But it stops here. If I catch them putting a rig up for Amber again, I will kill them.'

Bela got out of his bed, shuffled slowly over to her and then he said, 'Oh, please don't do that now, Eva. Because if you do that, then I may be forced to do something you don't like.'

'Don't threaten me, you old bastard,' Eva replied. 'I'd do time if it meant that girl was safe, and don't you forget that!'

The room was full of stuff. Not unlike Irving's house in Barking. Like that house, there was also a feeling of not so much neglect but of a stoppage of time. As if someone from the early twentieth century had just walked out of the door and left this room exactly as he or she had originally arranged it. It was impossible, of course. This house had to have been ransacked by Nazis and probably the Soviets. There was a fire in the grate, but it threw no heat.

'When the Nazis came to the house, my grandmother hid her,' Gunther said. 'I don't know where. The story my father told was that Rachel was with my grandmother in the coach house when they came. It was said that my grandmother, Maria, had a Jewish grandmother, but I don't know if that's true. She liked Rachel. Maybe it was because she couldn't get on with her own daughter. Adeline had joined the Party. Maybe she saw it as a way to get ahead or maybe she was just like her father.'

'What happened to Rachel?'

Levy was so desperate to know. But should Gunther tell him? Of course.

'Maria hid Rachel in the cellar of the house for a long time. Years.'

'Did Adeline know?'

'Of course. She and her mother lived in the house too, by then. How could she not?'

'But—'

'And Rachel bribed her. The Austerlitz women had jewellery, which the mother, Miriam, had hidden all over the house. They were so naive in the early days. They thought they might even return home. Rachel knew where it was and so she bartered with Adeline for her life using that knowledge.'

Levy said, 'But what did her mother say?'

'Maria was on a knife edge. Between her Nazi daughter and the girl she wanted to save. While Adeline was using the Austerlitz jewellery to fund her life going to plays and bars with good Aryan boys, she was keeping her mouth shut. Still, however, the house was searched. Again and again. And it was a problem. Rachel coughed; she had tuberculosis and so Maria walled her up in an alcove like a character from an Edgar Allen Poe story. A few bricks could be moved to feed her. Jews hid in cupboards, in drains, in spaces like coffins all over this city when the fascists were in charge.' He looked at Sara. 'We, the DDR, we tried to make sure it would never happen again. But people wanted to be free, apparently, to abuse Jews, which is what we see today.'

'It was more than that,' Sara said. Her face was

white with rage. 'You know this, Herr Beltz. How can people live with the knowledge that having a product from a foreign country, for instance, can have them put into prison for ten years? You know this happened.'

'I know that is how fascism creeps inside,' he said. 'A box containing a cake mixture from the West, is not just a box . . .'

'And Rachel?'

Irving had to interrupt. He'd never been a political person and he didn't care about the struggle between communism and fascism.

Herr Beltz cleared his throat. 'My father returned to Berlin with the Red Army when they liberated the city in 1945. He found Maria, but not Adeline.'

'In this house?'

'In what remained of the coach house. The Nazis had used the main house as a brothel since 1944.'

'What happened to Rachel?'

He walked over to the fireplace and positioned some more logs in the grate. Flames first died down and then rose to lick the untouched wood.

'She had died in 1944,' he said. 'I expect tuberculosis killed her. But I don't know. How could a person, even when well, survive being locked into a dark alcove?'

'Where was Adeline?'

Irving felt his heart pound. Was he close to discovering something significant?

Gunther Beltz sighed. 'Gone,' he said. 'In '44 we know she "entertained" in what had become

180

a brothel. But then, according to Maria, one day she just wasn't there. I don't know when. But my father used to say that his mother believed that Adeline had killed Rachel. How a person does that to one who is walled away, I don't know. Poison? Maybe. But when my father opened that alcove in 1945, Rachel was long dead.'

Outside, on the street, the day was progressing and the traffic building up as people made their way to work and school and college. There was a smell of sugar in the air from the bakery at the end of the street, which specialised in the small German doughnuts called Schmalzkuchen. Irving had always had a sweet tooth, but this made him feel sick.

There was nothing to see.

'The alcove was here,' Beltz said.

Lee looked at Irving, who was beyond white, almost green.

'I think we should go upstairs again,' he said as he took one of Irving's arms. 'It's cold.'

'Cold as death.'

If you looked closely, there was an outline of what could have once been a wall. The only feature that marked that alcove out from others in the cellar was that there was a ledge on the inside, about two feet from the ground. At a pinch, a small person could have been able to sit down, which was probably why this space had been chosen. Lee recalled a story he'd once been told as a child about a nun who had been walled up for supposedly having fallen in love with a priest. His father had said, 'Bloody Catholics! What do you expect?' and then gone back to his copy of *The Sun*.

Then there was the story of Anne Frank. It had been the one book from his youth that had really affected him. Lee had always wanted to go and see the secret annexe in Amsterdam and be where Anne had once lived. But maybe after this experience, he didn't. Then he felt a pressure on the arm that was not holding up Irving.

Mumtaz.

Beltz made more coffee and produced a plate of Schmalzkuchen. But nobody wanted to eat. Still cold from the cellar, the ex-Stasi officer suggested that everyone move their chairs closer to the fire. And because it was so dark in that room, the atmosphere began to take on the characteristics of a group of people telling ghost stories at midnight. Only one person sat outside the circle around the fire: Sara Metzler. But it was her to whom Herr Beltz spoke.

'I know it may be hard to believe, but the reason my father insisted upon owning this house . . .'

Sara said something in German.

Beltz countered in English. 'Think what you like, Frau Metzler,' he said. 'But my father preserved this place as a memorial to the Austerlitz family.'

'And made money.'

He ignored her.

'My father arranged for Rachel to be buried with her grandparents.'

'That grave is not recorded.'

'Because it was 1945 and the world was still burning,' he said. 'He did his best.'

How did someone in Berlin, whatever the subject under discussion, not become embroiled in the subject of East–West politics? Mumtaz remembered when the Wall had come down and what their teachers at school had said about that. A unified Germany, they'd parroted, was going to be so much better than the fragmented mess it had been before. But was it? And had true unity ever even taken place? Indeed, could it while all these old suspicions and beliefs about the West or the East were still in place?

She heard Irving say, 'And Adeline?'

Beltz shrugged. 'Never heard of since 1944. Maybe, Mr Levy, you have been thinking that Adeline was your mother, but I don't think so.'

Lee cut in. 'We reckon that Irving's father met his mother in September 1945. Because he was in the 131st Infantry Brigade he would've been in what the Russians call the "Forgotten Parade" . . .'

'Yes, the victory celebration at the Brandenburg Gate,' Beltz said. 'The Soviet Union and the US sent their top generals while the British and French sent people no one had ever heard of. They didn't want to contribute to something organised by a communist nation. A case of what you would call sour grapes, I think. You think that Mr Levy's father came to this house at that time?'

'It's known that the troops from all sectors got together then,' Lee said. 'He could've come here.'

'Why here?'

'I don't know.'

'Berlin was in ruins,' Beltz said. 'Why come here?'

'Because this house wasn't in ruins?'

'But it was. My father had fifty per cent of it rebuilt. The top two floors, the facade.' He turned to Irving. 'Do you have a photograph of your mother?'

Lee had them on his tablet. Beltz put his glasses on and began to flick through the images on the screen. He shook his head. 'I never knew Adeline and no photographs exist. This house was ruined, remember. But this woman doesn't look, to me, like my father or my grandmother.'

'We know she dyed her hair black,' Irving said.

He shrugged. 'Even so . . .' Then he stopped. He showed the screen to Irving. 'Who is the child?'

'That's my sister, Miriam,' he said. 'Why? Do you recognise . . .'

'No, just curious.' He looked up and smiled. 'I think maybe the child is you.'

'Oh no. My sister is another mystery I must try to solve before I die.'

'Oh really.'

'She was abducted when she was one year old,' Irving said. 'In a park where there was a fairground.'

'Ah, we used to have such a thing here in Berlin,' Beltz said. 'At the Spreepark. Frau Metzler will recall . . .'

'It was popular in the DDR; there was little else to do,' Sara said. 'Now it is abandoned.'

Mumtaz couldn't help noticing how Herr Beltz merely glossed over the abduction of Irving's sister, apparently to make a political point. In spite of the fire in the grate, it made her feel chilled.

Beltz handed the iPad back to Lee. He looked at Irving.

'I wish I could tell you that I know where my father was in September 1945, but I do not know and he is dead,' he said. 'He was a soldier by then; he would have been with his comrades. He told me he took my grandmother with him into the care of the Red Army. The house would have been empty again, or taken over by squatters. Maybe your father met one of those.'

'She called herself Rachel Austerlitz.'

'Did she have anything in her possession that had belonged to Rachel Austerlitz?'

Irving bowed his head. 'According to Dad, she came with nothing. I don't think she had anything. My father, like me, was a diamond cutter back home. Mum had a lot of jewellery, but it was given to her by him.'

He shook his head. 'I am sorry, Mr Levy, but I do not think there is a connection between us. I fear your mother was someone who lived in this house and maybe knew a little about the Austerlitz family.'

'Mum knew how to be a Jew.'

'Then maybe she was one?'

He told him about the DNA test and the German's face seemed to darken. Then he said, 'I cannot help you and I am sorry for that, Mr Levy. Your father, it would seem, met a lady here with whom he fell in love. But she was not Rachel Austerlitz and she was not, I believe, my aunt.'

Mumtaz watched Irving's face, but he gave away nothing about how he felt at that moment, which had to be, she knew, an ending.

If you live in a city all your life, you get to know the places where you can talk undisturbed. As a former East German, Sara Metzler had always felt she had a keen nose for such places. She just hoped that Irving Levy didn't find her choice of venue disturbing.

'It was a pharmacy,' she said, as she pushed open the door that led from the elegant, tree-lined Oranienplatz to a wooden-floored space, scented with coffee and cinnamon. On the left, a bar that had once been an ornate nineteenth-century shop counter was overshadowed by hundreds of polished wooden shelves bearing bottles that, in a former life, had contained substances like 'Arsenic' and 'Aspirin'.

And there were mirrors, brightly polished, set into dark wood frames. Unfortunately, they reflected how tired Mr Levy looked.

Sara took them to the comfortable chairs in the

small back room that was lined with drawers that had once contained herbs, powders and potions. There was always a slight smell of basil in that room . . .

'Coffee?'

Levy shook his head. 'If I drink any more I will be found on the ceiling,' he said. 'Tea. I'll pay.'

But Sara paid, in spite of Lee Arnold's insistence that the least they could do was buy her a drink.

Once she'd sat down, Sara said, 'You know you can't trust a man like Beltz.'

'Why would he lie about something that is really nothing to do with him?' Mumtaz asked.

'In the Stasi they were trained to lie.'

'Yes, but about this?'

They all looked towards Irving. He said nothing until his tea arrived; he'd let it brew, poured it out and then consumed his first cup.

'I'm sorry,' he said, 'I am really very English when it comes to hot drinks. Tea! What a blessing! But also, for me, Herr Beltz what a blessing too. I know, Frau, that you cannot put aside his past . . .'

'His father was in the Politburo. They made our lives like death!'

'Which I can appreciate, if not empathise with,' he said. 'But what Herr Beltz said made sense. And as Mumtaz has pointed out, why would he lie? Saying that all Stasi men lied doesn't, I think, work here. This is nothing to do with who he was, or even who his father was. It's to do with a house where terrible things happened and where two people met – one known and one unknown.'

'He was not welcoming when we first went,' Sara said.

'But he was today.'

'He has an agenda.'

'I didn't feel that,' Lee said.

'With respect,' Sara replied, 'you have never lived with such people. You've never had to keep the fact that you know a banned language a secret.'

'His dad was a communist fighting fascism . . .'

'Communism means something different here,' she said. 'To you it is something that you have never lived with and so can seem a nice idea. To us it was a catastrophe. It made us look at each other with hatred and suspicion. I have seen my Stasi file. Imagine someone watching everything you do – for years. Imagine a wall you know is meant to keep you somewhere you would rather not be. That was my life.'

He felt drained. Strangers didn't come, he made sure that they didn't. But he'd let the Jew and his people in. What they hadn't known was that Gunther Beltz had hoped to find out as much from them as they had hoped to discover from him.

The man could have been some distant Austerlitz relative, maybe even someone who might be able to explain why his father had taken Rachel's death so badly. Gunther's mother had never been able to compete. She'd died knowing she was second-best.

It had been like living in a funeral home. It still was. For good reason.

CHAPTER 15

Bela felt the caravan begin to move. He was supposed to be in the truck with Eva and Gala, but he'd refused to move from his bed. Back in the old country, caravans had been pulled by horses and nobody ever thought about getting out or riding up front.

There had been ten in his family. His parents and eight children, five of them fliers; Tibor, Viktor and Miklos wire-walkers, like their mother. Such happy times, flying through the air with his father, three brothers and their sister. Then falling in love . . .

All gone. Bela felt his eyes begin to moisten and stopped himself short before he gave in to tears. Watching him from the sofa at the end of his bed, their little made-up eyes searching for any sign of weakness. He could feel the Twins, thinking.

Irving had wanted to go home to the UK immediately – he was worn out and drained – but Mumtaz had managed to persuade him to stay one more day. Their flights didn't leave until Friday and she wanted to see more of Berlin if she could.

Sara, although still smarting from having to spend time with a man she despised, had nevertheless offered to show Lee and Mumtaz some of the sights of the city. Irving was spending the day in bed.

Sara said she'd arrive at ten and, because she hadn't seen him at breakfast, Mumtaz went to Lee's room to find out if he was ready. As she knocked, she felt her heart pound.

He opened the door and stared at her. Had he forgotten?

Then he said, 'Got some work to do. Sorry. You go on your own.'

Not sure whether she was pleased or not, Mumtaz joined Sara in the lobby. Was being around Lee ever going to get any better? As she followed Sara to the nearest bus stop, Mumtaz remembered reading letters in girls' magazines when she was a teenager about being friends with your 'ex'. It never seemed to work out and most of the agony aunts she remembered from back in the late eighties and nineties, advised against it. Probably with good reason.

Sara led her onto a bus and told her to register the transport ticket she'd bought at the hotel in a machine. That, so it seemed, was the only time she had to show it, unless she was pulled over by an inspector.

A bus journey and a short walk later, they arrived at Checkpoint Charlie, the old dividing point between East and West Berlin. It had a carnival atmosphere. A shed, surrounded by sandbags, not authentic according to Sara, stood in the middle of a road called Friedrichstrasse. You could, for a consideration, have your photograph taken with two Germans dressed as American GIs. Everyone smiled, especially small kids. Mumtaz herself smiled, in spite of knowing that people had died at this juncture. Where hadn't people died? Taking the poison out of a place that had once been so toxic had to be a good thing, didn't it?

'Charlie should, I think, have remained a warning,' Sara said as they watched a phalanx of kids have their photographs taken. 'You know this place became like the Stasi Headquarters for us. We wouldn't look at it. You never knew what horror you might see.'

There was a story about a man who had been shot and not died at Charlie. Mumtaz had read about it on the plane. He'd bled to death amongst the barbed wire.

'The Cold War may be over, but one does not trust the Russians,' Sara continued. 'The man Putin was a KGB officer. He came here with them in 1989. He saw the Wall come down. It's said that is why he's like he is now, intent on running the world.'

'Well, I don't—'

'And he is short.' She laughed. 'He feels bad about that, I think!'

Mumtaz had thought when she'd arrived in Berlin that a city of glistening spires had taken over completely from the old, paranoid, grey city of the past. But she'd encountered little that didn't echo back to a past that still seemed to reverberate and, in some cases, damage the present.

They had coffee at the Checkpoint Charlie Cafe. Like Irving, Mumtaz had never drunk so much coffee in her life. Bengalis didn't. It was all tea.

'Sara,' she said, 'do you think that Herr Beltz was telling the truth about Rachel Austerlitz?'

'That she died, yes,' Sara said. 'But how she died? I don't know. You have to understand, Mumtaz, that it's very difficult for me to separate the man from the Stasi officer. Those people lived and breathed lies. Some of them did so because they truly believed it was for the greater good. But some just wanted to get rich. If you were in the Politburo, like Beltz's father, your life was more comfortable than most. You had goods from the West, you could travel, you could learn banned languages, like English. Of course, they all said they had to do these things for the good of the country, but we lived always in fear. We were given apartments, cars, healthcare, but we could not have our own thoughts. In the end that becomes more important than anything.'

Sara couldn't know how much her words chimed with Mumtaz. Living with her husband had been like being a hostage. Not allowed out, unable to contact friends, being abused – and owing money to the Sheikhs was a continuation of that.

'Do you remember Herr Beltz's father?'

193

'Joachim Beltz? A little,' she said. 'But I took small notice of any of those people, if I am honest. They were just a collection of old waxworks who applauded whenever Erich Honecker, the General Secretary of the Central Committee, spoke, opened a factory or did anything, in fact. I think that like most people in the DDR I was too busy trying to outwardly conform while trying to hold on to something of myself.'

'It must have been exhausting.'

'It was. Which is why so many of us cannot forgive,' she said. 'You know when siblings fall out over something, it can be a terrible thing. I don't have brothers and sisters, but my friends who do have told me. People go to their deaths with these differences unresolved. The same is true of people who were comrades in systems like the DDR. We were all in the same boat, as you say, but some used the boat just for themselves. And that, for many of us, remains unforgivable.'

Lee's room was the one next door, Irving's was sandwiched between his and Mumtaz's bedrooms. Irving could hear him on his phone, probably to colleagues back in Upton Park. He couldn't make out any words. Mumtaz had gone sightseeing with Frau Metzler. She was a nice woman but, he felt, her very obvious problems with Herr Beltz's previous profession had maybe rendered their dealings with him less fruitful than they could have been.

In spite of what Beltz had said, Irving wasn't convinced that the Stasi officer's aunt could not have been his mother. She had disappeared sometime in 1944, but who was to say that she didn't return to her home in 1945? The war was coming to an end, why wouldn't she go home? Where else did she have to go? And yet Beltz had not recognised her from any of the photographs he'd been shown.

Irving lay on his bed and looked up at the ceiling. He'd left it too long. For years he'd wondered. He'd always felt there was something he didn't understand, or had missed, about his mother, but he'd never spoken to her or his father. Maybe it was because they fought all the time. What had they fought about? Things that were nothing, like whose job it was to clean the windows, whether to get a gardener. But sometimes they argued about him. They'd rowed mercilessly about him. Rachel had wanted him to go to the local grammar school so that he could have friends who lived nearby. His father had insisted he went to a Jewish school, and he got his way, which was why Irving had been required to schlepp from Barking to Hendon every day for six years. He'd hated it but, once he was there, his mother seemed to forget about the local grammar and just told him he had to put up with the place. She rarely defended her son and, when he finally went to work with his father, she treated them both with what was probably contempt.

Had losing Miriam made her cold? The way she had screamed when the baby was taken had stayed with him. It had been like the cry of an agonised animal. He had no idea what his father had felt. If he closed his eyes all he could see was his father either shouting or giving his mother diamonds. He'd done the same as she'd aged. Every time Rachel had seemed upset he'd brought her something from the Garden – earrings, brooches, sometimes emeralds from one of the Pakistani dealers in later years.

Herr Beltz's aunt had taken the jewellery Miriam Austerlitz had hidden in that house. Those had been terrible times, but had his mother's dependence upon jewellery to regulate her mood started then? Did diamonds do more for her than just look pretty? Did they make her feel safe?

When the Soviets had invaded Berlin in April 1945, the hidden Jews had begun to surface. The women thought that being Jewish would save them from the mass rapes visited by the Soviets on the German population at large. But it didn't. Reports from the time proved that the Red Army didn't care who its soldiers assaulted. There must have been exceptions, though. Maybe Irving's mother had used being Jewish – even though she was not – to confound the Soviets. And it had worked.

Then she'd met his father.

Adeline Beltz could have been his mother. Working in a Jewish household must have taught her how to be a Jew. What if he asked Herr Beltz to take a DNA test? Would he?

Irving knew that he wouldn't and why would he? A negative result would waste everyone's time and a positive one would do him no good. Or would it? He had to have opened his house to them for a reason.

Maybe there were things Herr Beltz had wanted to know from him?

Mumtaz took a lot of photographs, mainly for Irving, but also for her own family. Her dad would be interested to see how strongly Islamic architecture had influenced the building of a nineteenth-century synagogue.

'This is where you work?' she asked Sara.

'In the centre attached to the building, yes,' she said. 'One of the good things the DDR did was to restore this building. The Nazis took the dome away for safe-keeping because of the gold.'

The dome gleamed in the thin, autumn sunlight.

'It was repaired and reinstated by the DDR. But the building is very delicate and this facade is just held together by metal.'

'It's not in use.'

'No. It's also much smaller than it was. There is a space at the back where you can see just how huge it was. Now we have a small, mixed prayer hall, in line with Liberal Jewish tradition. Like the family of my mother, the Austerlitz family came here to worship. Liberal Jews were common in this city. The Austerlitzes would not have been overtly religious. They would most probably have celebrated Christmas and it is doubtful they would have committed to things like fasting on Yom Kippur. I think Herr Levy is Orthodox.'

'Yes.'

'So discovering his mother was a Gentile is a big thing for him.'

'Yes.'

Sara shook her head. 'So sad.'

'What is?'

'To be so wrapped up in a certain identity that you cannot see the life you could have if you let that go,' Sara said. 'My father was a Red Army commander and yet I still consider myself Jewish. I know that our religion is passed on through the maternal line . . .'

'Which is the point,' Mumtaz said. 'It's his mother.'

Sara shook her head. 'And so?' she said. 'If I were him, I would be using what time I have left to enjoy myself. He has money. Why drag up a past you will probably never find the truth about? Why chase the dead who cannot speak?'

'We all need to know who we are,' Mumtaz said. 'If we don't know that, we know nothing.'

'And if we refuse love because of who we are, we make God or whatever runs the universe weep,' Sara said. Then she moved her head close to Mumtaz's and whispered, 'You must go to Lee. If you don't you will break both your hearts.'

*   *   *

This had been a bad idea. To be fair, Lee had counselled against it. But Levy knew his own mind, or thought he did.

'There's no bloodletting, they just take a few cells from inside your cheek.'

Lee saw the way that Beltz looked at his client and he wanted the floorboards to swallow him.

Beltz said, 'I think I know how DNA tests work, Herr Levy.'

'Then surely that would solve this mystery.'

'Mystery? What mystery? That we may be related? We are not,' Beltz said. 'My aunt is dead. Maybe underneath this city, possibly in a mass grave somewhere. It is not anything to do with me, not now.'

'Then why let us in yesterday?' Irving persisted. 'You didn't the day before – and don't try to deny it, we knew you were in. Frau Metzler told you why we'd come when she left you her number, so you knew what we wanted when we returned.'

'I was curious.'

'Only that? I don't think so.'

Of course, Irving was right. Someone like Beltz had to have a good reason to let strangers into his house and then tell them what Lee imagined had to be family secrets.

The ex-Stasi officer sat back in his chair. Once again they were arranged around his fire. It still gave off little heat.

'Alright,' he said, 'I did hope you may have known something that I could use. I thought that if you were some distant relative of the Austerlitz family or you had access to information I don't have that maybe you could help me.'

'With what?'

He deflated his lungs as he looked at the floor and then he said, 'My father was a sad man. People saw him as a member of the Politburo and as a war hero, but they never knew how damaged he was. This house meant more to him than I ever did. Not just because Rachel Austerlitz died here or because he owed his life to her father. He loved Rachel and he never got over her. This house was her mausoleum. It remains so. My mother, my brother and I, we suffered for it. We were like ghosts passing through his life without touching him.' He shook his head. 'And when my mother died he had that woman's body brought back to this house and laid underneath the alcove where she hid from the Nazis. My brother would never speak to him then. Such an insult to our mother. I knew he was damaged and he was dying by then. I let it go.

'But I've always wondered whether Rachel loved him too. Did they sleep together? Did they maybe make plans to marry one day? Did her father put him on that train to Hungary, not to save his life, but to get him away from his daughter? They were just children, really, but he never forgot. He damaged his only family because of Rachel and now I find myself keeping this house for him and for the dead body in my cellar.

Madness? Maybe. I have a corpse in my cellar. But what else can I do?'

He didn't cry or scream or even raise his voice, but Gunther Beltz was in pain. He must have kept part, if not all, of this to himself for most of his life. Not that Lee was surprised. Secrets were what he dealt with every day. No secrets, no need for private investigators. They paid his bills.

Eventually, Irving spoke.

'I'm afraid I know nothing about your father and Rachel Austerlitz,' he said. 'The Rachel Austerlitz that was my mother was not that girl your father loved.' He stood up. 'I should not have come here. I apologise for disturbing you.'

Lee stood and pulled his coat tight around his body. Christ, what a bloody cold house! Maybe it was the corpse in the cellar . . .

Lee had left the room and Irving was just about to leave when Gunther Beltz called them back.

While the rides and the generators went on ahead, the caravans pulled into a field just outside Dartford. The fair had used it as a staging place and wintered there for decades. They'd spend one night and then push on to Barking in the morning. As soon as the vans were secured the women began connecting up the gas supplies and getting water.

Eva and Amber came to make sure that he was alright and the kid made tea.

'God, you look like a bag of rags!' Bela said when he saw his daughter. 'Tidy yourself up!'

She shook her head. 'I look like you, Papa,' she said. 'And, anyway, what do you expect? I've just packed my life away for the millionth time. This life gets no easier, I shouldn't have to tell you that.'

She did look like him. Brown as a Gypsy, her black hair, dyed now to try and hide her age, a long rope of thick coarse wire down her back. She'd passed her looks on to her daughter, Gala, another child from the dark side.

'Here you are, Nagyapa, a nice cup of tea.'

Ah but the little one was different. Unlike most of the girls her age she didn't need to dye her hair blonde. It shone like gold even in dull weather and it made the old man smile. But this time he resisted the temptation to do that and said, 'And you, Amber, I don't want you flying now. Not for a while.'

'Not ever,' his daughter said.

The girl pulled a face, but said nothing and left the caravan to go and help her mother. When she'd gone, Eva said, 'What are you playing at, Papa? It's you who have been encouraging the girl.'

He sipped his tea. 'I play at nothing,' he said. 'I'm just tired of trouble.'

'I don't believe you,' Eva said, 'but I'm still grateful you said it. She does what you say even if she ignores the rest of us.'

Later, Amber came to see him when he was alone. She said, 'Nagyapa, did you mean it about not flying?'

She looked hurt, which made his heart sting and

he said, 'For a while only.' And then he beckoned her close. 'I will give you money to go to Camden instead. How is that?'

Her eyes lit up. He had to work hard not to look sad. She was the only one who had ever listened to his stories. It was a pity her parents and her grandmother had discouraged her. It was sad that she was like so many young people inasmuch as she wanted every material thing. It broke his heart. And yet, poor child, she still wanted to fly and he could deny her nothing.

'You may fly again when we leave Barking,' he said.

'That's a long time. I'll get out of practice!'

She would never be good enough. Not really. She didn't have the discipline. He'd tried to tell her, but he couldn't be cruel. He'd never been cruel to that face and he never would be.

CHAPTER 16

There was no reality in her mother's obser-vation. 'Oh, you look thin!' was Bangladeshi shorthand for 'You've been away and only your mother can make you normal again.'

Mumtaz sat at the table of her mother's kitchen and watched helplessly as Sumita heaved pans around, chopped vegetables and ground spice.

'Amma . . .'

'It's just a biryani,' her mother said as she ground nutmeg, mace, pepper, cloves, cardamom, cinnamon, coriander and ginger. No wonder her arms remained strong even if her legs were sometimes weak.

Hopefully, Shazia would be home soon and they could talk. Mumtaz always felt guilty when she was in her mother's kitchen not helping. But her mother was adamant, she was a 'guest' now and so of course she couldn't be expected to help. Also, she'd just returned from abroad which, in Sumita's experience, was a very tiring thing.

'You should go and lie down, Mumtaz,' she said. 'You must be exhausted.'

'I've only flown from Berlin,' Mumtaz said. 'It's only one and a half hours.'

Her mother looked amazed. She only ever flew to see family in Bangladesh, which was a gruelling eleven hours.

Mumtaz heard the front door open and then close. Then she listened for the footsteps in the hall. If they were slightly heavy and halting it was her father, if light and fast, her stepdaughter. They were the latter and Mumtaz smiled.

They'd be setting up all weekend. Lesters was one of the biggest fairs in the country. Already he could see a few local kids were beginning to hang around the park gates, hoping for a look at this year's most daring rides.

Ever since so many people had started going to Disneyland and other huge theme parks in America as well as on the Continent, travelling fairs had needed to up their game. This meant new and ever more exciting rides every year. According to posters on the park railings, this year's main attraction was something called the 'BigO'. But there was no picture or description of this thing and so Irving was left to create his very own fairground monster in his mind. But he was too tired.

The flight from Berlin hadn't taken long, but the taxi back to Barking had got caught in traffic on the A13, making the journey home much longer than it should have been.

He sat in his chair and switched on the TV, which he immediately zoned out. The news was never pleasant these days. But at least he had been to Berlin, he'd seen the house where his parents had met, supposedly, and Herr Beltz had assured him that he would take a DNA test. Lee was going to look into how they would proceed with a comparison.

God, what a grim place that house had been! So cold and grey and so full of its own tragic history. Even, according to Beltz, a corpse under the cellar. A product of obsession, that. He couldn't understand; he'd never been in love. It reminded him of Ruben Abrahams, who had briefly lived next door when they were both children. He had once dug up the budgie his dad had buried in their garden to see what it looked like. Its beak had fallen off and then its legs. And it had been alive with maggots. Irving had almost been sick.

But at least the woman Beltz's father had exhumed hadn't been his mother. He was certain of that now. Rachel Austerlitz, however she had died, had breathed her last in 1944. This left a void where whoever his mother was should have been. And if he wasn't related to Beltz, what then? He would die without knowing who he had been. Did it really matter? World War II had taken not only lives, but also identities. Sara Metzler said there were thousands of people walking about who didn't even know they were Jewish because of what had happened between 1939 and 1945. He was just one of those. Nothing special; he should accept it.

And Irving knew he could do that if it wasn't

for Miriam. Not knowing one's past was one thing, but not knowing if one's only blood relative was alive or dead was unbearable. He'd encased his life in diamonds to blot it out.

Human flesh could disappear in a heartbeat, but diamonds, as the De Beers diamond company had first said back in the 1940s, are for ever.

'He looked right at me and, even though I know he probably still feels hatred towards me about Naz, I began thinking there had to be more to it than that,' Shazia said. 'His family killed Dad.'

'Your father owed them money. That is how such people operate. You owe them money, they take your life. It's an object lesson for their other debtors.'

Mumtaz had never questioned why the Sheikh family had killed her husband. They were gangsters and he had owed them money.

Shazia swung her legs up onto the bed and lay down beside her stepmother. Her bedroom was the only place in that massive house they stood a chance of getting away from the old people. And even there she had to make sure she put a chair against the door or her didima would be coming in with tea.

'Shazia . . .'

'Now you tell me that Wahid-ji is asking you for money again . . .'

'He has cancer; he needs treatment . . .'

'He's rich,' Shazia said. 'They all are. And

anyway, why make you pay for that? They must have people way richer than us indebted to them. They own property all over the East End; they own lawyers for God's sake!'

Still trying to absorb the fact that Wahid Sheikh had been seen around her stepdaughter, Mumtaz felt both relieved that they were talking again and anxious. If the old man was just lurking that was one thing, but what if he did something more drastic? What if he took Shazia? People like the Sheikhs were a law unto themselves. People who had friends in high places were, and the Sheikhs had very good lawyers and, it was said, police officers on their payroll. However, Shazia had made a good point: had they actually killed anyone apart from Ahmet Hakim?

'There has to be something else,' Shazia said.

'Like what?'

Why had she said that? Mumtaz had been careful never ever to think about such a possibility, even though she had always known it had to exist. To kill Ahmet had been a huge risk to take. After all, the Sheikhs couldn't have known for certain that she wouldn't go straight to the police with a description of her husband's attacker the night he died in a pool of his own blood on Wanstead Flats. The risk had to either be worth it or unavoidable, and if it were unavoidable, that probably meant that Ahmet had hurt the family in some way. She felt herself shiver.

Shazia, looking down at her painted fingernails, said, 'Lee could find out, couldn't he?'

Lee had been trying to find a weakness in the Sheikh family's armour for some time. And, although they rarely talked outside work now, she knew he was in all probability still looking. He loved her.

Mumtaz said, 'I don't want you going out on your own until you leave for uni.'

'I rarely am on my own. It's annoying.'

'Annoying it may be, but it's necessary,' Mumtaz said. 'And I will take you up to Manchester myself. I can't let your dadu do all that driving.'

'You were going to,' Shazia said. 'Before I phoned you in Germany.'

'Yes! Yes!'

She had been prepared to let her father take on a journey to Manchester, it was true.

'Shazia,' she said, 'I don't know what I can do to make things better between us. But really that is all I care about. If the Sheikhs want money from me then so be it. I don't know what finding out if your father had other problems with that family will achieve.'

'Speak to Lee.'

The girl didn't know what had happened between them and how both ashamed and confused she now felt about it. Hopefully, she would never know.

'He loves you, you know, Amma,' Shazia said.

Irving would need the weekend to recover from Berlin, then Monday, the fair was closed. Things got going on the Tuesday with the first of two half-price wristband afternoons. Then they'd go. Hopefully, Irving would be up to being walked through what he could remember about the day Miriam had gone missing. In the meantime, Lee had a shit-ton of calls on the office answerphone. He'd had casuals covering the office all week, except the Friday, and so they had to have all come in that day. Someone was keen to get hold of him. He was just about to listen to them when the bloody thing rang again.

'Hello, Arnold Agency.'

The caller cleared his or her throat, then an elderly voice said, 'Mr Arnold? That you?'

'Yeah. Who's this?'

'It's Tommy Askew from Thames View.'

The old bloke who'd been a copper when Miriam Levy had gone missing.

'Oh hello, Mr Askew,' Lee said.

'Been trying to get hold of you,' the old man said. 'Always goes to answerphone. Where you been?'

'Berlin,' Lee said. 'On a job.'

'The Levy baby?'

Lee said, 'What do you want, Mr Askew?'

'My oldest daughter come to see me today,' the old man said. 'She lives down Dorset; her husband's a doctor in some little village down there, I dunno. Second marriage, it is. Anyway, she can't get here much so when she turns up this morning I had tea and Mr Kipling ready for her. Don't want your kids to think you can't do nothing, do you?'

'No.'

Lee was tired and, if he was honest, he felt in two minds about the Berlin trip. Sara Metzler had been more proactive than he had, and it had been Mumtaz who had contacted her. He'd done sod all. And what had they learnt?

'So anyway, we're jawing,' Tommy Askew said. 'This and that, the old days. I told Suzy, that's me daughter, about how people'd come to talk to me about the Levy baby. She was the only kid I had then. She was five. Upset her at the time.'

'What did?'

'The baby going missing,' Tommy said. 'It was on the telly. I was on the telly. The missus pointed me out to her. Daddy was gonna find the little baby girl for definite, according to Suzy. Except I never did.'

There was going to be a point to this but, to Lee, it seemed a long time coming. God he was impatient! Since when had he joined the iPhone generation?

'But any case,' the old man continued, 'you're probably wondering what this has to do with your investigation. Now I'll tell you. You know I said that we asked the baby's mother whether she had a toy in her pram with her, but I couldn't remember what it was? Well, Suzy knew. She said I told her it was a bear.'

'A teddy bear.'

'That's it, but it weren't no ordinary one. It was one of them . . . I'll have to get me daughter, I've forgot, bloody foreign . . .' He yelled, 'Here! Sue! Can you come over here and speak to . . .'

211

He heard the phone get passed over and then a very studiously cultured woman's voice said, 'My father means a Steiff bear. The ones that have a button in the ear.'

'That's it! That's it! Give us the phone back, girl!'

Lee had known that posh teddies had buttons in their ears. Even he was occasionally desperate enough to watch *Antiques Roadshow* on a Sunday night.

Tommy said, 'Apparently the kiddie played with it all the time. Brought it with her when she come from Germany, the mother. Only thing she brought, poor soul.'

The BigO, the world's tallest big wheel ride was certainly a big draw, but the rest of the fair was a bit bog-standard for punters accustomed to the thrill rides at Disney and places like Alton Towers. If travelling outfits wanted to survive they had to be prepared to evolve. David Sanders knew that but, even as he showed his boss, Roman Lester, a breakdown of their takings from Croydon, he could see the old man disagreed.

'This is all about lack of pre-publicity,' Lester said. 'If folk knew we were on our way, they'd look forward to our appearance and come along. Anticipation is what fairs are all about, David – always has been. We need to get bodies out on the street handing out leaflets, like we did in the old days.'

They'd had this discussion before, many times.

Roman wouldn't or couldn't see the value of putting their advertising efforts onto social media, which frustrated the hell out of David. Knowing they had a largely empty website all ready to be filled with show details and offers broke his heart. But however often he told Roman about how 'kids these days' looked everything up online, he wouldn't have it. So David just said, 'Yes, boss,' and the conversation moved on.

Once they'd discussed the move from Croydon and how that had gone, David tried another tack he'd never tried before. They were getting close to the end of the year and so the time had come to think about the next season.

'I want to really bring in the older generation,' he said.

Roman frowned. 'We're about parents and kiddies,' he said. 'Don't want the place gummed up with old farts like me. Unless it's grandparents with their grandkids.'

'Yeah, but who's got money?' David said. 'The Baby Boomers. Youngsters don't have a pot to piss in these days. Middle-aged people do. And what do they like? Something new and unusual and weird. A lot of them grew up in the sixties and in the punk era. You look at what they like to do for entertainment and it's stuff like Cirque du Soleil, immersive theatre. And there's hipsters, the rich kids from places like Shoreditch. Christ, Roman, the stuff they're into!'

'Like what?'

'Anything vintage, tattoos, taxidermy, weird stuff.'

'Don't like the sound of that!'

'You might not, but they do, and if we want to attract them as opposed to a load of kids bunking off school, we have to think about them. People like this are moving into places like Croydon and especially Barking. If we want to get them in, we have to think about what they might want to come and see and do.'

'And what's that, then?' Roman asked.

'Something weird. Something that harks back to the old days of travelling shows.'

'Like what?'

'Like some of our old stuff,' David said. 'That old steam carousel we keep in storage down in Kent. Proper vintage glamour that, if we can paint it up a bit, have a girl in a crinoline and a bloke in a top hat running it. Proper Dickens.'

Roman shook his head. 'I don't know,' he said. 'We spent a fortune on the BigO.'

'Yeah and refurbing some vintage stuff won't cost a fraction of that,' David said. 'Look, let me put together an old rig for you so you can see what I mean. I know we've got a couple of defunct attractions onsite, we use them for storage. Let me give them a lick of paint and show you what I've got in mind.'

Roman Lester thought for a moment, then he said, 'Alright. Just don't spend real money on it.'

David smiled. 'You won't be sorry,' he said.

★ ★ ★

214

'I don't remember any such thing,' Irving said. 'And if that was the only thing my mother brought with her from Germany, I would.'

He had no memory of a Steiff teddy bear! His mother had been too unsentimental to have something like that.

'Your mother told the police your sister had it with her when she went missing,' Lee Arnold said.

'I've said before, there was no toy,' Irving said. 'Not a bear or anything else.'

'There's nothing like that in the house?'

He looked around his living room as if expecting to find something in the jumble of 'things' on every surface.

'No . . .'

'You're sure? I know you can't have gone through everything when your parents died, nobody ever does.'

'I did,' he said. He was tired and wanted to just fall asleep in front of the TV. 'Anyway, if mother told the police that Miriam had this bear, then it would be with her, wouldn't it?'

'Yes. But because you couldn't remember it from that day, maybe it wasn't with her. Maybe your Mother was wrong and the bear was at home.'

'I don't know.'

'Well, can you give it some thought?' he said. 'Constable Askew's daughter was very sure about this.'

'Alright, I will.'

He put the phone down. God, wasn't it enough

to have just come back from Germany empty-handed and now this? But Lee Arnold meant well. He was doing his job. Left to Irving himself nothing would happen. And maybe this business about a Steiff bear meant something?

But he'd been through the house since his mother had died and he'd found nothing that pertained to Germany or to Miriam – not even her birth certificate. That continued to bother him. When he'd first realised that he couldn't find it, he'd gone mad, tearing the house apart. Then he'd got ill and so any tearing had stopped. And, of course, he didn't know what was in every nook and cranny of his house. Who did? There was the garage, for a start. Semi-derelict now, it looked like a shack that might be found in a Brazilian favela. He couldn't even remember whether his father's old car was still in there or not. All he knew was that the last time he'd been in there the poor, drunken structure had been jammed to the rafters with who knew what.

CHAPTER 17

Lee had given her the weekend off, which was nice, especially now that Shazia was speaking to her again. It gave her time to wash the clothes she'd taken away with her and do some housework. Mumtaz also thought that she might look at some of the paperwork she'd brought with her from their old house. Some of it was hers, but much of it had belonged to Ahmet. Maybe if she looked through it she might be able to find a clue as to why the Sheikhs had singled him out particularly for death.

It was unlikely he would have committed anything inflammatory to paper. When she had gone looking for evidence of his debts, she'd found nothing. Everything Ahmet had done had been furtive. That included his abuse of his wife and his daughter. It had only been the drinking that had been obvious to people outside the house, and that very rarely. At home he would get slaughtered, rolling around the house screaming abuse and taunting Mumtaz with tales of his infidelity. Not that she ever knew who he'd been unfaithful to her with, or even if those stories were true.

She cleaned a space on the dining table and began to move unpacked boxes that still almost filled the hall into the middle of the living room. She wasn't sure which ones contained paperwork and so she'd probably have to wade through lots of useless ornaments and crockery first. Mumtaz took a deep breath. But then maybe now was the time to get rid of the mountains of 'stuff' she no longer used. Why did someone like her even have a twelve-place dinner service?

'It's the Sabbath.'

'I know that,' Lee said. 'Which is why all I want you to do is sit in a chair and watch. I'll clear out the garage. Look we're in September, but today the sun's shining; tomorrow it could be pissing it down with rain. Irving, mate, you gave me a job to do; I'm trying to do it.'

Irving Levy shrugged. 'What can I say?'

Lee Arnold had turned up at the house in Barking early. Irving hadn't even showered. Now wandering around in tracksuit bottoms and a pyjama jacket, he just wanted to be alone.

'It's terrible in there,' he said. 'Like a junk shop. And I think there's a car.'

'What kind of car?'

'I don't know. It was my father's. I never learnt to drive.'

It was a Morris Oxford Farina. Lee's Uncle Wol had one in the seventies. Big tail fins, smaller but similar to those seen on cars in old American films.

Uncle Wol's had been green, this one could be red, but then maybe that was just the rust. From the way the shelving full of God-knew-what sagged around it, the car was probably all that was holding the garage up.

'Christ!'

'I told you,' Irving said.

Lee had brought a wicker chair out of the conservatory for him to sit on. The garden was still damp from the overnight rain and so he spoke from inside a thick covering of blankets.

'I'll need a hand with this,' Lee said. He took out his phone.

John Shaw, fag hanging out of the corner of his mouth, trudged across the wet morning grass and said, 'I reckon you can see that bastard from space. But it can definitely be seen from Dagenham.'

David Sanders smiled. 'That's what we like to hear,' he said.

The BigO, billed as the tallest big wheel in the world, had cost Lesters a fortune and, although it still had a long way to go before it paid for itself, at least the bloody thing could make an impact. In Croydon, the BigO could be seen from Kenley, which had been good going. Dagenham in Barking was equally gratifying. It was just a pity the fucking thing wasn't proving the draw Roman Lester had imagined. But then, as David knew, big rides that didn't offer any new thrills were not what people wanted from fairs. There was nothing exotic about a big wheel, especially when riders were trapped in bloody great perspex pods. No risk, no romance, no nothing.

David pulled the tarpaulin off the roof of the old rig and tossed it to one side. Christ, it was filthy! If he hadn't known what it was, there was no way he would have been able to work it out now.

John shook his head. 'What the fuck is that?' he said.

'Ah, this is my big idea,' David said.

'What big idea?'

'Back to the future,' he said.

'They got that ride at Universal Studios,' John said. 'My brother took his kids.'

'I'm not talking about the film, muppet,' David said.

They both looked at the filthy old wagon, but only David smiled.

'People like experiences these days, think about Harry Potter World and that winter fair thing they have in London round Christmas. Bit of candyfloss and a go on the ghost train don't cut it any more. I want to give people a fair experience.'

'Candyfloss and a go on the ghost train is a fair experience.'

David shrugged. 'In one sense, yes. But it's a shit experience. It's still stuck in the seventies. Toffee apples, bumper cars, boys with mullets shagging girls round the back of the helter-skelter. It's childish and it's sexist and people don't want to eat the shit we sell no more.'

'People who come to fairs do,' John said.

'Then why are our takings down?'

'I dunno. Recession?'

'Over, officially,' David said. 'People want more sophisticated entertainment. What I want to do is try out some old Victorian attractions.'

'Like what?'

'We've got an old carousel in storage down in Kent, for a start. Powered by a steam engine, which we've also got, but which may need some work. We can adapt some of the sideshows with a lick of paint, get some animals in . . .'

'People don't like to see animals caged up these days.'

'Not caged up, in a petting zoo, donkey rides . . .'

'You'll get complaints from animal rights nutters.'

But David ignored him. He looked up at the old wagon and said, 'And then there's this.'

John shook his head. 'What the fuck is it?'

A voice that wasn't David's answered, 'It's something you should cover up and not even think about using. It's a bloody horror,' Eva Horvathy said.

Lee Arnold had always had a lot in common with Jasvinder Patel. They'd both worked out of Forest Gate nick, they'd both believed that many of their superiors' attitudes towards Muslim communities in the East End were ill-informed and fucked up, and they were both tall, thin and wiry.

Jas had given the Job a couple more years than

Lee, but that was because, at the time, she'd needed the security of a regular wage while she paid off the mortgage on her flat. Now a freelance PI and part-time personal trainer, Jas was a happy, carefree singleton, living a dream her permanently worried Hindu parents in Ilford found hard to fathom.

Lee and Jas pulled the old car backwards no more than a foot. They heard unnamed things clank to the floor and onto the bonnet.

'It's holding the whole thing up,' Irving said. 'I told you!'

Having him around kvetching like an old woman wasn't helping. But it was his garage . . .

'Mr Levy—'

'Irving!' he said. 'Call me Irving, Miss Patel!'

'Then please call me Jas,' she countered.

The day was getting lost amid Irving's constant anxiety that the garage would collapse and Jas's irritation that 'Mr Levy' seemed to think she shouldn't be lifting old cars about because she was a woman.

Lee, hands on hips, said, 'This is getting us nowhere.'

'I told you, leave it!'

'And if there are things in this garage that might lead us to your mother or your sister . . .'

Irving looked down at the ground. Although Lee knew he wanted to find his mother and his sister with a passion he couldn't even begin to appreciate, he could also see how tired and ill he was.

'I know, I know,' Irving said. Then he hauled all the blankets piled on top of him to one side. 'I'll go and make us all some tea.'

'No, I'll—'

'Lee, no,' he said as he moved slowly across the garden to the house. 'So it's the Sabbath, but what you're doing is important. I know this. For God's sake pull the car out and let the bloody garage collapse. What's the point?'

Once he'd gone, Lee and Jas sat down on the remains of an old rockery and had a fag break.

'Does he mean it about pulling out the car?' Jas said.

'I dunno.' Lee shook his head. 'He's supposed to be in remission, but he was tired when we went to Germany and knackered after. It's tough, because everything that happened did so such a long time ago. Everyone who could have told us anything about his mother is dead and I can't believe that his sister can be alive. You know the score. First twenty-four hours are crucial; if the kid's not rocked up after seventy-two hours, chances are the worst has happened.'

Jas had always been a practical woman. 'It's a job, Lee,' she said. 'You mustn't get too involved.' She shrugged. 'But then it's you and so you do.'

'A fucking freak show!'

Almost blasted backwards by the force of her words, John Shaw said, 'Whoah!'

David, who, as a member of the Horvathy family

by marriage, was a little more used to such behaviour, shook his head.

'Yeah, the same wagon where Ping and Pong used to work,' he said. 'If you can call it work . . .'

'Exactly!'

Eva Horvathy flung her arms in the air.

'Be good if they done something to earn their keep instead of living off your dad,' David said.

'No it wouldn't!'

'Yes, it would.'

'You don't understand,' she said. 'You've never seen a freak show. It was disgusting. To exploit people because of the way they look . . .'

'Yeah, it's weird,' he said. 'But, believe me, Eva, it's what the punters want these days.'

'These days? These days people are, what do they call it, politically correct . . .'

'Some are, but look online and you'll see that most aren't,' David said. 'Like I told old Roman, people are mad for the unusual these days. Don't ask me why. But if they can see a kid with a massive birthmark all over its body, a giant blackhead or a bloke with an arse for a face, they're happy.'

'They're sick!'

'Maybe. But look online and look on telly and you'll see I'm right,' he said. 'Fucking hell, Eva, there's even a late-night show about extreme tattooing. I've seen it. Geezers with tattoos between their toes, for God's sake!'

She shook her head. 'My father won't like it,' she said. 'Not if Ping and Pong are involved.'

'So we won't involve them,' David said. 'I'll advertise.'

'You what?' John said.

'I'll advertise.'

'For freaks?'

'For unusual people with unusual skills,' David said.

Eva walked away, shaking her head. John, if he was honest, rather sympathised.

Strictly, the car didn't come out in one piece. All the hub caps fell off, one door and part of the bonnet. But it didn't bring the garage down with it. And, crucially, Irving wasn't watching them when Lee and Jas pulled the car out. However, the stuff that remained in the building looked precariously balanced and was uniformly filthy.

'Where the fuck do we start?' Jas said.

Lee said, 'I've no idea.'

'So we're looking for a teddy bear . . .'

'And photographs and documents, particularly if they're in German and anything that looks unusual.'

'It all looks unusual.'

'You know what I mean,' he said. 'Personal things, stuff you wouldn't expect to find in a garage.'

'What wouldn't I expect to find in a garage, Lee?'

He shrugged. 'I dunno. Jewellery, knickers, jazz mags . . .'

'Oh, now you as a copper should know that a garage is a wonderful place for illicit jazz mags!'

She laughed. 'In fact, porn can be and is found anywhere.'

'Yeah, well forget the jazz mags, then,' he said. 'But anything else – personal.'

The dining table, which was far too big for her only living room, was covered in paper. Bills, bank statements, certificates, letters, things so old Mumtaz couldn't make out what they were. She'd only emptied two boxes and there were nine more to go. Just looking at it all exhausted her. Ahmet had only been forty-five when he died and yet he'd accumulated so much!

She made herself a cup of tea and sat down. At this rate she'd need to hire a skip to get rid of it all. And still she was none the wiser about her husband's activities. Of course, most of what should have been his fortune had been gambled away. Poker had been his game and he'd been hopeless at it. But he'd also been an addict, which meant that even when he lost big time, he couldn't stop. It was a state of mind she couldn't understand. She looked at the pile of papers on her table again and shook her head. In a way it was an emblem for modern life. Too much, too complicated, too desperately sad in its profusion.

And yet sometimes, data, for want of a better word, was exactly what was missing. Irving Levy had nothing that could throw light on the identity of his mother and that was partly because so much 'data' had been lost. Entire families had been excised, meaning that even when a connection was established, it was at best tenuous and at worst a lie. Or worse.

When Irving had told them that Gunther Beltz's father had exhumed Rachel Austerlitz and re-buried her in his cellar, she had felt as if she'd just slipped into a pool of madness. What had prompted him to do that? And how did he even know for sure that the body he'd taken out of the cellar was Rachel? She'd died sometime in 1944, he'd buried her the following year. She must have been unrecognisable. And for what? Why had he done that?

Irving said Beltz believed his father had loved Rachel. But had he? She knew that Christian Europeans, which Joachim Beltz must have been in his youth, had a different attitude towards the dead. In Islam, bodies had to be buried quickly because the soul was in pain until it was under the earth. There were practical considerations connected to hygiene as well. The same applied to the Jews. The Christians alone, as far as she knew, venerated dead bodies. The corpses of some saints were actually on display, while 'relics' or pieces of body, blood or clothing from Jesus, Mary or any number of saints were looked upon as magical talismans, able to perform miracles in their own right. Had Rachel been a talisman for Joachim Beltz or had his removal of her body had a darker purpose?

She suspected his son veered towards the latter. She considered how, when things were hidden, they could sometimes sour. It was then that it occurred to Mumtaz that if she wanted to know why her husband had been murdered by the Sheikhs, she could do worse than ask them.

'*Wien*. That means Vienna,' Irving said.

Jas had found the photograph. It had been in a side pocket of an old handbag she'd found on the back seat of the Morris Oxford. Items that had been with it included an empty perfume bottle, an almost full box of 'Guards' cigarettes and a gold lighter.

'My mother smoked well into old age,' Irving said. 'Guards were her brand. My father disapproved, but he did so in silence. It was the one issue between them that he accepted without comment. He smoked himself, but I know he felt that women shouldn't.' He pointed at the photograph. 'I've no idea who that is.'

Pasted onto a stiff backboard, the photograph was of a young man standing to attention in a suit. From details stencilled onto the backboard, as well as the unnatural background of what looked like a garden of artificial flowers, it had been taken in the Viennese Photography Studio of one Zalan Kovacs. It was old.

'It looks a bit Victorian,' Jas said. 'Standing like that. Victorians often looked as if they had rods up their backs. But the suit doesn't look that old. Looks quite modern to me.'

'Maybe it was a friend,' Irving said.

'Of your mother's?'

'This is one of her old bags,' he said as he looked at what remained of the brown leather handbag where the photograph had been found. 'He doesn't look like anyone I know.'

'You never met anyone from your mother's side of the family?' Jas asked. 'Did she ever show you any photographs?'

'No and no,' he said. 'She only ever spoke about her family as all dead. I knew nothing about them and I never asked.'

Lee, who had been wondering about this, said, 'Why not?'

'I don't know, to be honest. My parents fought a lot. Not physically, but they argued. Then after the arguments came the silences, which could go on for days, weeks.'

'What did your mother do while your father was at work and you were at school?'

'She kept the house,' he said. 'In the sixties this still happened in a lot of middle-class families. My mother didn't need to work and so she didn't.'

'What about friends? Or rather,' Lee said, 'what about people you invited to her funeral?'

'My father's family came,' he said.

'Only your father's family.'

'Just them. My dad's sister, Auntie Evelyn, my cousins Robert and Dawn, and their families. My mother had various cleaners over the years, but they never stayed or became friends of the family. My mother was a difficult woman. She looked down on people, she was a snob. Because, through my father, she had money she had nothing but contempt for those who didn't. She judged people, I think, on what they had and not who they were. That was why I sometimes fell out with her. She had no education and always failed to appreciate those who did.'

Lee got an image in his mind of an old woman dripping in diamonds, watching daytime TV.

Jas, still looking at the photograph, said, 'Is there any resemblance between this man and anyone you know? What about the Vienna connection?'

'No Vienna connection that I know about,' Irving said. 'But then maybe that was where this woman who was my mother came from. The man looks, to me, more like an Italian than a Jew. Or maybe a Gypsy. I'm sorry if you think my assumptions are racist, but that's just how I see him.'

Lee crossed his arms over his chest and frowned. 'What I can do is ask my artist contact to compare this photo to one of your mum and see whether she thinks they're related. Not foolproof, and it will cost you . . .'

Irving shrugged. 'Money?' he said. 'What's that to me? I can't take it with me.'

CHAPTER 18

The punters dripped onto the site through the drizzle. Such as they were. A small parade of the long-term unemployed, kids bunking off school and the occasional fat man on a disability scooter. They depressed the hell out of all those taking money at the entry booths. But David Sanders was elated. A low turnout for a half-price wristband day proved his point about the need for change. If they ran a Victorian-themed funfair, lots of the attractions could be put under canvas or wood and they'd do a roaring trade on food and drink. Just one look at the face of a bloke in a shell suit morbidly sucking on soggy candyfloss was enough to convince David. How much more grub could they sell, admittedly to a different type of punter, if they could offer mulled wine, hearty soup and home-made bread?

The old sideshows didn't interest anyone. Dismal and grubby, full of soft toy 'prizes' they'd had for donkey's years, they looked like relics from the 1970s, which of course they were. How much better if the shooting gallery and the hook-a-duck stalls were done up in Victorian splendour complete with new quirky prizes that people could actually win. Maybe each stall could be run by a Dickens character? That was a good idea.

David watched far fewer people than he would have liked climb onto the BigO. He suspected most of them just wanted somewhere to get in the dry. Who, after all, wanted to see a view over a naff old fairground and Barking Station? Things would pick up in the evenings and, once he got his way and the Victorian Fair was up and running, they'd make real money.

But in the meantime he had a problem. Old Bela Horvathy had called Roman Lester to complain about the resurrection of the freak show van. Gala's bloody mother had seen it, nearly had a conniption, and then told her old man. Apparently, Bela had gone on to Roman about how the old freak show would bring back bad memories for him and especially for Ping and Pong. He felt it was cruel.

But then if David knew the Twins, they'd relish the chance to display themselves and appal people. Old Horvathy could think he had control of them as much as he liked, but since they'd stopped working, back in the seventies, they'd taken every opportunity they got to frighten the punters. David had complaints. The only reason he never acted on them was because he knew his missus's family would all gang up against him and he couldn't be arsed with that. But now Ping and Pong might as well earn their keep. In fact, given the financial fragility of the organisation, it was essential the fair had no passengers.

She saw him through the window. Tall and handsome, he nevertheless looked like a bad thought as he stood, a man in grey, beneath a grey umbrella, in the street outside Sara's office. He looked as if he was waiting for someone, which could, Sara knew, be her. What did he want? Was it about the DNA test he'd agreed to have? Had he changed his mind?

'No, I have agreed to do that and so I will do it,' he said when she went outside to join him in the rain. 'I want to speak to you, though. Would you care to join me for lunch?'

They went to one of Berlin's many vegan restaurants where Sara allowed herself to be led by Beltz, who ordered them both aubergine and pesto pizzas with a side salad that looked like a small garden.

'I'm not a full-time vegan,' he explained. 'But I like this place.'

Now she was alone with him it was even harder for Sara to be with Beltz. Not only was he an 'enemy' he was also attractive and really rather charming. And he was using that charm to great effect. What did he want?

And so she asked him. She knew she sounded like a nervous fool, but Sara didn't care.

He put his fork down. 'Frau Metzler,' he said, 'I fear that the English people may have told you something I told them in a moment of, well, let's call it unwise self-disclosure.'

'What?'

Sara thought she knew, but she waited for him to carry on. He leant forwards. 'About the place my father chose to bury Rachel Austerlitz.'

'Oh.'

In his cellar. So that she'd be close. It had been on Sara's mind.

'I should never have spoken,' he said. 'It's not like me.'

Given his background, it probably wasn't.

'Of course, should you decide to go to the authorities, I can't stop you,' he said. 'And given what I used to do for a living, my words may fall on deaf ears. But I should like to ask you not to do so. It's my belief that my father loved Rachel with a passion. I don't know that, and I had hoped that maybe Herr Levy would be able to illuminate me about that. But sadly he knew nothing.'

She didn't know what to say.

'You know,' he said, 'this country is not the same as it was when Mutti came to power. Many of the young people are tired of Frau Merkel's politics with no highs and no lows. This is not a dynamic Germany. They seek other, some would say, older ideologies.'

Sara began to feel cold. She'd heard this language before. Contrary to what foreigners always seemed to think, those who had held the DDR together for forty-one years hadn't always done so with an

iron fist. There had, she recalled, been 'conversa-
tions' too.

'I find,' he said, 'unwittingly, that such people
sometimes seek me out.'

He was a writer, he'd told her, but she'd never
read or even seen any of his books.

'Passionate young people who feel that maybe
Germany needs another alternative.'

Sara looked into his eyes and saw nothing. In
the mouth of almost anyone else, his words would
have been benign. Ordinary political speculation.
But from a man who used to be in the Stasi they
were ominous and threatening. He would know,
as all Germans did, that discontent with Chancellor
Merkel's administration was higher than it had
ever been. Inconceivably, to Sara, some people,
particularly the young, had started to embrace
both far-right and far-left ideologies in recent
years. And where the far right and the far left met,
at the extreme ends of those ideologies, lay madness
and, she now felt, Herr Beltz.

Feeling exposed and scared, she looked around
for a way out of this conversation. Even if what
she perceived as a threat wasn't, she wanted to go.

And then she saw a friendly face outside the
window. Thank God!

She stood.

'Frau—'

'I'm so sorry, but I've just seen one of our
young workers,' she said. 'I'm mentoring him. I
have to go.'

She waved to attract the young man's attention and began to work her way through the crowds and out of the restaurant. At the door, in a moment that was in truth a reflex, she turned back to Beltz and said, 'I'll say nothing. You don't have to worry.'

He smiled. What she didn't see was the way he then also smiled at the nice young voluntary worker she was so keen to be with.

He was called Rolfe.

The rain had stopped, but the ground was still wet underfoot. Mumtaz took Irving's arm to steady him. Lee, walking ahead, turned and said, 'You sure you came in this way?'

'After over fifty years? I can't be certain, but this is the quickest way in from the house,' Irving said. 'My mother was pushing Miriam in the pram; she wouldn't have wanted to go out of her way.'

'Did you hold your mum's hand?'

'I don't know,' he said. 'My mother was not a demonstrative person. Probably not.'

They'd entered Barking Park through the main entrance, nearest to the town centre. Irving's house was almost opposite.

'My mum had me on reins,' Lee said.

'Your mother probably cared for you,' Irving said. 'The more I recall my mother, the more it occurs to me that she was only really interested in herself.'

As usual the fairground had been set up in the open, grassed areas of the park nearest to Longbridge

Road. As they had been the previous year, the entrance booths were to the right of the path.

Mumtaz asked, 'Was the fair always set up here, do you know?'

Irving smiled. 'Yes,' he said. 'That I do know. But that's mainly because there's really no other place for it to be.'

They paid a bored-looking woman for three wristbands and entered a churned-up, muddy space surrounded by sideshows festooned with large soft toys. The site smelt of cooked onions, toffee and fag smoke.

Lee said, 'Christ, if you took that big wheel away, we could be back in 1972.'

There was even a young boy floating around wearing a tank top and sporting a mullet. However, the BigO, the largest big wheel in the world with its enclosed seating, in futuristic blue-lit pods, was something that would have amazed and probably frightened people back in the seventies. Very much along the lines of the London Eye, but bigger, or so it was claimed, it completely shadowed the entire site, blocking out the little light being thrown by a very weak afternoon sun.

Irving stood. 'So what now?'

It was highly unlikely he'd remember anything except the most salient points from that awful trip to the fair back in the sixties and so Mumtaz suggested they start by getting a cup of tea. Encouraging context-dependent memories, especially memories that were so old, took time. She

237

had suggested that if all else failed, Irving might benefit from hypnosis, but he'd said he wasn't comfortable with that. Like a lot of people, he distrusted a technique he saw as not much more than a magic trick.

Mumtaz watched Irving watch the fair. They'd managed to find some tables under cover where they sat and drank their tea. There were very few punters. Most of the people she could see were fairground people talking to each other. But then un-glamourised by the multicoloured lights that illuminated the place at night, it was a pretty shabby affair. Most of the rides and the sideshows looked distinctly dated. The rain didn't help.

After a few moments, Irving said, 'To be honest with you it all looks about the same as it always has. I know that's no help at all, but a fairground is a fairground. Unless I see the freak show, which I won't, it's all much of a muchness. Even as I child I wasn't really interested in anything much except the freak show. Oh, and the animals. They had a tiger and a monkey. But I don't suppose they have animals any more. I think there are laws about such things now.'

'Cruelty to animals,' Lee said, fully aware that he was probably breaking some sort of animal cruelty legislation by keeping his mynah bird, Chronus, chained to his perch. But then at least he could see what was going on outside and had a great view of the telly. Fairground and circus animals had been notoriously ill-treated.

'When we've finished our tea, we'll walk the site and see what you can remember,' Mumtaz said.

'And if I remember nothing?'

'Then maybe you'll remember later,' she said. 'Context-dependent recall isn't always instant. You may even have a significant dream in the next few days.'

She saw Lee turn away. The context-dependent recall she knew he could get on board with. But the dreams . . .

And yet sometimes they really did mean something. Sigmund Freud hadn't been a complete fool.

Eva watched her father sleep. His chest sounded like a bag of nails these days. When he did die, she'd be lost. Only Bela had loved her – inasmuch as he could love anyone. There had been Gala's father for a while, and Gala herself, before she met David. Only Amber came close and it was for the young girl that she'd hold her tongue even when her father died. Far better he died as he had lived, ignoring what he couldn't bear.

Bela had built a whole new identity when he left mainland Europe. Unable to fly by that time, he'd found a new purpose, which he had maintained ever since. He'd taken care of his family, sometimes by means that were not kind to others. But he'd looked after his own without judgement. Eva knew she couldn't do that. She knew that she still found it hard to like him even though she loved him.

Amber entered the van and Eva put a finger to her lips.

'He's sleeping,' she whispered. 'What do you want?'

'I came to see if Nagyapa knows where Ping and Pong are?'

'Why do you want to know?' Eva asked. 'You heard what Nagyapa said: no flying. Not until we leave here.'

'Yeah, but why?' Amber said. 'Why here?'

'We don't like you flying anywhere,' Eva hissed.

'Nagyapa does.'

'And he is wrong,' Eva said. 'Silly old man. You won't fly here, and in fact, you won't fly anywhere from now on. I'm sick of how worried you make your mother!'

Amber pouted. Then she said, 'Well, actually, I wasn't getting the Twins to help me, but Dad. Ask him, if you don't believe me.'

Eva frowned.

'For the freak show,' Amber said. 'Dad's put it all back together. He wants to pick the Twins' brains about how it used to look in the old days.'

They walked in silence. Both Lee and Mumtaz watched Irving as he trudged slowly past shooting galleries, a haunted house and a hall of mirrors. As a child, Lee had always wanted to believe in something beyond what he could see. Raised with little concept of religion, he'd always secretly wanted life to offer a bit of fairy dust. Not that he'd ever told anyone.

Ghosts had been his thing, as he remembered. He'd dearly wanted ghosts to be real. And Father Christmas. He'd once 'seen' him out of his bedroom window flying with his reindeer above Tate and Lyle's sugar factory. He'd never told a soul.

Irving said, 'I know there was a smell of animals back then. There won't be now. Also, I recall a machine men would hit with a big mallet to test their strength . . .'

'I haven't seen one of them for years,' Lee said.

Irving shrugged. An eerie laugh echoed out of the haunted house as a gaggle of blokes in saggy tracksuits walked past smoking fags and holding glow sticks. They all looked as if they were going to an appointment at the Job Centre. Lee thought, *poor buggers*.

Irving, who had also obviously seen the men, said, 'I'm not one of those who believes this borough will gentrify. There's too much poverty.'

'I would've said the same for Spitalfields. I was born just off Brick Lane and it was a dump, I can tell you,' Mumtaz said. 'Now you can't move for Trustafarians and artists.'

'Yes, but Spitalfields has the benefit of historical buildings. A closed-down arts and crafts police station and a lot of ex-council housing doesn't cut it, I think,' Irving said. 'Barking will always be a poor place.'

'I have to agree with Mumtaz,' Lee said. 'Housing's so short now, a place like this, so close to London, can only get more expensive. I think it's a shame. If the poor can't live in Barking and Dagenham, where can they afford to live, eh?'

They turned a corner and came across the dodgems. Time was when the 'job' of being on the dodgems had been to hit as many other cars, usually containing your mates, as possible. Now, or so a sign in the corner said, deliberate bumping could see you thrown off the ride. Where was the fun in that?

Lee was just thinking, not for the first time, about what a moany old sod he was becoming when he saw that Irving had stopped moving.

Just for a short time, he'd probably been about four at the time, Irving Levy had a nanny. Why Bronagh came, and why she left, were mysteries to him. And although he couldn't remember what she looked like, he did remember that she had been what his mother later called 'superstitious'. She'd also called her 'bog Irish', which had struck Irving as not very nice and undeserved.

He'd liked Bronagh; she'd told him about all sorts of scary things that had made him giggle with frightened delight. She'd been full of tales about the Banshee, about malignant fairies and about the walking dead. A lot of the characters in her stories had been strange and freakish. Maybe that had been why he had wanted to visit the freak show at the fair all those years ago?

And now here it was again. Battered by time, its paint peeling and bubbling, and yet it was unmistakable.

In the years since Miriam's disappearance, he'd tried to recall exactly what it had looked like but he couldn't. In his head it had sometimes been a converted Gypsy caravan, sometimes a large shed. What it was resembled a goods van from an old steam train. A small ladder led up from the ground into an opening in the middle of the structure, the name 'Freak Show' was picked out in red on a board above this aperture.

'The Tattooed Man greeted you at the door,' he told Lee and Mumtaz as he pointed at the thing. 'I think the others stood around the walls, the Siamese twins were at the back. And there were a couple of exhibits in cages. I don't know that I even looked at those, I think I was too frightened. And there were snakes, but then they might have been somewhere else.'

He felt Mumtaz grip his arm.

'I can't believe they still have it,' he said. 'God, but it must be empty, surely!'

And slowly they went to take a look. He was right, it was empty – save for a middle-aged man sitting on the floor smoking. When he saw them, he smiled.

'Now, that's what I like to see,' David Sanders said. 'People with an appreciation for vintage fair craft.'

CHAPTER 19

It had to be in her head. When she thought
back on their conversation, Sara couldn't find
anything Gunther Beltz had said that was
actually threatening. After all, a lot of people were
talking about the rise of far-right politics in
Germany. They had been for some time. Mainly
disaffected middle-aged former East Germans, as
far as Sara could tell; the far-right party, the AfD,
did have young followers too.

Maybe it had been the way that he made a
comparison between the far right and the old DDR
communists? Had she been wrong when she had
interpreted this as a warning to her that he, or
people like him, may get into power again? How
could she know? She'd hardly stuck around to find
out. Young Rolfe had been her way out, a dear
young man who was writing his doctoral thesis on
the Hidden Jews of Berlin.

Now she couldn't sleep. Ideally, she'd go out and
try and walk herself into the mood for sleep, but
she didn't want to leave her flat. She felt unsure
of herself in a way she hadn't experienced for
years. She'd known all along that she shouldn't

have any dealings with anyone she knew had been in the Stasi. But the English people had got at least some information from the encounter and that had to be the main thing.

She just wished they had never told her about what lay underneath Beltz's house. Sara knew she should tell the police, but she also knew that she wouldn't. Old habits died hard and Beltz had been right about one thing, and that was that anyone could come to power in the twenty-first century. Everybody she met these days said that Mutti Merkel's time was coming to an end and they were probably right.

And there were people aiming to take her power who did not bear thinking about.

Gala had chosen to make goulash of all things. She used way too much garlic, even for the old man's tastes, and it stank the van out. But she liked doing it and Amber was a fan.

Eva watched her son-in-law put the takings in the safe and lock up.

'How did we do?' she asked.

'Not bad,' he said.

She knew that with only a small amount of pressure, she could get him to talk about how much interest the old freak show van had inspired. Just before they'd started the evening session, he'd come in full of it.

'And not just hipsters either,' he'd said to no one in particular. 'All sorts. Kids and old people, black and white, some Muslim woman with a coupla Jews.'

Eva had looked up and said, 'How do you know the woman was a Muslim or the other people Jews?'

'Woman had her head covered in that way they do.'

'In what way?'

He'd waved his hand at her. 'You know, like they do!' he'd said. 'The Jews . . . Well one was a bloke about my age, he might not've been a Jew to be fair, but he was dark and looked a bit like the older bloke who was wearing one of them hats.'

What hats? Eva knew, but at the time she'd left it at that. Now she could have pressed for more information, but she didn't. Her papa could be listening. Even though he was apparently making jokes with Amber in his bedroom, she couldn't be sure. He wasn't to be trusted and, if she was right about what Amber had been planning to do that afternoon with the Twins, neither was she.

Shazia had decided to stay.

'There's no point going back to Brick Lane now,' she'd said once she'd finished the meal Mumtaz rapidly cobbled together for them both. 'Do you mind?'

Mumtaz had said, 'This is your home. Of course I don't mind.'

And so the two of them had sat around chatting

and watching TV. Shazia told Mumtaz about the books she'd bought for her course and Mumtaz told her about the fair.

'They bill this BigO as the biggest big wheel in the world, but I don't think it is,' she said. 'I'm sure the London Eye is bigger.'

Shazia laughed. 'That's fairgrounds,' she said. 'It's all a con. Fun, but these days . . .' She shrugged. 'I don't know how they carry on.'

'Why?'

'Well, we have theme parks, don't we?'

'They're expensive.'

'Yeah but they're always rammed. I dunno, maybe Barking's the right sort of place for a fair . . .'

'Because it's poor?'

'I guess,' she said.

Mumtaz shook her head. 'Such a shame.'

'What is?'

'We met a man, connected with the fair, and he said they were planning to theme it next year.'

'Theme it?'

'They want to make it an "experience",' Mumtaz said. 'A Victorian fair with steam-driven carousels, mulled wine, great big swings and all the people on the stalls dressed up in crinolines and old-fashioned corsets.'

'Sounds cool. Sort of steampunk.'

Mumtaz wasn't sure that she knew what steampunk was. It probably didn't matter. Then she said, 'He also talked about reinstating the old freak show.'

Shazia frowned. 'That sounds a bit . . . well
. . . dodgy. Do you mean like bearded ladies and
elephant men?'

'Yes.'

'Don't like that much,' Shazia said. 'Mind you,
you can see worse on YouTube these days, I
expect.'

'I try to avoid it.'

'Oh, there are some good things on there, and
some of the weird stuff can be interesting, but it
does give you the impression there are a lot of
weird people out there who will do anything to
get themselves noticed.'

'Including exhibiting their deformities?'

Shazia shook her head. 'Amma, you are naive
sometimes,' she said. 'You just have to look at
some of the celebrities flaunting their new noses
and bums to realise this is OK now. It's fun to be
a freak in some people's eyes. It's appalling.
Anyway, do you have to go back to the fair?'

Shazia didn't know who Mumtaz was working
for or why.

'Yes,' she said. 'What of it?'

'Grace is going. Might go with her,' Shazia said.
'Especially if you're going to be there.'

If he slept, what would he dream about? Irving
looked at the bottle of co-codamol on the table
and then looked away. If he took a couple of those
he'd begin to feel drowsy and then he'd drop off
in the chair. His whole body ached and he knew

he'd feel better, physically, if he slept. But if he dreamt about that freak show, he could lose his mind.

What a terrible thing this journey he had embarked upon had been. That awful macabre story that Herr Beltz had told about his father would haunt him for a long time. Even if it was proved he was not related to Beltz, that story would remain with him. How strongly did someone have to feel about another person to exhume their body and bury it underneath their house? But then, maybe Beltz's father had just simply felt misplaced guilt over Rachel's death? Not that he could have done anything about it.

Irving had never felt strongly about anyone. But then had anyone ever felt strongly about him? His parents may have done, although they never showed it. His father had been distant and his mother inscrutable. He'd often wondered what had happened to her to make her so cold, but he never dared ask. Maybe it was because she never once volunteered any information about herself. She would tell him about her day, if he asked, but nothing more. It had been as if she lived only in the present. Maybe she could only live there?

He tried to remember whether he'd ever been back to the fair as a child. He felt that he probably hadn't. He'd been a few times as an adult, just after his mother died, but he'd not seen the freak show van that time. That time, he'd just wandered around in the rain on his own, recognising nothing.

Only his own imminent death had caused him to go back to the park at all. And then, for reasons he couldn't fathom, he'd started to dig. Did he really think he'd find Miriam's body amongst the marigolds and sweet peas?

Stiff from sitting too long in front of some 'reality TV' nonsense, he got up and walked over to the front window. The outside light was on, illuminating the garden, which looked like a quagmire. Lee and Jas had cleared up after themselves when they'd cleared out the garage, but it still looked like a piece of unkempt waste ground. Who had the man in the photograph they had found been? Had he ever been anything to his mother? Just because it had been found in a handbag, did that mean it had to have belonged to her? It was as he was thinking about this that he noticed a figure standing in the street, looking at him. Muffled up against the rain in what could be a waterproof coat of some sort, Irving couldn't work out whether it was male or female.

He went back to his chair to get his glasses, but by the time he returned to the window, the person had gone.

Gala snored. She sounded like a pig. But then she didn't look that much different from one. Maybe she was like her father? Whoever he had been.

Eva had been in the midst of her 'wild' phase when she'd given birth to Gala. Running around with all sorts of men. Bela had beaten her so many times, but it had never stopped her. She'd taunted him, hinting at things she could reveal, which she could not possibly have known. But it had given him pause and so, in the end, he'd just let her do what she wanted. She was like him in every possible way. She looked like him, spoke as he did, thought the same thoughts. Sometimes it made him shudder. To have someone so in tune with you was unnerving. Bela tried not to think about the Twins, but failed.

CHAPTER 20

They showed her the ropes, literally. But Amber shook her head.

'I've promised Nagyapa I won't fly for a bit,' she said.

Their small, painted eyes looked at her with disdain. Amber was aware that her friends were watching her and said, 'I'm going shopping with Lulu and Misty. We're going up Camden.'

Then she turned and walked away. Eva watched until the girl was out of sight and then walked over to the Twins. Addressing them in their own language, she said, 'I don't know why my father tolerates you. That is something about which I've no idea. But what I do know is that you can be hurt, and if you carry on encouraging Amber to fly, I will hurt you.'

One of them went to speak, but Eva silenced it with a raised hand.

'And don't say that what you do, you do with the approval of my father,' she said. 'Because I don't care. And yes, I know that if it came down to you or me, he would choose you. But whatever you are to him, you can die just like other people.'

She walked away. Not sure whether she believed what she had just said or not.

Mumtaz had left for Barking as soon as she'd ended the call from Irving Levy. Now sitting in his dark, slightly damp living room, she took the cup of tea he offered from his shaking hands and said, 'What happened?'

'In the real world, nothing much,' he said. 'Last night I looked out of that window about midnight and saw somebody standing in front of the garden, in the street. Couldn't see whether it was a man or a woman, but I had the feeling it was looking right at me.'

'Did you feel threatened?'

'No, not really,' he said. 'More curious than anything else. And not about that person, about myself.'

'How so?'

He leant back in his chair. 'I'm finding I'm not afraid,' he said. 'After a lifetime of timidity I find it hard to credit, but there it is. Whatever I discover about my mother or Miriam is alright because it has to be. I can't change what was.'

This, Mumtaz knew, was a new way of thinking for Irving.

'I had a dream last night,' he continued. 'A dream, a vision – something. I'd been trying not to sleep. After seeing that freak show van, I was unnerved. I wondered whether, if I closed my eyes, I'd dream things that would make me go mad. I didn't. At least I don't think so.'

She smiled. 'I don't think so either.'

'But, in the end, something like sleep happened,' he said. 'I don't know who they were, but I was with people who loved me.'

'In the dream?'

'Yes. I'll be honest, it was so nice, it's shaken me. Neither of my parents ever showed affection. I always felt on edge with both of them. But these people – we were having a picnic on grass – they were nice. They worried about me. I could tell.'

'I've no answers for you, Irving,' Mumtaz said. 'I'm not sure how much credence I would personally give to dreams. But I do believe that sometimes they can reflect what maybe we have missed, but which has been noted by our unconscious.'

'I really felt as if these people loved me. But there is no love in my life.'

'Maybe it's the simple fact that, although Lee and I are working for you, we do care,' Mumtaz said. 'Because we do. We really want you to find, at the very least, some closure. You're a nice man . . .'

'Who has wasted his life in the company of diamonds.'

'No,' she said. 'A skill like that is never wasted. You work in a most extraordinary trade in a most extraordinary place.'

He smiled. 'I am flattered.'

Mumtaz said, 'Lee is taking the photograph he found in your garage to the artist today. So, although Lesley's opinions won't be definitive, we may get some idea about whether your mother was related to him. In the meantime, do you want to tell me about your impressions from yesterday? I know that seeing the freak show van was a shock, but did it provoke any memories you'd not had before?'

'No,' he said. 'It was shocking, as you say, but I didn't feel afraid. The van was clearly older than it had been the last time I saw it, and it was empty.'

'Would it have been different had some of the "acts" been inside?'

'Oh, yes,' he said. 'And I admit I was horrified when that man said he'd like to bring the freak show back. I know that logically it is unlikely to feature any of the freaks that were exhibited when I saw it – most have to be dead by now – but I found it distasteful.'

'Me too.'

'And sad, to think that people still have to resort to such cruelty just to make money. I don't understand. Money has never been important to me. But then of course, I have never wanted for anything.'

'Only things money can't buy,' Mumtaz said.

He paused for a moment and then he said, 'You know, I find that I don't even care what Miriam is like. Just that she exists. Just that my blood is not alone in this world. She can like me or not, it's of no importance.'

Mumtaz felt her heart squeeze. The chances of Miriam being alive were so slim.

*   *   *

Vi didn't drop Lee off outside Lesley Jones's vast gothic house. She pulled over at the other end of the street.

'Any man that bloody woman knows is her personal property – in her head,' Vi said.

Lee laughed. He knew what she meant. Lesley was unnerving, especially if she thought a man she fancied was sleeping with someone else. And she fancied most men she met.

'She's bloody good at what she does,' Lee said. 'And I'm a big boy now.'

Vi raised an eyebrow and then said, 'Thanks for last night, love. It was fun.'

He shook his head as he got out of the car. 'Don't be daft, Vi.'

Lee hadn't meant to spend the night with Vi, but when she'd turned up at the flat to offload about the impact the so-called legal high known as 'Spice' was having on the borough's poorest people, she'd needed more than a hug to make her feel better. Spice was everywhere – on the streets, in clubs, even flown in over prison walls using drones. It made users incapable of thought and often motion, and whoever was dealing it was targeting it at the most vulnerable. Even someone as battle-hardened as Vi had been shocked by what she'd seen.

A boy he'd not seen before let Lee into the house. Lesley lay on a sofa in the middle of her massive living room, completely covered in a duvet. But when she saw Lee, she sprang to her feet.

'Just having a small power-nap,' she said. 'Do you want tea?'

'That'd be nice,' Lee said. 'Les, you can say no, but do you think you could have a look at this photo I told you about while I'm here? I'm a bit keen to get back to the client with something.'

She looked delighted, which was bothersome, on one level.

'Of course,' she said. 'You want me to compare it to that woman whose baby you had me age, yeah?'

'Yes.'

'Well, won't take me five minutes . . .'

'I know.'

Lesley shrugged. 'You'd better settle in on the sofa, then, hadn't you?' she said. 'I'll get you some tea, but if there's anything else you want . . .'

The boy was called Hubert and he was smitten. Amber hadn't wanted to go to a pub. She and Lulu had been up for a coffee, but now Misty had met Hubert they appeared to be trapped in this pub.

According to Misty, who had dragged her two friends into the toilets to speak to them, this Hubert was some sort of rich person's son. He talked posh and said he had a flat in Chelsea, even though he looked as if he'd slept the previous night in a bin. And he had a green beard.

'All the really rich boys have beards now,' Misty had said when Lulu had given it as her opinion that Hubert was full of shit. 'It's like, look at Prince Harry.'

'His beard ain't green.'

'Well, he's not alternative, is he?'

Lulu said, 'What does that mean? "Alternative"?'

'It's a look,' Misty said. 'It's, like, it's different, you know. Anyway, I don't care. He's buying the drinks.'

And so they were stuck. Amber had wanted to go round Camden Market and buy herself some clothes with the money her nagyapa had given her, but it wasn't happening. She'd only been allowed out as long as she stayed with Misty. If the girls went back without her they'd get into trouble. But as time went on and Misty got drunker and drunker, both Amber and Lulu realised that they'd have to get back soon. Eventually, Lulu said, 'If we miss the evening session we'll get in trouble.'

At first Misty ignored her. She was kissing Hubert now and he had a hand up her skirt. Lulu punched her arm. 'Oi,' she said, 'we gotta get back!'

For a moment the girls thought that maybe Misty had seen sense, but then she said, 'Well, go back, then, I ain't stopping you.'

Wahid Sheikh hadn't picked up the phone when Mumtaz had finally got her courage up to ring him. The delay left her feeling anxious. She'd tried to distract herself with her work, but it was tough. Finding out who, apart from Vi's Uncle Bill, had worked for an organisation like a travelling fair was going to be difficult, especially when the details you needed were fifty years old. Fairground workers, even now, could very well be casual employees, which meant that they paid no tax or national insurance.

The current owner of the fair was a man called Roman Lester, but tracking him down was proving difficult. He had an office in Hitchin, but every time she tried to call, the line just rang out. Then her mobile rang.

'Mrs Hakim,' a familiar voice said, 'you rang me?'

Even his voice made her cringe. Mumtaz pulled herself together.

'Wahid-ji, yes,' she said. 'Thank you for getting back to me.'

'It's no problem.'

He was always polite. It made him even more sinister.

But it was now or never. She'd not feel she could do this again. She said, 'Wahid-ji, I'd like to ask you something about my husband.'

There was a moment's pause and then he said, 'What about him?'

If she alluded to Ahmet's murder he'd just put the phone down. They both knew what had happened to her husband, but neither of them could say that on the phone. Who knew who might be listening?

She said, 'I know that a lot of people have been in debt, as Ahmet was . . .'

'It was a shame,' he said. 'A man in thrall to a gambling habit is a sad sight to see.'

'Indeed.'

'And yet debts must be paid.'

'Of course. I'm not disputing that,' she said. 'However, what I find difficult to understand is why so many people are gambling addicts and yet only Ahmet is dead.'

'Ah, well when it comes to addiction, some live and some die.'

Her heart was hammering now. She said, 'You know what I mean, Wahid-ji.'

And now there was a long silence. He knew what she meant. And he also knew she knew that.

When he did finally speak, his tone was much graver than it had been before.

'I fear,' he said, 'that the answer you seek is much more complicated than a humble man like myself can give you. Let me consult and get back to you.'

'Very well.'

She put the phone down and sat still for a moment, taking in some long, calming breaths. What did he mean by 'consult'? Consult who? The rest of his family? Then she began to berate herself. Why had she even asked the question? Why hadn't she just agreed to pay the old bastard more money and have done with it?

What kind of can had she opened? And did it contain worms?

* * *

Amber stared at the Tube map and said, 'We need to get to the District Line.'

'We came on the District Line, didn't we?' Lulu said.

'Yeah, till Embankment, then we got the Northern Line up here,' Amber said. 'Here you see, from Camden Town down to Embankment and then on the District back to Barking. It's easy.'

It would have been had the girls caught the right train. But they took the Morden Branch instead of the Kennington train and ended up at Borough on the South Bank. Chatting, mainly about Misty, they didn't realise where they were until it was too late. Then, instead of looking at the Tube map, the girls ascended to Borough Station. Panic was setting in and, when Amber suggested she phone her mother to tell her what was happening, Lulu stopped her.

'They'll never let us out again if you tell your mum,' she said. Then looking down a road she didn't know the name of she said, 'Look there's a sign there for London Bridge. If we go over that, won't we be on the right side of the river again?'

Amber said she thought they would and so the two girls began to walk in that direction.

It took Mumtaz a moment to realise that the incoming call was not from Wahid Sheikh. It was Farzana, one of the workers with the Asian Refuge Sisters. What she said made Mumtaz go round to the refuge immediately.

261

Farzana was in her office. A small woman in her thirties, she was a pretty, covered lady who looked delicate, but was as tough as boots.

'She went out this morning and hasn't returned,' Farzana said.

'Did she take anything with her?' Mumtaz asked.

'What, apart from her Prada handbag? No,' Farzana said. 'I wasn't on this morning. Rukhsana signed her out, but she didn't think much to it. Said that Shirin was no different.'

'Meaning?'

'She's always reserved, doesn't really communicate with the other women unless she has to. With the exception of little Bijul.'

'Who is she?'

'Little Sikh girl,' Farzana said. 'Comes from a family of doctors, so class-wise she and Shirin have a lot in common. They also both dress in designer gear. If Bijul hadn't come and had a word, I wouldn't be so worried about Shirin.'

'What did she tell you?'

'Apparently Shirin thinks she might be pregnant,' Farzana said.

Mumtaz felt a hole open up in the pit of her stomach. The reason Shirin's husband had wanted to move a second wife into their home had been because Shirin had been unable to get pregnant. Or rather, that was the story he told to justify sleeping with another woman.

'So, do you think that Shirin has gone back to

her husband to tell him the good news?' Mumtaz asked.

'I don't know. I've asked Bijul, but she's not in a good place and I can't get much out of her.'

'Can I talk to her?'

'If she'll speak to you,' Farzana said. 'She's just seventeen and she's suffered the kind of abuse that could make your hair stand on end . . .'

'But we have to try and find Shirin.'

'I know.' Farzana stood up. 'I'll take you to her,' she said. 'Just don't expect a great conversationalist.'

The refuge only reported women who left them to the police if they strongly suspected that they had either been kidnapped or had quit under duress. Mumtaz doubted whether Shirin came into either category. If she thought she was pregnant, Shirin had probably gone back to her husband of her own accord.

'How did she know she was pregnant?' Mumtaz asked Farzana as they walked up the stairs to the women's bedrooms.

'I don't know,' Farzana said. 'What bothers me is that she may have just taken the cessation of her periods as a sign. A lot of our women have menstruation issues when they come in here. It's the stress.'

Mumtaz remembered it well. She too had been unable to have a child by her husband. And the more he brutalised her, the smaller her periods had become.

Farzana knocked on one of the doors on the top floor of the house and called out, 'Bijul. It's Farzana. Can I come in?'

A small voice said, 'Yes.'

CHAPTER 21

'If the woman dyed her hair black, then it's difficult to imagine exactly what her real hair colour was,' Lesley said. 'But if we assume it was mid-brown – most European hair is mid-brown – then it's only her hair dye that looks anything like the man in the photo.'

Lesley had a range of photographs up on her computer screen. Those she'd scanned in for the comparisons Lee had asked her to do originally and the latest picture rescued from Irving Levy's garage.

'You wouldn't say they're related?' he asked.

'I couldn't swear to it, but no,' she said. 'The bloke's features are thick and heavy. He's a looker, but he's not going to win any medals for refined features. The woman's a bit more refined and she does have those down-slanting eyes. I'd say they're not related.'

Lee sighed. 'Thanks.'

'Oh, but I'm not done,' Lesley said. 'While you were getting your beauty sleep, I performed some more measurements.'

'Yeah?'

'Yeah,' she said. 'He could be related to the little kid.'

'Miriam?'

'Maybe,' she said. 'Like a lot of babies, her hair could've darkened, probably did – if she grew up. I know this because her skin is dark, unlike her mother's, much more like that of her father. The kid as an adult has those big features.'

'Like her father, Manny Levy.'

'Indeed. I'd say that this photo could well be someone who came from the paternal side of that kid's family,' Lesley said.

They'd assumed that the man in the photograph had a connection to Rachel because it had been found in her handbag. But maybe it was a picture of someone in her husband's family? Possibly, unknown even to Irving, did his father had relatives on the Continent?

Lee nodded. 'Thanks, Les,' he said. 'You'll have to let me know how much I owe you.'

She shrugged. 'No probs.'

'Which means what?' Lee said. 'Three hundred quid? Four?'

'Or you could go out and get a biryani for us and stay over,' Lesley said.

Jackie Berman still looked askance at the Asians who had come to work in the Garden donkey's years ago. Irving ignored it because Jackie was old and set in his ways. He thought about getting the old man to meet Mumtaz – she was probably the nicest woman he'd ever met – but then he decided against it. Jackie didn't like change and being around women – any women – was, for him, change.

It wasn't raining for once and so he'd left the house and crossed the road. He couldn't sleep anyway and so a walk around the park might do him good, provided he didn't get mugged. Although he wouldn't take the risk of walking down South Park Drive on his own and so limited himself to a stroll along Longbridge Road to Faircross and back.

He ended up standing in front of the main entrance to Barking Park. The fair had shut down for the night and, although the site was far from quiet, there were no more flashing lights, bangs, whizzes and general hubbub. The main gate was closed and so even if his unconscious mind had wanted to get in and have another look at the freak show van, his body wouldn't have been able to do so. But he walked up to the gates and was going to rattle them to make sure, but then he saw the padlocks and so he just stood there, looking.

Nothing inside moved, or rather it didn't move at first. To begin with it was just voices, whispering. Beyond the gates, a little conversation in sibilant expirations rather than words caught his ear and held it. Like snakes in conversation, it was a communication in the letter 's' and it fascinated him. Irving pushed his head a short way through the bars of the gate and strained to hear what was being said.

267

Then it stopped.

For a moment he thought that his ears had tuned the sound out, but then Irving realised that the snake whispers had gone. He was about to leave and go home when he saw a movement in a bush beside the path. He quashed the urge to say *Is anyone there?* as it really wasn't his business. Whoever was there was in the park; he was outside. It was none of his concern.

But he carried on looking anyway. For a bit.

Then as he turned to go he saw, just out of the corner of his eye, a face that he knew.

'I don't know for sure,' the girl said.

Bijul, apparently seventeen, looked about twelve. She sat stiffly on the edge of her bed, her tiny, stick-like legs encased in black skinny jeans, her body swamped in a red, petal-print top. Her hair had been cut into a hard, asymmetric bob. To Mumtaz, she looked not unlike what she had always imagined an elf to be.

'She missed her period,' Bijul continued. 'But I don't know whether she actually did a test.' She looked from Mumtaz to Farzana and then back to Mumtaz again. 'She didn't say where she was going.'

'Today?'

'Yes. She just went out.'

'And yet you were the only person Shirin talked to.'

'Shirin is the only person I can speak to,' Bijul

said. 'Some of them, the other women, don't speak English. My Punjabi is basic, to say the least. Shirin was the same with Urdu. Some of these women in here come from villages in India and Pakistan.'

Mumtaz couldn't work out whether Bijul thought badly of the other women in the hostel or not. She was clearly very young and had to be frightened to find herself in such a place. Like Shirin, she wasn't accustomed to 'village' women. It wasn't her fault or theirs.

'All Shirin said was that she was going out,' Bijul said. 'She didn't say where and I didn't ask. As I say, she's like me, she's used to going out.'

Most of the other residents didn't budge from the hostel, afraid that their abusers might see them. But for all her fragility, Bijul, according to Farzana, did go out and so, of course, did Shirin. They were used to the world outside the home and missed it when they were confined. Mumtaz knew how these women felt.

Mumtaz said, 'When Shirin told you she was pregnant, was she pleased?'

'I don't think she knew what to feel about it,' Bijul said. 'When her period didn't come she was afraid at first, but then I think she was happy about it. She told me she hadn't really wanted to leave her husband, even though he'd hurt her.'

'Do you think she may have gone back to him?'

'Oh, I don't know,' Bijul said. 'She was frightened

269

of him. She was frightened of her own family too. Her marriage was important to them.'

Mumtaz looked at Farzana, who said, 'We can't report her missing until she's been gone for twenty-four hours because she's an adult.'

She was right. For the police to be involved a missing adult had to have not been seen for a whole day.

When they left Bijul's bedroom, Farzana said to Mumtaz, 'Do you know where Shirin's husband lives?'

Mumtaz nodded.

Amber wasn't even through the van door, when her mother smacked her round the head.

'Where the hell have you been?' Gala yelled at her.

'Ow!'

'Where? I let you have your way and this is how you repay me? I almost called the police!'

She hit her again.

'Mum! Stop it!'

Her father pulled her mother away and said, 'That's enough!'

It took Amber a few moments to get her breath and then she said, 'It was Misty. She met this boy and she wouldn't leave him and so Lulu and me had to come home on our own and we got lost on the Tube . . .'

'She met a boy where?'

'In Camden Market.'

'What boy?'

'I don't know. He was called Herbert or something; he was posh. He took us to this pub . . .'

'You got drunk!'

'No!' she said. 'But Misty wanted to stay with him. Me and Lulu, we said we had to get home, but she took no notice. So we left on our own and then we got all confused on the Tube. We got the wrong train and then we had to walk, then we couldn't find the right station. We ran from Barking Tube and then the park gates were shut and we had to climb over, then we heard some boys coming and so we hid in a bush and Lulu ripped her coat . . .'

She was covered in leaves and her tights were ripped.

Gala sat down and shook her head. After a moment she called out, 'Mama!'

Amber's grandmother came out of her room and stood in the doorway. 'What's the matter?'

'Young Miss Flier here tells me that Misty Dobos has gone off with some boy. Left her and Lulu alone in the wilds of Camden. Can you go and tell Milos and Amalia their precious daughter is a whore?'

Amber said, 'Mum, I don't know she *went* with him!'

'She went with him, trust me,' Gala said. 'Is Lulu home?'

'Yes. We came back together.'

Eva slipped on her coat. 'What do you want me to tell Amalia?'

'I don't know!' Gala said. 'What's the Hungarian for slapper?'

Eva shook her head. 'I will make sure that Lulu's alright too,' she said.

'Do what you like!'

Eva left the van.

Gala turned on her daughter. 'And you, get to bed,' she said. 'And don't ever ask to go anywhere again. Remember, miss, I will be watching you like a hawk!'

Lee had sounded groggy when she'd called him. As if he'd just woken up, which was possible. It had been two o'clock in the morning. But he'd understood her fears for Shirin. With no phone on which to contact her, she was effectively incommunicado and, he agreed, she could well have returned to her husband or her family.

Mumtaz's first urge had been to go to the husband's swanky place in Holland Park, but Lee had cautioned her against this.

'If she left the refuge of her own accord, there's nothing you can do until twenty-four hours have elapsed,' he'd said. 'Then it's a job for the coppers. The refuge will need to report it. Have you given them the husband's address?'

'Yes. I'll phone Farzana and tell her.'

Farzana had said she'd take it from there.

Now alone in her flat, Mumtaz couldn't sleep. Although Wahid Sheikh had said nothing to confirm her fears, he'd not dismissed them either.

And who did he have to 'consult' before he could get back to her about Ahmet?

Her husband had done something beyond simply owing the Sheikhs money. But what?

She made tea. As she waited for it to brew she wondered what, if anything, Irving Levy's dreams about being with people who loved him might mean. He didn't know who they were, only that they made him feel warm. It was probably nothing, but she hoped, for his sake, that there was some truth in it. He was a nice man and was, she'd noticed, becoming ever more weary. Maybe Berlin had taken it out of him? She wouldn't be surprised if it had. Even for her, the whole experience had been incredibly harrowing.

For anyone not to know who he or she really was made her shudder. And if Sara Metzler was right, then there were possibly thousands of people all over Europe who lived in ignorance of their true identities. Jews who were not Jews, Gentiles who were not Gentiles, people whose fathers had been Nazis . . .

To be so cut adrift from one's culture was something that filled Mumtaz with horror. But then if a person didn't know they were cut adrift, what did it really matter? It mattered in case they found out – like Irving Levy. Now on a quest to find his true 'blood' before he died, was he wise to be doing such a thing and was the Arnold Agency correct in assisting him?

Theoretically, Irving's case was just another job.

He was paying them handsomely to do it. He wanted to know. But was it right, for him, that he did know? And then Mumtaz thought about her dead husband again and realised that she, just like Irving, *had* to know the truth.

Whatever the cost.

'He'll get her married off to her cousin up Liverpool soon as he can.'

Britannia Lee, like her husband, Ron, was a Romany Gypsy. More Eva's age than Gala's, she'd had her youngest girl, Lulu, when she was forty. Eva had delivered her.

'I know it's your business and your way,' Eva began. 'But marrying a girl in haste . . .'

'It's the only way to tame 'em,' Britannia said and that was that.

The two women shared a cigarette in silence until Britannia said, 'Amalia Dobos call the police, did she?'

'No,' Eva said. 'Milos has gone up Camden looking.'

Britannia shook her head. 'How he gonna manage with no English?'

'He can speak a bit.'

'A bit, yeah, but . . .' She coughed. 'Anyway, how do we know our girls told the truth about Misty? Silly tart could be anywhere. Bloody Lulu's coat's a rag, tore when the two of them climbed them gates, so she says. Ron thinks she's been got.'

'By a boy?'

'So he thinks,' she said.

'You don't?'

'I dunno. Whenever that one makes stories they're always like a fucking novel – elaborate and that.'

'How'd'ya mean?'

'Well, going on about how they run from the station and got stitches in their sides. Then all that malarky getting over the gate, then boys some-where so they had to hide . . .'

'Amber said that.'

'Some bloke looking at 'em from outside the gates . . .'

'What bloke?'

Britannia shrugged. 'I dunno. Some geezer peering in through the bars at 'em.'

Eva frowned. 'Amber never said nothing about some bloke peering in,' she said.

'Probably never noticed,' Britannia said. Then she stood up and went back into her caravan. 'Night.'

'Night,' Eva said.

But she didn't go back to her van. She went for a walk.

CHAPTER 22

'Roman Lester here.'

It was a cheery voice, annoyingly so. Although he hadn't taken a drink for well over a decade, Lee Arnold felt hungover. Maybe it was that bloody awful biriyani Lesley had made him eat. Or the guilty sex.

'Lesters Travelling Fair,' the voice continued. 'Your Mrs Hakim wanted to know about employees. That is Mr Arnold, isn't it?'

'Yes,' Lee said. He cleared his throat and sat up straight. 'Yes, er, thank you for getting back to us.'

He wanted to add the word 'eventually', but didn't. Instead, he told Lester about the disappearance of Miriam Levy and asked whether any of his current employees had been with the fair at that time.

'Of course, the fair wasn't owned by us then,' he said. 'It was Mitchells back then. I was ten in '62. Doesn't time fly when you're having fun?'

Lee almost said that he wouldn't know. But then Lester ploughed on.

'When my father bought Mitchells he bought it lock, stock and barrel, including the employees,' he said. 'Of course, not all of them liked the change of management and so some left there and then. But a lot stayed.'

'Are any of them still with the fair now?'

'Now? Not many. Although some of the families of those original employees have stayed with us.' Then he said, 'I have to admit that I knew a kiddie had gone missing on the site donkey's years ago, but my understanding is that all the fairground staff were cleared.'

'The case was never solved,' Lee said. 'But you've nothing to worry about, Mr Lester. The reason I contacted you was so that maybe I could talk to anyone you still employ who was around at that time.'

'I can't force anyone to talk to you, Mr Arnold.'

'I know, and if you don't want to help . . .'

'Well, of course I want to help, but . . .' He paused for a moment and then he said, 'I can think of a few. A bit long in the tooth now and not all of them can speak English . . .' Then Lee heard him murmur, '. . . or speak . . . But look, let me contact my foreman on the site and I'll get him to talk to you. He's down there on the street, as it were . . .'

Irving took his morning pills, as usual, on automatic. There were ten of them and so even with a foggy brain he could count them out with ease.

After he'd taken his tablets he sat, motionless, as if shocked he was still alive, then he drew a cold, dry hand down his lined, stubbly face. What the hell had the previous day and night been about?

First of all he'd woken from a dream in which he was apparently loved by a group of unknown people. This, after seeing a figure of some sort standing outside his house at midnight. Then a day of lack of appetite, a kind visit from Mumtaz Hakim and then a walk in the moonlight. Why he'd done that, he didn't know. He wasn't one of life's walkers. He remembered he'd been thinking about Jackie Berman, for God's sake. About how Jackie would never accept women working with diamonds, much less Asian women. Silly old fart.

So nothing to do with his mother. Nothing. And yet just for a second he thought he'd seen her. Or rather he'd seen an idealised picture of her in his mind. He'd certainly never seen her like that in life.

Maybe he needed a change of medication? Or maybe his life was starting to flash past his face as it was rumoured to do when a man was drowning.

The noise coming from the Dobos's caravan was enough to wake the dead. In spite of Milos's best efforts he hadn't found Misty and had returned to the site at six o'clock that morning determined to call the police.

Five minutes later a very tearful and mud-stained

Misty had turned up. Nanny Eva said Milos and Amalia were threatening to kill her.

Amber, alarmed, said, 'Don't you think we should stop them?'

'She's their daughter; it's their business,' her grandmother said. 'Let what happens to Misty Dobos be a lesson for you. You defy your elders at your peril.'

Misty screamed and Amber ran in to her nagyapa's room.

'The Dobos are killing Misty!' she yelled. 'You must stop them! They'll listen to you!'

Her great-grandfather turned over in his bed and fixed her with his black-currant eyes.

'They won't,' he said. 'They're just being what your mother calls "Hungarian". A lot of noise, meaning nothing. They may beat her . . .'

'Nanny says they'll kill her!'

He smiled. 'Your grandma exaggerates,' he said. 'And she doesn't understand.'

'Understand what?' her grandmother said.

He didn't look at Amber when he spoke, but at Eva.

'Killing her will call attention to them,' he said. 'And they wouldn't want that.'

It was only later, when the noise had calmed down and Amber had managed to persuade herself that her friend was alright, that his words seemed so strange to her. Surely the Dobos wouldn't kill Misty, because they loved her?

* * *

279

'If Irving's with me, they might not talk,' Lee said.

Mumtaz looked at him over the top of her computer screen. 'They might not want to talk to you,' she said.

'They might not.'

He looked terrible. She hoped he hadn't started drinking again. He didn't smell of drink, but then alcoholics were well-known for their guile. Her husband had rarely smelt of booze even when he'd been drinking all night. A shower plus some liberally applied cologne had always taken care of that.

An e-mail arrived with an attachment. It was from Berlin. She opened it.

'Herr Beltz has sent through his DNA test results,' she said.

'Good. I'll tell Irving.'

'We'll have to have a comparison done. On their own they mean nothing.'

'I'll e-mail him,' Lee said.

Then his phone rang. She heard him say, 'Hello, Mr Lester.'

The owner of the fair. Then her mobile rang. It was Wahid Sheikh. She picked it up and walked into the small kitchen at the back of the office.

'Wahid-ji,' she said. 'Good morning.'

Her heart raced. What was he going to tell her?

'Good morning to you too, Mrs Hakim,' he said. 'I trust you are well?'

'I'm fine,' she lied. The niceties of South Asian communication were sometimes hard to bear. *Get to the point!*

'Good. Well,' he said, 'I have spoken to my brother Rizwan and he would like for you to come and meet him.'

Mumtaz felt sick. 'Meet him?'

'Yes, at his daughter's house in Dalston. I will text you the address.'

'Yes, but . . .'

'My brother will tell you what you wish to know about your husband, but he prefers to do it in person,' he said. 'In spite of his illness, Mrs Hakim, my brother still wishes to pay you the courtesy of discussing your late husband's case face-to-face.'

Her late husband's 'case'? So, there was more than just money. Of course there was.

Her throat dry now. She croaked, 'When?'

'Again, my brother is generosity itself,' he said. 'When it is convenient for you, Mrs Hakim. Call me and I will arrange it. After all, my brother, since his unfortunate health problems in the wake of his son's death, is not going anywhere, is he?'

She ended the call and sat down. Did she even want to know what that ghastly toad, Rizwan Sheikh, was going to tell her? If anything. That family still believed that Shazia had killed Rizwan Sheikh's precious thug of a son, Naz, and they were never going to be disabused of that opinion. Especially since Rizwan had suffered a stroke. That, she knew, he pinned on Shazia too. If Naz hadn't died maybe the old bastard would have had a stroke anyway, but that was not, Mumtaz knew, the Sheikh family's choice of interpretation.

'Mumtaz, I'm off out.'

She walked back into the office to see Lee putting on his coat.

'The fair people are going to speak to you?' she said.

'One or two.' He put his cigarettes into his pocket and opened the office door. 'I've not e-mailed Irving yet. Can you do it?'

'Of course.'

'Ringing him up first might be a good idea,' he said as he left the office. 'If I don't see you before, I'll pick you up tonight at six.'

He left.

There was to be one more visit to the fair with Irving that evening. Neither Lee nor Mumtaz felt that he could take much more. Seeing the freak show van had shaken him considerably and he was beginning to experience rather gentle, if disturbing, dreams.

One didn't prod the leaves of the past and not expect to find rats, but this was a man who, though in remission, was still gravely ill.

To see one's parents for some time after their deaths is not an uncommon phenomenon. Irving still sometimes saw his father hunched over his old bench in what was now his workroom in the Garden. He'd seen his mother several times since her passing. Usually in the living room, sitting in her old chair, half asleep.

What he'd never, ever seen before was his mother

as she was when he was a child. Young Rachel was such a dim and distant memory, even looking at old photographs failed to conjure in him little actual recognition.

So why had he seen just that in Barking Park, through the bars of its closed main gates? The same eyes, same pale skin, a look that could have been fear crossing her fine features. What did it mean? In recent days his dreams had become almost idyllic, and yet now – this vision. And vision it had to have been.

He'd always had the odd hallucination, even as a child. According to his mother, there had been an invisible friend when he was a toddler, followed by a woman who would sometimes walk out of his wardrobe. Irving could still see her face if he concentrated. His mother had even taken him to see a psychiatrist at the London Hospital when he was about ten. The doctor, who was short and thin and had warts on his head had told her that Irving would 'grow out of it'. And he had, mostly.

Perhaps it was the drugs. His latest cycle of chemotherapy had been tough and some of the drugs he had been told to take since the treatment had finished were pretty toxic. It was well documented that corticosteroids could cause confusion and blurred vision. He'd been on those for months.

The phone rang, but he ignored it. He even shut the door into the hall so he couldn't hear the answerphone. What good was conversation if he was going mad? *If* he was going mad . . .

His father had never been good with craziness. His opinion had always been that one only went mad if one wanted to go mad. And, in spite of his adherence to the laws and dictates of Orthodox Judaism, he'd never had any time for the supernatural. The only time Manny Levy even became remotely fanciful was when he was looking into the heart of a diamond. Only in the stones, according to him, could a man see the infinite face of God. Diamonds were, he occasionally maintained, windows into reflections on realms humans were not meant to fully comprehend. Looking at them so intently also, as Irving knew to his cost, ruined your eyesight.

To think that a tiny flash of what could have been a hallucination was a sign that he was going mad was overdramatic. What he was, was tired, ill and upset. Although he would never have said anything to either Lee Arnold or Mumtaz Hakim, he was disappointed in what he, and they, had found out so far. He still didn't know who his mother had been, and Miriam appeared as illusive as ever. Had he expected too much? Probably, but then wasn't that the purview of all dying men? To leave everything important in life too late and therefore impossible to fulfil?

Irving sat down in the chair that had once been his mother's and lay his head back. He wasn't mad, he just wanted the world to do what he wanted it to. And it wouldn't.

★　★　★

Grace had decided not to go to Barking Park Fair with her boyfriend.

'Thought we could just go together, yeah?' she said to Shazia.

They were in Shazia's bedroom at the top of her amma's parents' house in Hanbury Street. The vast weavers window, which took up the whole of the front wall, had a very good view of the street below – and all the tasty young boys on it. Shazia suspected that Grace had become a bit bored with her goody-goody latest boyfriend and was up for going out on the pull.

'That's cool,' Shazia said. 'But I'm not up for getting chatted up.'

'What? Not for free drinks?'

'I don't drink, dumb-ass.'

'I know,' Grace said. 'But I do. Be jokes getting a coupla hot fairground boys to give us free rides and that.'

'Oh, they'll give us free rides!' Shazia said.

Grace clicked her tongue. 'Not like that, man!'

Shazia took a pair of black skinny jeans out of her wardrobe and threw them on her bed. Grace looked at the trousers with disdain. She'd already told Shazia what she was going to wear and there wasn't very much of it.

'I'm off to uni,' Shazia said. 'Last thing I want to take with me is some fairground boy's foetus.'

'Oh man!' Grace looked disgusted. 'Do you have to?'

'What, talk about getting pregnant? It happens.'

'Yeah, but . . . *You* sayin' it . . .'

Shazia knew that to so many of her friends she was, and probably always would be, the epitome of the chaste Muslim virgin. Except that she wasn't. Or rather she was chaste, by choice, but she was no virgin. Her father had put paid to that many years ago. And if she was chaste, it was because she wanted to be. As far as Shazia could see, very little that was good came out of what could loosely be called 'romance'. Mainly because it involved men and, although she knew there were good men in the world, she also knew that finding one of those was very difficult.

'I just want to go to the fair with you and have a laugh,' Shazia said. 'Just us.'

'Me too,' Grace said. But then she looked down at her long, manicured nails with an expression of desolation on her face. 'It's cool.'

Grace would go on the pull whether Shazia joined her in that quest or not. That was just Shazia being real about the situation. She loved Grace and so she wouldn't cramp her style, even if some of the men she tended to hook up with were well dodgy. Shazia would never leave her friend alone with strangers, but she would also make sure that she had enough cash on her to jump in an Uber if the two of them needed to make a quick getaway.

CHAPTER 23

Lee had no idea how old the man he was looking at was. Although apparently confined to his bed, what he could see of his skin did not have the consistency of crocodile hide often associated with the ancient. Only the eyes, like coal-black currents, gave a clue as to just how much this man had seen in his long life. Lee, instinctively, didn't like those eyes.

This was, he was told, the grandfather of the frowzy woman who had let him in to the caravan. Tired and unkempt, Gala Sanders was the wife of the good-looking man who ran the site.

David Sanders placed a chair down beside the old man's bed and said, 'This is Mr Arnold, the man I told you about.'

The coal-black eyes looked at him with something that could have been hatred.

'If you've changed your mind, tell me now,' David said. 'Mr Arnold's got better things to do than be pissed about by you.'

'I said I'd see him, so I'll see him.'

The old man sat up.

David said, 'Make yourself comfortable, Mr Arnold.'

Lee sat in the chair.

'This here's Bela Horvathy,' David continued. 'He was here when the kid went missing in '62, so he says. I weren't born, meself. But basically he's been with the fair since the dark ages. Wanna cup of tea?'

'That'd be nice.'

David Sanders left.

'Mr Horvathy . . .'

'Bela,' the old man said. 'And I know it's a girl's name in this country, but that's not my problem.'

His accent was thick, which, to Lee, made him sound like the old film star, Bela Lugosi – also Hungarian.

'Bela . . .'

'When David told me Roman Lester wanted me to talk to you . . .'

'All I did was ask Mr Lester whether he knew anyone still with the fair who was around in '62,' Lee said. 'Your name wasn't mentioned. Although I must tell you that I've heard your surname before.'

'You have?'

As soon as David Sanders had said it, Lee had remembered.

'At the risk of bringing back bad memories, I believe your wife died in an accident here.'

'You are correct,' the old man said. '1968.'

'A fire . . .'

'A lot of change was happening back then,' he said. 'Both my wife and I came from a circus background. We felt at the time that maybe we'd like to return to the circus. Irenka, my wife, was practising an escapology act she used to perform when she was a girl. It was cold; there was a fire. We could make fires in those days. She fell.'

He showed no emotion. Then, as if to explain this, he said, 'It was a long time ago.'

'I'm sorry.'

He smiled. Although discoloured and misshapen, he still had his own teeth. In view of the fact that he was, according to David Sanders, 'ninety-something', he appeared to be in reasonable shape. Lee wondered why he was confined to his bed.

After a pause, the old man said, 'But you've not come to ask about me, have you?'

'No.'

'You want to know about the child.'

'Miriam Levy, yes.'

'Yes, so tell me what you know,' he said. 'And I will try to remember.'

'She said she was happy to stay with him.'

Mumtaz shook her head. Shirin had been terrified of her husband. When she'd arrived at her palatial Holland Park home to take her to the refuge, Shirin had been shaking with fear.

Farzana, on the other end of the phone, said, 'That's what she told the police when they went round first thing this morning. They told me there was nothing more that they could do. She's an adult. And I know that even adults don't always know what's best for them, but what can we do?'

Mumtaz leant back in her chair.

'Nothing,' she said.

'She's even left a load of stuff here, which, she told the police, she doesn't want,' Farzana said. 'I've put it in a cupboard in case she changes her mind.'

'She may well do that,' Mumtaz said. 'I think she's confused. I've never been pregnant, but I know it affects hormones, which can affect a person's judgement. If she's pregnant, that is. Just missing a period isn't proof.'

'I know.'

'I fear she's clinging on to that because, in her mind, being pregnant is the answer to all her problems. If she's having a baby, her husband will stop beating her, he won't get a second wife and she'll never have to tell her parents what she's been through. But even if she is pregnant, I don't believe that her husband will suddenly no longer require another wife.'

'Me neither,' Farzana said. 'Once that issue comes up, it rarely goes away. If not now, then he will try again later. Maybe when the child is born.'

'If there is a child,' Mumtaz said. 'To suddenly fall pregnant at this time seems so unlikely to me.'

'But if she doesn't go ahead and have a baby, the abuse will start again . . .'

'Exactly. It may already have started, for all we know.' Mumtaz shook her head. 'I feel I want to warn her, tell her that if this is just a ploy to try and make things better, it won't work.'

'I fear we were to blame, at least in part,' Farzana said.

'You? Why?'

'Shirin just hated it here,' she said. 'She cried all the time. The fact that she made friends with Bijul was a minor miracle, but that was the only positive. She was horrified by this place. All the poor, broken women . . .'

'Not your fault, Farzana.'

'I know, but—'

'Not your fault,' Mumtaz repeated. 'It would have been impossible for you to accommodate Shirin in the way to which she was accustomed. I didn't go into her apartment when I went to pick her up, but I could see it was huge. She had servants. She couldn't adapt.'

'I know.'

By the time their conversation ended, Mumtaz felt that she'd probably made Farzana feel a little better about Shirin. Her decision to leave the refuge really was more about how she couldn't adapt to what everyone knew was a stressful situation. And of course, Shirin didn't want to be a 'failed' wife. Who did?

But Mumtaz remained uneasy. Ahmet had put pressure on her to get pregnant and she remembered that she often missed her period because of the strain it put her under. She couldn't believe that Shirin was magically pregnant any more than she'd ever thought she had been with child. But what could she do?

Legally there was nothing. She'd gone back to her husband of her own free will and had told police officers that she was fine. Mumtaz was certain that she wasn't. She knew the syndrome too well. So much of what women like Shirin did was done to retain their dignity and please their families. Involving herself in Shirin's life again could do more harm than good. But that didn't stop Mumtaz feeling bad. That woman was in danger in ways those police officers would never have been able to detect.

Mumtaz stood up and put on her coat. So going out meant leaving the office unmanned for a while, she didn't care. She had to see Shirin for herself.

'I don't remember the little girl's brother,' Bela said. 'A lot of children used to scream when they went inside the freak show. In those days tattooed men and big fat women were rare.'

'Mr Levy was really frightened by the Siamese twins,' Lee said. 'Ping and Pong.'

'Oh, Ping and Pong!' He laughed.

'Not real Siamese twins . . .'

'No!' he said.

'And are they still . . .'

Horvathy's face became grave. 'They remain with the fair, but they don't speak English,' he said.

'What do they speak?'

He looked away briefly. 'Hungarian.'

'So you could translate . . .'

'For the Twins? No,' he said.

'What, you don't speak the same dialect or . . .'

'The Twins, as the Levy boy has told you, were in the freak show when the little girl went missing,' the old man said. 'They can tell you nothing.'

'They might have seen something.'

Lee took a swig from the mug of tea David Sanders had brought him. It was so dark, it was almost black. Just how he liked it.

Horvathy shook his head. 'You have clearly looked into this,' he said. 'You know the police questioned people at the time.'

'Yes . . .'

'The Twins included,' he said. 'I translated for them myself. Now they're old men, they do odd jobs for the fair. Leave them in peace.'

Bela Horvathy had told Lee nothing he hadn't known before about Miriam's abduction. She'd been left in her pram by her mother while she went to the toilet and then she had vanished. Every van and attraction on the site had been searched as well as the park outside the fair.

'Small children were paraded for the mother to see, but she identified none of them.'

This was new, however.

'What do you mean?' Lee said. 'What? Babies were shown to Mrs Levy?'

'My own young daughter too!' Horvathy said. 'But the woman identified no one.'

'You had to parade your kids?'

'If they were babies, yes,' he said. 'But only us, only travelling folk. I never heard of any people in these streets around here having to do that.' He smiled. 'But that is the story in so many countries, isn't it, that the Gypsies take the children from the people who live in houses?'

'I think we've moved on from that.'

'You think?'

Lee knew he'd said a stupid thing. What was all the hysteria that had accompanied the Refugee Crisis, if it wasn't fear of the 'other'? He shrugged.

'The child disappeared and I was sorry for that,' the old man said. 'People who lose children or cannot have them are sad souls. I wouldn't wish that condition on anybody.' He paused, then he said, 'You work for the girl's brother?'

'I'm working for interested parties,' Lee said.

'They lived close to here, I remember. Do they still?'

'I can't say,' Lee said.

'You won't?'

He changed the subject back to one the old man seemed reluctant to address.

'I'd like to meet the Twins, anyway,' he said. 'By your own admission, you weren't anywhere near the scene of the crime when the little girl was taken. But they were. The old freak show van was close to the toilets. That was why Mrs Levy went to those toilets, because they were close to where her son was. The Twins are, as far as I know, the only living connections we have.'

Last time Mumtaz had come to Academy Gardens, Shirin had been waiting for her. Now she had to contend with a uniformed man who called himself a 'concierge'.

'Mrs Shah doesn't know you,' he said, once he'd put the internal telephone down.

'Yes, she does,' Mumtaz said. 'My name is Mumtaz Hakim. We're friends. I've been here before.'

'Mrs Shah is adamant that she is to have no visitors.'

Knowing that Shirin had servants, Mumtaz said, 'Did you actually speak to Mrs Shah?'

'Mrs Shah is not to be disturbed . . .'

Which meant that he hadn't.

'Speak to Mrs Shah in person and tell her that I am here,' Mumtaz persisted.

He paused for a moment, took a breath and then said, 'My instructions are that Mrs Shah is not to be disturbed at this time.'

'Instructions from her husband?'

'Instructions.'

Shirin and her husband lived on the first floor of what was an extremely exclusive red-brick mansion block. It was one of those properties that had been built in a square that overlooked the very neat communal gardens Mumtaz could just see through a window at the back of the entrance hall. Apart from the sound of her own voice and that of the concierge, there was absolutely no sound at all.

'Well, can you please tell Mrs Shah that I came,' Mumtaz said. 'Not her husband or any of her members of staff, Mrs Shah herself.'

'Certainly.'

But he didn't smile. Nor did he write down her name. What he did do was stand. A tall, white man wearing the type of uniform more suited to Honduras than Holland Park, he loomed over Mumtaz until, eventually, she left.

Once outside the manicured front gardens, which, though well past their best, still smelt fragrant, Mumtaz looked at her watch. She had to be in Barking at six to meet Lee and Irving. Walking out of the idyllic ambiance that surrounded Academy Gardens, she went back to her car and rang her boss, but Lee didn't pick up. She wondered what, if anything, he was learning from the fairground folk about Miriam Levy's disappearance. She also found herself longing for the days when he would have picked up a call from her whatever he was doing.

Lee Arnold had learnt many things about the mysteries of life during his time in the army, then in the police and now as a private investigator.

One of the most valuable lessons he'd learnt was that you could get a lot of information out of people who said they'd given up smoking if you offered to share one of your fags with them. He passed the cigarette to David Sanders who said, 'I don't pay them no wages and I've managed this fair for the last fifteen years.'

David inhaled and passed the fag back to Lee. Then he said, 'That's good.'

'Your wife's grandfather told me that Ping and Pong do odd jobs. I think he was implying they were employed,' Lee said.

'Well, they're not.'

'So how do they live? On pensions?'

'Pensions? I'm not even sure they're allowed to live in this country,' David said. 'They came over here with him.'

Lee smoked and then passed the cigarette. 'Bela? When?'

'Yeah. After the war. I don't know the story, but what I do know is that he pays them.'

'Bela pays the Twins?'

'Yeah.'

'Why?'

He shrugged. 'There's another Hungarian family on the site and they do a lot of things that make no sense. Can't work 'em out.'

Lee lit another fag and told David he could finish the first one.

'So what is the connection between the Twins and Bela Horvathy?'

'I dunno,' David said. 'And to be honest with you, I've never asked. Gala don't speak Hungarian and don't know much more than me, I don't think. As for her mother . . .'

'What about her?'

'Her and her old man are always talking in their own language,' he said. 'Then there's my girl, Amber.'

'She speaks Hungarian?'

'No, but she's always in with the old man, listening to his stories about the old days in the old country when he was a flier, a trapeze artist, with a circus.'

Maybe if he'd been a trapeze artist Bela had broken his back or his legs. That could explain why he was in bed.

'Stupid kid thinks she can fly too,' David continued. 'And he encourages her.'

'Dangerous, isn't it?'

'Yeah. Which is why I don't like her doing it. Listening to him all her life has given her ideas she shouldn't have. I've told her, you have to grow up in the circus to be a flier. Old Bela was born into it. Amber was born here in the fair. It's a different thing. Anyway,' he said, 'this is their van.'

'The Twins'?'

'Yeah.'

He knocked on the door. 'Oi! Ping and Pong, it's David; open up!' He smiled at Lee. 'They understand a knock,' he said.

And they may well have done, but no one came

to the door. David walked around the caravan trying to look into its windows.

'Got the curtains drawn,' he said. 'Could be hiding in there, could be out. Who knows.'

'Could your daughter be with them?' Lee asked.

He shrugged. Then he said, 'If she is, I'll give her what for. After last night's shenanigans.'

'What happened last night?' Lee asked.

'Me and the missus let her and some mates go up Camden,' he said. 'They never got back until the middle of the night. Kids, eh?'

One of them showed her, while the other one held onto the end of the rope. Just in case. The rig was, as far as Amber could see, securely attached to the bar across the top of the old Big Swing set. It had been a long time since oversized swings were fairground staples, but this was one of the attractions her father was looking to bring back into service.

The Twin not holding the rope swung and then let his backside slip over the trapeze, then he let go. Although he was only four feet from the ground, Amber gasped.

He slipped fast, but he stopped abruptly, his feet breaking his fall as they caught the ropes and held his body. The Twin's head, only at most a foot from the ground, miraculously retained its satin 'Thai' style cap.

Amber clapped. She couldn't do that move anywhere near as quickly as either of the Twins and they were ancient. But she'd get there in the end.

All she wanted was to be a flier like Nagyapa. She'd do it even if it killed her.

CHAPTER 24

Mumtaz felt slightly awkward. She could tell from the expression on Lee's face that he wasn't easy with what Irving was telling them. And although she knew he didn't pooh-pooh psychological explanations out of hand – he'd employed her, in part, because of her psychological knowledge – such things were hard for him to accept.

'I know what I saw was just in my head,' Irving said as he placed teapot, cups and milk jug down on the coffee table. 'But to see my mother as a young woman is odd, isn't it?'

'Maybe you were remembering happier times,' Mumtaz said.

'Happier times?' He sat down. 'When? I can't say I had an abusive childhood; I didn't. But my mother was quite indifferent to me. She wasn't a warm person. Maybe the loss of Miriam made her feel as if it was too dangerous to love anyone in case she lost them? My childhood was spent listening to my parents fighting. Not that it ever got physical, unless she threw something at him . . .'

'What I mean is that when your mother was young, so were you,' Mumtaz said. 'You weren't ill. The mind doesn't always present us with the most obvious symbol of its distress. These few weeks have been hard for you. The strain of going to Germany and, in some ways, the disappointment you had to bear . . .'

'And yet we have those results from Herr Beltz now and so maybe something will come of that,' he said. 'Maybe I am related to a man who was once a spy.'

He smiled.

Mumtaz smiled back. But she couldn't help feeling that was a remote possibility.

'You don't have to come to the fair again this evening,' she said. 'We can postpone until tomorrow or . . .'

'Perhaps you did see someone who looked like your mother,' Lee said. 'We're assuming it was in your head, but maybe it wasn't.'

'My mother is dead, Lee,' Irving said.

'Yeah,' he said. 'And maybe you did see some sort of hallucination, I dunno. But then isn't it said that every one of us has a double somewhere . . .'

'A doppelgänger?'

'Why not?' he said.

But then Mumtaz saw what she thought was something cross his mind. It wafted briefly over his face like a veil.

★   ★   ★

'That ain't the biggest big wheel in the world,' Grace said. 'London Eye's, like, twice the size.'

'Maybe they mean the biggest one in a fairground,' Shazia said as she looked up at the big wheel.

Like the London Eye, the BigO's passengers were transported in pods rather than on precariously swinging seats. And although it went faster than the Eye, the girls could see that the pods were shabby. When people got on, the doors were manual as opposed to automatic and, as the girls looked up at the attraction, they saw a woman pull her little boy's pants down and encourage him to piss on the floor.

'Oh! What?'

'Look,' Shazia said. 'There's no law that says we have to go on it.'

Grace popped a small piece of candyfloss into her mouth. 'Yeah, but everything else here is so lame,' she said.

'No it's not. There's a massive great waltzer . . .'

'So I'll throw my guts up, yeah. Next?'

'Helter-skelter?'

'Going down a slide so the world can see my pants?' Grace shook her head.

Shazia looked at her friend and smiled. Grace always looked sensational. But she didn't know how to do casual and, while Shazia wore skinny jeans and a jumper, Grace was hampered by thigh boots, a leather mini dress and fishnet tights.

'So what do you want to do?' Shazia asked.

'You're the one going to uni, innit,' Grace said. 'What you wanna do?'

Shazia thought for a moment and then she said, 'Dodgems.'

Grace looked up into the darkening night sky and shook her head. 'Man,' she said, 'we could be on the pull and you want to go riding in a likkle car with no brakes!'

Shazia laughed and took her arm. 'Come on,' she said, 'it'll be a laugh!'

Eva ignored the girl. David had caught her out with the Twins that afternoon, attempting to fly, and now she was confined to the van. But Eva did pay attention to the old man.

Speaking in Hungarian so the girl couldn't understand, she said, 'What's the use of my telling the girl she must behave when you don't?'

Bela said nothing. Stupid old fool.

'Telling some stranger our business!' she said.

'What do you mean?' He sat up in his bed. 'The disappearance of that child didn't have anything to do with us. I told him what I remembered.'

'Did you? Did you really?'

Amber said, 'What are you talking about?'

When the girl spoke, he smiled. His little 'angel'!

Eva said, 'Nothing.'

'You sound so angry,' Amber said.

Bela stroked the girl's face. 'I'm sorry,' he said. 'Our language makes us sound angry. But we are not.'

'Everyone's always angry with me,' Amber said.

This was too much for Eva. 'Oh, don't whine!' she said. 'You always end up getting your own way!'

'No, I don't!'

'You do!'

'I don't!

'You—'

'Stop behaving like children!' the old man said. 'Eva, for God's sake, you are a grown-up!'

Infuriated, Eva returned to Hungarian.

'I am, but you're not!' she said. 'You, who give her everything, who lets her do whatever she wants!'

The way he looked at her, just for a moment, made Eva feel fear. But she managed to squash that down.

'And I know why,' she said as she loomed over him.

Bela said nothing.

It was then that Eva noticed that Amber had gone.

'Christ!' she said.

Perhaps it was because more people tended to visit fairgrounds in the evening, but they always smelt more 'fairgroundy' at night. Quite what made up that distinctive odour was complex and could be highly individual. For Mumtaz the smell of sugar from the doughnut and candyfloss stalls was dominant. But for Lee this was overlaid with the tang of frying onions, engine oil from the vehicles and also the odd waft of cannabis.

Then there was the noise. Screams of excitement, tinny, fairground music from some of the older attractions, the pounding beat of Beyoncé's 'Crazy in Love' played so loud it was distorted and that characteristic whizzing noise that always seemed to accompany fairground and British seafront activities.

Irving, clearly discomforted by the sounds around him, said, 'You know, when I was a child I'm sure all this wasn't so noisy or bright.'

'Nobody had glow sticks in those days,' Lee said. Back in his 'day', fairgrounds had been lit by very basic coloured bulbs, when they worked, and all the boys operating the rides had looked like David Essex. Now most of the blokes on the rides looked like washed-up boxers. And there were women.

'Irving,' Mumtaz said, 'do you think it might help if you could look down on the site?'

So far, only the discovery of the old freak show van had even begun to activate Irving's memory. And, to Lee's way of thinking, nothing new was going to occur to him now.

'I'm not going on that thing that is winched up and then dropped to the ground,' Irving said.

'The Sky Drop? No,' Mumtaz said. 'I wouldn't go on that myself. I was thinking about the big wheel.'

He looked up at the BigO and said, 'Maybe later. I think I'll just walk around now, and on my own.'

306

He patted Mumtaz's hand. 'You understand, don't you, my dear?'

Lee knew that Mumtaz wouldn't like this. She had, right from the start, cosseted the diamond cutter. He was dying and vulnerable – why shouldn't she? Lee felt ashamed that he felt jealous.

Mumtaz squeezed Irving's hand and said, 'Alright. But I'll wait here for you, in case you need me.'

He smiled.

Amber ran. Ping and Pong would be in their van. Her grandmother would know that's where she'd go, but if she was quick, she could get inside the van and hide until the old girl went away.

Knocking on the door, she yelled, 'It's me! Amber! Open up!'

They must have seen her because the door opened immediately and she jumped inside. People said the Twins didn't understand English, but Amber knew that they did.

'You have to hide me!' she said. 'Nanny Eva wants to keep me prisoner and she's coming!'

Not many people ever entered the Twins' van, but Amber knew it well. As a child she'd loved the wild profusion of stuff they hoarded. There was always something strange and fascinating to find in their van, which was less like a home and more like an enclosed car-boot sale.

Without saying a word, one twin took a large box out from underneath a bed and opened the lid.

It was dark brown, looked a bit like a coffin and smelt of camphor.

'You want me to get in there?' Amber said.

And it was dirty.

The Twin nodded.

Amber held her nose and got inside. Once the lid was closed she felt the whole thing move backwards and then she heard what sounded like things being piled on top of the lid. Then she heard her grandmother's voice and a lot of knocking. In the utter blackness of the box, she closed her eyes.

Then more of that furious Hungarian. Her grandmother shouting, the Twins mainly silent, interjecting just the odd word. They might have the same face, but they had different voices. It was the one with the high-pitched voice who did what passed for most of the talking.

Something that felt like an earthquake followed. Her grandmother opening cupboards and hurling blankets, clothes, crockery, everything – looking for her. Amber began to sweat. If she found her, she'd thrash her. She did that. Apparently, her mother had been a wicked old woman and it seemed that Eva had taken after her.

But if she didn't find her, Amber knew that her nagyapa would be pleased. He really wanted her to fly, in spite of what he told her mum and her grandma. He wanted her to follow in his footsteps. It was only those bitches who didn't and that was because neither of them had ever been pretty enough to fly. Men had to be handsome, as Nagyapa had been when he was young, but girls who flew were meant to be beautiful. And Amber knew she was beautiful because her nagyapa had told her she was all her life.

'He'll be alright,' Lee said.

'He's so alone,' Mumtaz said.

She didn't look at him. Her eyes were still fixed on the point between a row of sideshows where she'd finally lost sight of Irving Levy.

'I have my family,' she continued, 'and my friends.'

Lee couldn't help himself. He said, 'Am I one of your friends?'

Now she looked at him, her dark-green eyes turned emerald by the pulsing fairground lights.

'Of course,' she said. 'Your friendship is really important to me and to Shazia.'

'But not my love?'

She stood, open-mouthed in front of him.

'This is not the time to be talking—'

'So when is the time?' Lee said. 'Eh?'

She turned away, then she looked up at the biggest big wheel in the world and tried to concentrate on the people inside the slowly moving perspex pods.

Lee, infuriated, pulled her round to face him. He heard Mumtaz gasp. But he didn't care.

'I am in love with you,' he said. 'I always have been, since the first moment I saw you! And you know it!'

His breath was laboured now and he knew his face had drained of all colour. He'd held this in for far too long and now he was coming on to her like some sort of scary nutcase.

She shook her head.

'So tell me you don't feel the same?' Lee said. 'Tell me! That night, Mumtaz, I made love to you and you made love to me. Tell me what I felt from you was just desperation or a sudden rush of lust and I'll sod off and leave you alone, but . . .'

'It's not right!' she said. 'We are different!'

There were tears in her eyes.

'Oh the "you're a Muslim and I'm not" thing? I don't care about that!' he said.

'I do!' She glanced around nervously. 'People are watching!'

'I don't give a shit!' he said. 'If you love me, I'll change me religion! If you don't . . . But I don't believe that you don't love me! I don't! Maybe I'm being arrogant, but . . .'

Now he was sweating and he knew his face had probably gone from white to red. He probably looked like some sort of oily old perv, watching a woman whose arm he held tremble in front of him.

She was about to speak when suddenly a familiar voice broke whatever spell had existed between them.

'Amma! Lee!' Shazia said. 'Didn't think I'd actually see you here!'

★　　★　　★

310

The last sideshow was a shooting gallery where, if you were fortunate, for these things depended on nothing but blind luck, you could win a fluffy *Sesame Street* soft toy. But that didn't happen often, as the stained and tired-looking toys at the back of the attraction showed.

Beyond the shooting gallery was a defunct carousel – complete with some headless, some tail-less prancing horses – and then a lone caravan. A woman stood outside ranting in a language Irving couldn't understand. He felt his skin crawl. In spite of the fact he knew that Romany Gypsies, as well as Jews, had been sent to concentration camps by the Nazis, he found them hard to like. He didn't even know if this woman was a Gypsy, but she looked like one and that was enough for him. And she was staring.

Gypsies or not, people did sometimes stare at Irving. Even though he didn't have the side-locks denoting a member of the ultra-Orthodox Haredi sect, he knew he looked like a religious Jew, which was what he had always been. But that didn't mean he was comfortable with starers. He wasn't, and this woman, this Gypsy, was giving him the creeps.

Irving turned his back on her and went off around the back of the fair, towards the old boating lake.

'We're three girls all on our own; we need a man to look after us!' Shazia said with her tongue very firmly in her cheek.

311

Grace, who didn't always do irony, said, 'Man, I know you're old enough to be me dad, but you're fit, right? And I need something to look at.'

Lee had to smile. The girls were sweet; he was fond of them.

'Sorry,' he said. 'Me and your mum are waiting for someone.'

'Ah. Work stuff?' Shazia said.

'Yeah.'

'Oh.'

Grace nudged her. 'I told you we should've gone with those sorts from Dalston. They would've paid and that!'

Mumtaz raised an eyebrow. She didn't like the idea of the girls going on rides with boys they didn't know. 'If money's the issue, I will pay,' she said. 'Or maybe . . .' She looked at Lee. 'I can wait for Mr Levy . . .'

He sighed. He liked Shazia and her mate, but they had spoilt his chance of getting the truth out of Mumtaz. It had taken him months to work up enough courage to do that. But it was what it was.

'Okay,' he said. 'I'll take you on . . .'

Both girls jumped up and down squealing.

Lee, smiling in spite of himself, shook his head. 'Provided you don't do violence on me ear'oles by squeaking,' he said.

Both girls put their hands over their mouths, still squeaking behind their fingers.

'Good!'

Mumtaz tried to give Lee money, but he wouldn't take it.

'Oh, for Christ's sake!' he said as he pushed her away. Then bending down to whisper, he added, 'Whatever you feel for me, I love you.'

And then he put his arms around the girls and joined the queue for the BigO.

CHAPTER 25

One or more of the women had bad dreams most nights. Even if the conscious mind could deal with the horrific abuse most of these women had suffered at the hands of their partners or families, the unconscious mind wasn't having it. Farzana could make out Bijul's groans of agony as her brother beat her again in her dreams. And then there was a new voice, probably the tall woman whose family had tried to make her kill herself when her husband had died. Even if past horrors could be suppressed during the day, night-time brought them back, often with a terrifying intensity. Five years of working in the refuge had taught Farzana many things, one of which was that the past may be another country, but it was very close by. Like France. One could easily just slip across the English Channel or hop onto a Eurostar.

Usually when women came to the refuge they were in distress, they were afraid and they knocked on the front door so hard some of them made their knuckles bleed. So when Farzana first heard what wasn't much more than a light tapping on the front door, she ignored it. Sometimes local kids would knock on their door and run away. Sometimes, more worryingly, the caller was a furious husband, intent upon removing his wife from the premises. That was why they had an intercom. Farzana went back to looking at the dire state of the refuge's accounts. They were currently spending what was turning out to be an unsustainable amount of money on food. She shook her head. So much of the food they bought came from pound shops already, it was almost impossible to economise. Basically, there were just too many residents.

The tapping started again and this time Farzana picked up the intercom and said, 'Yes? Who is it?'

Only when no one answered did she look at the intercom screen. But when she did look, she put her hand over her mouth to stop herself screaming.

She was following him. He'd become convinced of this when he'd strolled back into the fairground and then out again. Why hadn't he let Mumtaz come with him? After all, he'd had no meaningful memory or moment of enlightenment on his solo walk. He'd just picked up this Gypsy woman who was making him nervous. Maybe she meant to mug him at some point? But then if she did, she was going about it in a very strange way. He'd already got a good view of her face – which was none too pleasant.

That was unfair, but then wasn't she being unfair

by following him about? Irving left the fairground and began to thread his way through the jungle of caravans where the workers and show people lived. Many of them appeared to be empty, but there were a lot of vans where people were cooking, watching TV and strolling around. Of course, the fairground people were just ordinary folk, most of them, probably not Gypsies at all.

It had been his father who had told him they were all Gypsies and vagabonds. And why wouldn't he, after what had happened to his daughter? To be fair, his mother never had. She'd just never spoken on the subject at all.

Irving looked behind him and saw that the woman had gone. He breathed a sigh of relief. Then he kept on walking until he came to the place where he'd first seen the woman. But this time he could hear a voice speaking English. He walked behind the lone caravan in front of him and saw a strange and familiar figure, throwing a rope over a horizontal metal bar suspended between two, what looked like, castle towers.

Shazia looked at her friend's face and stated the obvious.

'Doesn't go very fast, does it?'

Grace said, 'Gonna take us half an hour to do one circuit!'

It hadn't looked this slow when they'd been on the ground. But Lee had known it would be. He smiled.

'I think this is for the old people,' Grace said.

'Doesn't make it shit,' Lee said. 'Look, you can see Ford's factory, if you squint hard and have a good imagination.'

Grace raised her eyes.

Shazia took his arm and squeezed. 'I heard what you said to Amma,' she said.

'Shazia . . .'

'I know it's not my business,' she said. 'But if you can't see she loves you too, you must be blind.'

Lee said nothing. He knew the girl was right, but that didn't make his life any easier.

Farzana ran to the front door and unlocked it. Not only could she now see what was staining the woman's clothes, she could smell it too. A sort of iron-scented, meaty aroma. She gagged.

'Shirin!' she said.

Her whole body rebelled at the thought of touching her, but somehow Farzana managed to pull Shirin Shah inside and close the door behind her.

'Shirin, how did you . . .'

How had she got there? She couldn't have come by public transport and Farzana knew she didn't drive.

A scream made her look away, as one of the other women, coming down the stairs, saw what she saw. Farzana said, 'Sssh! Sssh!'

The woman, a tiny middle-aged Indian, put a hand over her mouth.

God, what a state! And still Shirin's face didn't so much as flicker. It was almost as if she was sleepwalking. Dressed entirely in what had once been a full-length white nightdress, she was entirely soaked in blood from the waist down.

And her hands were covered too.

Farzana just managed to catch her before the woman collapsed. Holding her up underneath her arms, she said, 'Oh Shirin, what has been done to you?'

Some old man who looked as if he was going to a funeral was looking at her. Staring. Amber did get a lot of male attention these days and so she ignored it. The only man who meant anything to her, Nagyapa, would be so pleased she was practising and that was all she cared about. The Twins had taught her how to drop down from the trapeze, catching the ropes with her feet at the last possible moment. It was a common technique, but if she could master it, she could move on to going higher and, maybe, trying somersaults.

Of course what she really needed was someone to act as her catcher. There she met a dead end, for the moment. Soon she'd just have to approach a circus and see whether she could train with an existing act. Nagyapa, she knew, would be so proud. Once she was flying she'd be just like he had been when he was young.

The Twins pulled the trapeze into place and secured the ropes.

Why her grandma had stopped yelling outside their van, Amber didn't know or care. Once she'd gone, the Twins had retrieved a rig from a huge canvas bag. When she'd started they'd just cobbled something together with whatever they could find. Then they, or her nagyapa, had bought a proper rig. The Twins had always kept that in their van. But this rig wasn't that one. Amber asked, 'Where did you get this?' not expecting an answer.

She didn't get one.

She climbed up the side of what had once been part of the old Tunnel of Love and pulled the trapeze towards her.

The old man dressed in black shouted something at her, but she couldn't hear what it was above all the racket from the fair. And so Amber just waved. She mounted the trapeze, swung out into thin air, and waved.

She was just a girl. Not much more than a child . . .

And yet she had that look, that self-absorbed, almost haughty demeanour. Her lips pouting, eyes closed in ecstasy . . . His mother when she ate chocolate, when she wrapped her heart-shaped face around the filter of a cigarette.

Irving felt sick. What was it Lee had said? Everyone has a doppelgänger.

A boy of about sixteen was hassling her to buy one of his glow sticks.

'Every colour you can think of,' he said. 'For your kids. They'll love them!'

Mumtaz said, 'I don't have any children.'

The kid pulled a face and then said, 'Nah.'

Oh, so they were in the territory of 'all Asians have millions of children', were they? Mumtaz heaved a sigh.

'Think what you like,' she said. 'But I think I'd know whether I have children rather better than you.'

He left, but she saw him pull a face, mimicking the 'posh' way she spoke. But she didn't care. She was starting to get a bit worried about Irving, if she was honest. Either he'd been gone a long time or she was more bored than she imagined. The BigO may be large, but it in no way shifted itself. She couldn't see where Lee and the girls were, but she knew that Grace, at the very least, would be bored to death.

Mumtaz looked at her watch. It had been a long ten minutes since Irving had left. What was he doing and why the hell didn't he have a mobile phone like a normal person?

The BigO moved and Mumtaz could now see Shazia's feet.

Light from the powerful lamps on the BigO illuminated the girl, but not the figures behind her. Dressed in a tatty old tracksuit, she was far from glamorous, but she was beautiful. And, as she swung ever higher on the trapeze, she was also joyful. Which was something Irving's mother had never been.

He heard a noise behind him, but didn't know what it was until the girl said, 'You see, Grandma, I'm not doing dangerous stuff. I'm just practising.'

A harsh voice answered. 'Get down!'

It was the woman who had followed him. She was, it seemed, the girl's grandmother. She looked nothing like her.

The girl said, 'Nagyapa has always encouraged me and I don't know why you don't.'

'Because I don't want you to kill yourself!'

'I won't.'

The ropes creaked as ropes do.

'Who are you?'

Irving had almost come to believe he was invisible in this conversation between grandmother and granddaughter. So much so, he couldn't speak.

'Get down!' the woman repeated.

'I want to know who that man is,' the girl said.

'He's no one!'

Irving turned to the woman and said, 'Am I indeed. Then why were you following me?'

'Amma always tries to do the right thing,' Shazia said. 'Always! Even when she does the wrong thing, if you know what I mean.'

'Shazia . . .'

'Lee, you have to make her do the right thing,' she said. 'I know she loves you and you do her. If you allow her to throw you away because she thinks she must do the "right" thing and marry another man she doesn't know just because he's from Dhaka, then you're letting her down. She thinks her parents will be angry, but they won't; they really like you . . .'

'I'm not sure Mr and Mrs Huq would want me to be their daughter's boyfriend,' Lee said.

'Oh, they'll get used to it!'

'Here, come and look at this.'

Shazia had monopolised Lee to the extent that they'd almost forgotten about Grace. Their pod had just started to make its way down from the highest point of the BigO when she spoke, pulling their attention away from each other.

Lee and Shazia walked to the front of the perspex orb and looked out.

'What we looking at, Grace?' he asked.

It was a good view, but so what?

'Look, there's a girl on a trapeze over there.'

Grace pointed.

'Do you think there's gonna be circus acts and that?'

Lee squinted. The girl wasn't actually that far away, in a space just beyond the sideshows. But his eyesight was getting a bit dodgy – not that he'd tell anyone until he was practically blind. Just the thought of wearing glasses made him cringe. He knew they'd make him look like a thin Ronnie Kray.

'Isn't she just on a swing?' he said.

Grace punched his shoulder. 'No! Look! She's sitting on a stick, man. Since when did a swing get to be a stick? And look how high she's going . . .'

She was going high. A pale figure with what looked like long blonde hair . . .

'Don't go over the top,' Irving called out. 'My cousin Len did that on the swing in next door's garden and he broke his ankle.'

The girl ignored him. But the woman, who was now at his side said, 'She's on a trapeze, not a swing!'

And yet she was getting to the point where she would loop over the bar. Cousin Len, although he'd been in intense pain when he broke his ankle, had described it being like flying. That had been the whole point.

'I can do a few things,' the girl yelled. 'I learnt this the other day.'

She moved her body back and forth until the trapeze was level with the bar.

Then she let go of the ropes.

'Fuck me!'

Grace put a hand over her mouth, but she carried on looking. They all did. Not that they saw how it happened. It just did. One moment the girl was throwing herself backwards, presumably with the aim of breaking her fall using her feet against the ropes.

And then she hit the ground, head first.

The two girls screamed. Lee took his phone out of his pocket and called 999. Shazia, meantime, was calling Mumtaz.

Irving knew the girl was dead. Even if her head hadn't been at a ninety-degree angle to her body, he had heard a crack so loud and so sickening as she hit the ground, it had taken his breath away.

The Gypsy woman had gone to her; of course she had, she was her granddaughter. Now cradling her blonde head in her thick, dark arms, she said words he didn't understand while people ran towards her. For his part, Irving found that he couldn't move. The two figures who had set the trapeze rig up seemed to be afflicted with the same infirmity. Still holding onto the ropes, they stood in the shadows like a pair of Chinese vases.

Whether it was this image or whether the site was suddenly flooded with light, Irving wasn't sure, but when he saw the figures as they really were, he knew why he'd made that comparison. Older, clearly, but still wearing the same clothes he remembered from his distant youth, there were the Siamese twins, Ping and Pong.

'Irving! Are you alright?'

He didn't consciously fall into Mumtaz's arms, but that was what happened. His legs gave way. She held him up until he regained his strength.

'Irving, what happened?' she said. Then, looking around her, 'What is this?'

He wanted to say that a girl who had looked exactly like his mother had just died. But that wasn't what had shocked him to the core. That had been seeing *them*.

CHAPTER 26

Gala stood in the doorway and he knew. As soon as he'd heard the sirens, he'd known. 'What have you done?' she said.

His father had used exactly the same words to him a lifetime ago and he gave her the same reply, 'Nothing,' he said. And then he added, 'I never do.'

She turned and ran out of the caravan.

Bela wanted to cry, but he couldn't. He'd done all his crying a long time ago.

Mumtaz, her coat covered in mud, wrapped her arms around Irving as he sat on the ground. He couldn't move.

She looked up at Lee. 'Get the girls out of here,' she said. 'I don't want them to see . . .'

'They've already seen,' he said.

'Oh, God.'

'The coppers have shut the site.'

She put a hand to her head. 'Of course. So just go and be with them.'

She saw him gather the two girls into his arms and walk away.

The site was a blur of green and blue as

paramedics and police pushed people back from where the girl lay in the arms of a woman who screamed and screamed and screamed.

She looked at Irving, who said, 'She's dead.'

Her phone rang, but she ignored it. How could she take a call now? And yet all around people were interacting more with their phones than with each other. Talking into them, even taking photographs.

'The paramedics . . .'

'She's dead,' he reiterated. 'I was here. I heard her neck break.'

He put his head on her shoulder. The ground underneath her was soaking and she felt the wetness go through her trousers and into her underwear. But it didn't matter.

'Irving,' she said, 'what were you doing here?'

'I was walking . . .'

'Yes, but how . . .'

'She looked exactly like my mother when she was young,' he said.

He'd obviously had another psychological incident. He wasn't well.

'It's OK,' she said. 'You've had a terrible shock. Look, this is all going to take some time and I expect the police will want to talk to you . . .'

And then she looked up and saw two very strange creatures standing right in front of them. They wore black silk kimonos and had what looked like curling pieces of wood sticking out of their sleeves. They didn't speak, but Irving did.

'What did you do?' he said to them. But neither of them spoke.

Mumtaz looked at Irving. 'What do you mean?' she said.

'They were here when my sister disappeared,' he said. 'And now they've killed my mother.'

When the ambulance doors closed, Eva sat down on the ground and raked her fingers down her face. Why couldn't it have been her?

Blood mixed with mud. She lay in the wet and buried her face. But the reflex to breathe was too strong and Eva found herself rearing up, gasping for air. Then she felt hands on her and she screamed as she tried to pull herself away. She heard someone say, 'I'm sorry . . .'

Sorry? What did that mean? Why had it even been said? And why hadn't it been said by the man who had broken into their lives without a clue as to how much he was not wanted. Now cradled in the arms of some Muslim woman, Eva wanted to tear out his eyes.

A police officer pulled her to her feet. But she carried on looking at the man on the ground.

'You shouldn't have come here,' she said.

The man began to cry. But she felt only hatred.

'When you dig up dead things,' she said, 'you get poisoned.'

Farzana held Shirin's hand. Still stained with blood it wasn't pleasant to hold, but the young woman needed some human comfort even if she didn't acknowledge it.

Once the paramedics Farzana had called to the refuge had established that Shirin was not injured, the police had arrived. Shirin hadn't said anything. She'd even refused the sanitary towel Farzana had given her after her examination. When her period had arrived was impossible to say, but it was heavy and the floor of the day room was slippery with blood.

An officer called WPC Rhodes had taken down Shirin's address, which she had passed on to officers at Notting Hill Gate. They were on their way to the apartment now. Farzana hoped against hope that what she felt had happened hadn't. If Shirin's period had come and her husband had found out then she feared for both of them.

Another refuge worker, Tasneem, brought her a cup of tea and told her that the other residents had all gathered in the biggest bedroom.

'They're really freaked out,' she said.

'Is it surprising?'

'Have you managed to get hold of Mumtaz Hakim?'

'No,' Farzana said. 'I've given WPC Rhodes her number. Don't know what else I can do.'

'Nothing. Are you sure Shirin doesn't want a cup of tea?'

Farzana looked at the young woman and shook her head. 'I can't get a word out of her,' she said. 'No one can.'

⋆   ⋆   ⋆

It was going to be a fuck of a long night. The girl's death had almost certainly been an accident, but the coppers still wanted to take statements from everyone on the site. It was just a mercy that the tea and coffee vans were still open. Not that the coffee at least was exactly drinkable. Lee took a swig, pulled a face, and then lit a fag.

'Can I have one of them?' Grace asked.

'What? You wanna get cancer?' Lee replied.

His daughter, Jodie, smoked too, and he didn't like that either, but he threw his packet of Silk Cut at Grace.

She smiled and lit up.

He knew the girls shouldn't be left on their own, but he was worried about Mumtaz. As far as Lee had been able to see, what had happened to the girl, who was the site manager's daughter apparently, had been a pure and simple accident. The kid had tried to throw herself back on the trapeze while hooking her feet around the ropes and had screwed it up. Unless the coppers found any evidence of foul play, that was it.

Except that it wasn't. Irving Levy had been there when the kid died and he had history with the fair. What, if anything, did his presence mean?

Shazia nudged him in the ribs.

'What?'

'Over there.'

She pointed towards a small group of uniformed officers talking to what looked like a pair of comedy 'Chinamen' from a bad pantomime.

330

'You know when we came to the fair last year,' Shazia said.

'Yeah.'

'I got a bit lost looking for the loos and one of those women showed me where they were. She gave me the creeps.'

Lee saw two shrunken figures dressed in black satin. They had those really long curly nails he remembered seeing in the *Guinness Book of Records* when he was a kid. People who did that, back in those days, were usually Chinese. Could they be the 'Siamese' twins, Ping and Pong?

He said, 'How'd you know it was a woman?'

He'd always assumed that Ping and Pong were men.

'I don't know,' Shazia said. 'Maybe because she had a high voice?'

'You say you were with a man when the incident occurred.'

His manner was nice enough, but Eva automatically didn't like coppers. They didn't like fairground people and the feeling was mutual.

'Yes,' she said.

'You know him?'

The copper, Sergeant Harris, had a round, red face, which looked like a sunburnt moon.

'Not really.'

'Not really? What do you mean?' he said. 'Either you know him or you don't.'

'You'll need to speak to my father,' she said. 'He'll explain.'

331

'I wish someone would,' Harris said.

'My father will.'

And if he didn't – and she knew he wouldn't want to – she would, inasmuch as she could.

The police had set up a temporary incident room in one of the tea tents. Scene of crime officers were looking for evidence at the site of the girl's death while PCs like Kerry Paternoster were taking names and contact details of fairgoers as well as interviewing witnesses like Irving Levy.

'There was a lady with you when you witnessed the incident, I understand,' she said to him.

'The girl's grandmother,' he said.

An Asian woman held his hand. A private detective from Newham. Kerry had heard on the grapevine there was some covered woman chasing down errant husbands and kids meddling in drugs. She hadn't expected to come across her with an old Jewish bloke.

'Do you know her?'

'No,' he said.

'So why were you with her? The trapeze was set up outside the fair. What were you doing there?'

'I was searching my memory.'

'For what?'

'It's a long story.'

SOCO had only just started their investigation, but everyone she spoke to had been in no doubt that what had happened to the girl had been an accident. But there was a story here and she had a feeling it was important.

'Tell me,' she said.

'Back in 1962, when I was seven,' he said. 'I came to this fair with my mother and my one-year-old sister, Miriam. Miriam disappeared and has never been seen since. I have been looking for her, with the help of Mrs Hakim and Mr Arnold. We came here this evening to see whether being at the fair might jog memories I may have buried.'

'We've made several visits this week,' the Asian woman said.

'You're Mrs Hakim.'

'Yes. Mr Levy is a client of Mr Arnold's. I am Mr Arnold's assistant.'

'But you weren't with him when the girl fell from the trapeze?'

'No.'

'Was Mr Arnold?'

'No.'

'Why not? If you were supposed to be helping him?'

'Mr Levy wanted to be alone,' Mumtaz said. 'Sometimes, if someone is trying to recover lost memories, it's better they are alone. Sometimes not. It's a very individual process.'

'Where were you, then?' Kerry asked.

'Mr Levy left Mr Arnold and myself at the base of the big wheel,' she said.

'I was going to go back there later,' the old man interrupted.

'But then my daughter and a friend appeared . . .'

'You didn't know they were coming?'

'No,' she said. 'The girls – my daughter is eighteen – wanted to go on the big wheel and so Mr Arnold took them. I stayed on the ground waiting for Mr Levy. It was my daughter, Shazia, who used her mobile to contact me when the accident happened.'

'Your daughter saw it?'

'From the big wheel, yes. She told me what direction I needed to take. I was afraid that maybe Mr Levy had seen what my daughter had witnessed. Unfortunately, my fears were confirmed.'

'And did Mr Arnold and your daughter's friend see what happened too?'

'Yes. They're here somewhere. I told Lee, Mr Arnold, to take the girls away from the scene and look after them. That's a terrible thing for young people to witness.'

'Yeah.'

'She just threw herself backwards off the trapeze and then she fell to the ground,' the old man said. 'I heard her neck break . . .'

'What was the woman you say was the girl's grandmother doing at this point?' Kerry asked.

'To the girl? Nothing,' he said.

'To you?'

'She'd been following me. I've no idea why. I was trying to shake her off when I came across the girl. When she saw her, the woman lost interest in me. She shouted at the girl to get down, but she wouldn't. Then she swung very high and did what I suppose was meant to be a very clever trick.'

'Did you see anyone else around?' Kerry asked.

A couple of the blokes were attempting to talk to what had looked like two old Chinamen. They'd put the trapeze rig up for the kid. But she'd heard neither of them could speak English. Talking to a slightly confused old Jew paled into insignificance.

He looked at the Asian woman who said, 'You must tell the police everything.'

He sighed. Then he said, 'When my sister disappeared, I was in a tent watching what was called, in those days, a freak show. It featured Siamese twins called Ping and Pong. I believe the figures I saw at the back of the trapeze rig tonight were Ping and Pong.'

From 1962? Kerry leant forward and fixed the old man with her eyes.

'You serious?' she asked.

'Oh, yes,' he said.

He said he was Hungarian. He certainly had an accent, but what did Dave Harris know? Hungarian? Bulgarian? Romanian? What the fuck was the difference?

'So, Mr Horvathy,' he said, 'your daughter tells me you know this Mr Levy she was with when your great-granddaughter had her accident . . .'

He'd offered his condolences and, although Eva Horvathy had cried, her old man – and he was a very old man – hadn't.

'I don't know him, no,' the old man said.

'Yes, you do!' the woman said.

'I know of him.' He shrugged.

She said something to him, in his language, and Dave said, 'In English, please . . .'

'I said he does know him,' Eva Horvathy said.

The old man said, 'And so do you, it seems.'

'Oh yes,' she said. 'I've known about Irving Levy a long time.'

'How?'

'How'd you think?' she said. 'The Twins told me. Decades ago.'

'Did they tell you anything else?'

'Like what?' she said.

'Like how your mother died?'

'You killed her!' she screamed.

'No,' he said. 'That's what you like to think, Eva. But that is very far from the truth.'

She said nothing, but her face went white.

And suddenly Dave Harris felt very awkward, as if he were intruding on a private conversation.

The rich were another breed. What the fuck was the use of having a concierge if he didn't notice a woman covered in blood leaving his building? What was his purpose if he didn't realise the front door to one of the apartments was open? Not that Detective Constable Lockwood really gave a shit. The open door just made his life easier.

'So you've not seen Mrs Shah today?' he asked

the concierge, who was clearly shrinking with embarrassment.

'No,' he said. 'I saw Dr Shah come in at four.'

'But you've not seen him since and you didn't know his front door was open?'

'No . . .'

Lockwood could tell he wanted to stick around and see what was inside the Shahs' flat. If the hall was anything to go by, it wasn't going to be pleasant. Ghoulish twat. Lockwood told him to go back downstairs. When he'd gone, they entered.

Until they found the body, which was in the master bedroom, the hall was the only space that was affected. Blood on the floor, up the walls.

Dr Shah lay face down on the floor. He'd been stabbed in the back, but it wasn't until some time later, when SOCO arrived, that Lockwood realised the main mutilation had occurred to the doctor's face.

His wife, if indeed it had been his wife who had killed him, had stabbed him in both eyes.

CHAPTER 27

Dave Harris didn't know Lee Arnold, but he knew of him. A Newham lad, he'd been close with DI Vi Collins when he'd been a copper at Forest Gate. Now a PI, he was working for this old Jewish bloke Eva Horvathy had told him about. And, although there wasn't, as yet, any indication that Amber Sanders had died as a result of foul play, there was a problem. It centred around the death of a woman and the disappearance of a child back in the 1960s. The missing child was still, officially, unsolved.

Dave waited with Lee Arnold and the two girls with him at the park gates. One of the girls' grandfathers was coming to get the kids. Dave was looking out for DI Bateman from CID. Once the kids had gone, Lee began to walk back into the fairground.

'Don't go off anywhere, will you, Mr Arnold,' Dave said.

'I'm going to find my partner, Mrs Hakim, and Mr Levy,' he said.

'They're with my colleague, PC Paternoster, in the tea tent. We need to talk to Mr Levy.'

'He was nowhere near the girl when she had her accident,' Lee said.

'We need to talk to him,' Dave reiterated.

'He's my client.'

'Which means we may have to talk to you.'

Dave saw Lee narrow his eyes. 'This is about my client's past, is it?' he said.

Dave didn't reply.

Lee Arnold said, 'Maybe we should have a few words.'

One live child was all Gala Sanders had ever been able to have. She'd given birth to six dead children. Only Amber had survived. And now she was gone.

'Mama, I need you to stop this now,' she said to her mother. 'David has gone to the hospital. I need you to be here for me.'

But Eva Horvathy wasn't listening. Gala wasn't even sure whether her mother knew that Amber's body had been taken away. Looking through a pile of papers in an old hatbox, Eva was in a world of her own. It was only when Gala shouted at her that she looked up.

'Mama!'

'He did this!' Eva said. 'He encouraged her. He destroys everything he touches!'

Gala said, 'Nagyapa didn't know she would end up killing herself! He loved Amber!'

'Did he? Then why didn't he protect her, eh?' her mother said. 'I'll tell you, shall I, Gala?'

'Oh, Mama . . .' She'd heard things, crazy

339

notions, from her mother about her grandfather for years. What her mother had against him, she didn't know. Maybe she was mad? 'I know I blamed him but . . .'

'Because he is a murderer!' Eva said.

'Oh, Mama, not this . . .'

'Yes, this,' Eva said. 'This I should've dealt with years ago. Well, now I'm going to tell the police everything. May God forgive me I left it so long!'

DI Bateman was young, ambitious and adamant.

'I want him down the station, booked in, in a cell, let him call his brief.'

Dave Harris shook his head. 'With respect . . .'

'You're going to tell me he's old, aren't you?' Bateman said. 'He's also been accused of murder.'

'I'm not sure it's what it seems,' Dave said.

The trouble, according to Dave, with some of the new, young CID officers were that they were permanently champing at the bit for a 'collar'. Competitive with ordinary plods and their own, maybe going to university made them like this?

Bateman took a swig from his bottle of water and said, 'Explain.'

Dave told him the edited highlights of his chat with Lee Arnold.

When he'd finished, Bateman decided that, although SOCO were not yet finished at the accident site, he was going to have to meet with the bereaved family and Irving Levy.

★   ★   ★

340

Farzana let go of Shirin's hand.

The WPC who took her put the cuffs around her wrists as gently as she could. But Shirin didn't even seem to notice. Until she spoke or evidence appeared to the contrary, nobody could be certain that Shirin had killed her husband. But it seemed a safe bet.

What Farzana and everyone else involved with Shirin had feared had come to pass. Her period had arrived. Possibly when she was home alone. God knew how she'd dealt with it. Had that been the point at which she'd lost hold of reality? Because to kill her husband, however cruel he had been, didn't make sense. Far easier would have been to come back to the refuge. But then sense rarely had much to do with emotion.

Had she waited for him to come home, told him and then he'd attacked her? It was difficult to see where all the blood that covered Shirin's face and body was coming from. Maybe none of it was his? Although that was unlikely. Had he known her period had arrived, the chances were, he'd gone berserk.

Farzana watched Shirin go and then put her head in her hands. Had Shirin known she wasn't really pregnant all along? Or had her period simply been just late? Whatever the reason, it seemed that her husband had been less than understanding.

And even if Shirin had killed him, Farzana couldn't find it in her heart to condemn her.

Murder was a sin but, as far as Farzana could see, Shirin had already paid for her crime upfront.

When she was at university, Mumtaz had often played games with her fellow students. Some were board games, like Risk, while others were word games, usually played when her friends were drunk. Her favourite had always been 'Cheap Film Titles' where people thought up alternative cut-price titles to famous films. Things like 'Saturday Night Light Sweat' for 'Saturday Night Fever'. Now squashed into a small caravan bedroom with six other people, she felt as if she was participating in a downmarket denouement of an Agatha Christie Poirot novel. Try as she might, she couldn't think of an appropriate title.

'My daughter thinks I killed her mother, but I didn't.'

Bela Horvathy got in before anyone else could speak. Mumtaz could see that he was old but, considering he was over ninety, he looked extremely vital.

Eva said, 'Now he'll say that Ping and Pong did it. Watch him. Normally, he'll do anything for them, except when it comes to his own skin.'

'The Twins didn't kill her either,' the old man said.

There were two police officers in the room; the older of the two said, 'As I understand it, officially it was an accident.'

'No it wasn't.'

'No it wasn't,' the old man said. 'My daughter is right. What I think she also knows is that the woman who was my wife, wasn't her mother.'

Mumtaz saw Eva Horvathy look away.

Bela Horvathy looked at Irving Levy.

'Which is where you come in to this story, sir.'

'Me?'

'Oh, you have done nothing wrong, sir. Far from it: you are a victim.'

'I don't understand,' Irving said.

'Your mother didn't lose your sister back in 1962,' the old man said. 'She gave the child to me.'

Mumtaz put a hand on Irving's shoulder.

His voice, when it came, was weak. 'Gave her? To you?'

'Because she couldn't stay with your father,' Bela Horvathy said.

'Why not?'

'Because she was not his child. Look at her!' He pointed to Eva and smiled. 'My daughter looks like me. When the police came that day in 1962 and asked me who the baby laying in a cradle in my caravan was, I said it was mine and he believed me!'

In light of how entirely Miriam Levy had disappeared it made sense that she had never actually left the fairground.

'Now, sir, I don't know what your mother may have told you . . .'

'Nothing,' Irving said. 'She never told me anything.'

343

His words sounded bitter and he looked crushed. Mumtaz put her arm around his shoulders. He looked up at her and smiled.

'So why have you been coming here?' Eva Horvathy asked. 'Why did you hire these private detectives to come and ask questions?'

'Because I discovered that my mother was not Jewish and because I wanted, if I could, to find out what happened to Miriam before I died. Because I am dying.'

For a few moments that bald, passionless statement of fact took the breath from the room and everyone except Bela Horvathy looked to the floor for inspiration. Mumtaz wondered at how British they all were and whether the old man despised or admired them for it.

Irving, who had created the silence, broke it. 'And so you are Miriam,' he said to Eva.

She had his eyes. Nothing else.

'Yes,' she said.

He nodded.

'I don't want anything,' she said. 'I know you live in a big house and you cut diamonds, but I don't want what you have. I want everything to stay as it is. I want my Amber back . . .'

She broke down. Tentatively, at first, then more firmly, Irving put a hand on her back.

The younger of the two police officers shuffled his feet. Mumtaz allowed herself an internal smile. This was of no interest to him. Eventually, he turned to the old man.

'So,' he said, 'if your wife's death wasn't an accident and you didn't kill her, who did?'

The old man addressed his daughter.

'Irenka, my wife, and the only mother you ever knew, was a sad woman. She couldn't have children of her own; she couldn't be where she wanted to be. The war had broken all our lives and what we did to carry on hung heavily upon her. She was cruel to you and I did little to stop her. I take full responsibility for that. If an excuse for my actions exists it is that I was always too busy. Learning a new language, making a living, caring for my family . . .'

Eva raised her head. 'What family? Those freaks? They're not your family! I am your family. Me and my child and Amber, who you killed!'

'I didn't kill Amber.'

'You encouraged her to fly! You and those freaks of yours!'

Her words hurt him. When she spat them out it was as if she'd slapped him.

'When death comes, we tend to tell the truth,' Bela said. 'Listen and I will tell you. I'm sure that these police officers just want to do their jobs and leave . . .'

Dave Harris said, 'If it's relevant to what happened today . . .'

'In a way, yes,' he said. 'I think it may explain why my granddaughter wanted to fly and why I encouraged her.' He cleared his throat. 'You know,

Eva, when I came to this country, I had nothing except my reputation.'

'Yes, we know you fought with the Hungarian Resistance. We've all heard the stories.'

'Which are true,' he said. 'Together with my parents and my brothers and sisters I was a trapeze artist in the Magyar Circus, which travelled Europe until 1944 when the Nazis occupied Hungary. My family were divided upon what to do then. My father urged us all to resist. He, my mother and three brothers died doing just that. Only I survived. That is but one side of the equation. My brother Tamas and sister Szuszanna believed that working with the Nazis was the right thing to do. In October 1944, while I was hiding out in the cellars of Budapest, Tamas and Szuszanna were rounding up their fellow Hungarians and shooting them. On the Chain and Margaret Bridges across the Danube, the Arrow Cross Hungarian Nazi Party members murdered their opponents and threw their bodies into the river. I saw Szuszanna with my own eyes. There and then I vowed to kill her. But, as I have said all along, I have never killed anyone. My father always blamed me for not watching my young brother, Egon, when he was a baby. He died in his cot for no reason, but it happened when he was in my care and so I lived under suspicion from then on. But I did nothing to the child, just like I did nothing to Szuszanna.'

Bloody DI Bateman yawned as if he was bored.

The old man clocked it, but Dave, fascinated by this time, said, 'Go on, sir.'

'The next time I saw my sister and brother Tamas was here in London. Refugees from both the Nazis and the Soviets, just like me, or that was how they presented themselves. I wanted nothing to do with them. I had found work at Mitchells Fair. I wanted to start my life again. Let them fool what remained of the Hungarian community here in London! I didn't care. But then 1956 happened, the Hungarian Uprising against the Soviets and thousands of my countrymen came here seeking asylum. Among them were people who remembered the truth about Tamas and Szuszanna Horvathy.' He shook his head. 'You have a saying here that blood is thicker than water. It's true. I have never really investigated what I did next, but I imagine I did it not for my remaining brother and sister, but for the Szuszanna and the Tamas of my youth. But I punished them too.'

'How?'

'I was nothing at Mitchells. Too damaged and stiff to do a proper job, I ran sideshows, including the freaks. Two skinny creatures who couldn't speak English – what was I to do with them? And so Ping and Pong were born, a freak so bizarre no one could recognise them. I believe I saved their lives. What else is family for, eh?'

His face was dark; his lip curled into a sneer. He said, 'My wife, Irenka, hated them. She called them Nazis and traitors. They hated her too. But she was my wife and they respected that. But they were also full of joy when I met up with Adeline again.'

'Adeline?'

'Do you mean Adeline Beltz?' Irving Levy said.

'How do you know that name?' the old man replied.

Could Bela Horvathy be trusted? Maybe, maybe not. But the fact that he'd known the Stasi officer, Gunther Beltz's aunt, couldn't, Lee Arnold thought, be a coincidence.

'She was a maid in a big Jewish household in Berlin,' the old man said. 'In 1942 we played Berlin and she came with a group of German soldiers who had taken over her employer's house. But, in spite of all their warrior glamour, she only had eyes for me and I for her. It was just lust. What else could it have been, given the company she kept? She came back the following night and I took her for a drink, then we made love. The circus moved on the next day, but I didn't forget her. I never saw her again until she came here to this park with her small son in 1960. She told me she was in a loveless marriage to the man who had rescued her from the ruins of Berlin. She came back without the boy later and we made love for the second time. I didn't know she was pregnant until we returned to this park the following year. There she was with a tiny baby. Adeline gave her to me the following year.'

'How did you know the kid was yours and not her husband's?' Lee asked.

'Look at her,' was all the old man said.

And she was his image. All except her eyes.

'And the dates were wrong,' Horvathy continued. 'The diamond cutter couldn't be the child's father. Or so she told me.'

'And so the little girl, me, I had to go,' Eva said.

'To one who wanted you, yes.'

'You lied to me.'

'I meant to tell you the truth . . .'

'Is that why you still have a picture of her with me when I was a baby? Or have you kept that so you can fantasise about her? Oh yes, I know that photograph, Papa. I've looked at it many times—'

Lee interrupted, 'What did your wife have to say about it?'

He shrugged. 'She couldn't give me a child herself. What could she say?'

'She burned my head with curling tongs, she bit me, she used me as her slave. I was barely out of nappies. I remember it all. You let that woman abuse me so you could keep your fucking secrets!'

All heads turned towards Eva.

Then her father said, 'But you do not remember killing her. I have been grateful for that.'

'Why do people think that if they change what they are doing, everything in their life will fall into place? I have no answer to that. Like me, Irenka came from a circus background. She wanted to go back but, like me, she couldn't fly any more. So she began working on acts from clowning – but she was too fat – to escapology. Her father had performed some of Houdini's acts. She knew what she was doing. What she didn't know was that the child she had so reluctantly taken in was watching her.' He shrugged. 'Ping and Pong found her, but it was too late. They told me the child pushed her into the fire and held her there. When I found my Eva she was holding Irenka's legs, so that she couldn't move. She was seven years old and her face was quite blank. Like it is right now.

'And so we never told her. The Twins, as we call my brother and sister, may be destructive, but even they have a limit. I did not know they told my daughter about you, Mr Levy, and I am sorry for that. But you must understand that for all the kindness I have shown Tamas and Szuszanna, I have also never allowed them to have their own lives. I have been kind to be cruel, and so when my granddaughter and I wanted so much for her to fly, they helped because I believe they thought it would end in tears. And it has. But what can one expect of Nazis, eh? I wanted the world for my granddaughter, the only person in this family to look like my passionate Adeline, and I ended up killing her because I am an old fool.'

CHAPTER 28

When Mumtaz finally arrived home later that night, she sat down with a cup of tea and began to look through the messages on her phone. There were a lot from Farzana at the refuge. But then her phone rang and, seeing that the caller was Wahid Sheikh, she picked up.

'Wahid-ji,' she said, 'to what do I owe the pleasure?'

'You are a difficult woman to track down,' he said. 'I've been trying to find you for some hours.'

'Yes, well, I've been working . . .'

'If you look out of your window you will see that I am seated in my car outside your flat,' he said.

Mumtaz felt her face go cold. She ran to the window.

'It is a silver Mercedes C-Class Cabriolet,' he said. 'If you'd care to join me in it, we can sort out that enquiry you recently made about your late husband.'

Tasneem brought Farzana a cup of tea. All the women had finally gone back to bed and they'd cleaned as much of Shirin's blood off the floor as they could see.

Farzana said, 'What a night!'

Tasneem shook her head. 'What can you say?'

'I've seen many things since I've worked here, but nothing like that. Nothing. And the husband! Dead! God I do hope that she—'

'Oh, Shirin killed him,' Tasneem said quietly and, astonishingly, calmly. 'She told me when I took her to the toilet. She also told me what he'd done to her. He deserved it.'

'He has a right to know,' Irving Levy said as he allowed his body to fall into his chair.

'Could open up an even bigger can of worms,' Lee said, as he gave him a cup of tea. 'Can I leave you here for a minute, while I just pop out for a fag?'

'Oh, have it in here,' Irving said. 'I really don't care. There's an ashtray that belonged to my father on the sideboard.'

Lee retrieved a heavy multicoloured bowl he recognised as Murano glass and sat down.

'As Mr Horvathy said, blood is thicker than water,' Irving said. 'Look at what he did for his family. Mr Beltz is a member of my family, whether I like it or not.'

'He was in the Stasi . . .'

'And Mr Horvathy's siblings were Nazis. Family tests us.'

'Irving, you're Jewish, you can't forgive Nazis.'

'No, and I don't,' he said. 'Now that the truth is out, the wartime crimes of Tamas and Szuszanna Horvathy can be investigated. But I repeat, Herr Beltz has a right to know what happened to his aunt and why. I don't know whether Adeline, my mother, killed Rachel Austerlitz or not. Who can know that now? But at least the poor woman rests under the house where she was loved not just by her family but by Joachim Beltz as well.'

'God, you're a bloody saint if you ask me, Irving,' Lee said.

He smiled. 'Death gives one a view, Lee. Much of which is that life is too short to be bitter. I think that Mr Horvathy has lived his life in that way for a long time.'

'He's caused a lot of trouble in his time.'

'By trying to do the right thing by those he loved, whoever they were,' he said. 'And you know, Eva Horvathy was right when she said she wanted their lives to simply remain what they always had been.'

'What? Never changing? Not possible.'

'I mean going back to a past none but the old man could remember,' he said. 'To me that smacks of the fascism of the mythical "golden past" nationalists always refer to. But for Eva to not want to know me or even accept my help . . .' He shook his head. 'You know, I think she has wanted to know me, really. I think it is her I've seen sometimes standing outside this house. And I would give her everything.'

'She doesn't want it,' Lee said.

'Maybe, after what she did all those years ago, all she has ever wanted is some peace of mind.'

Lee nodded. 'Even if we don't remember something, it leaves a mark.'

He smiled. 'Doesn't it just.'

Rizwan Sheikh stank. Mumtaz, as one of his victims, knew that it was no more than the evil old gangster deserved, but as a human being, she pitied him. How could his family let him get into such a dreadful state? Lying on a filthy bed, in filthy nightclothes, surrounded by chocolate wrappers and stinking of pee?

She said, 'Why is he like this? This is awful!'

Wahid Sheikh frowned. 'Doesn't it please you? He is your enemy, isn't he?'

'He's a human being!' she said. 'And your brother! And that woman we saw downstairs is his daughter!'

The man on the bed tried to say something, but failed. But his eyes looked at her with hatred in spite of what she was saying. Mumtaz felt her whole body cringe.

'So say what you have to and let's have done with it,' she said.

Wahid Sheikh offered her a tattered, stained chair, but she refused to sit.

He sat on his brother's bed.

'As you can see, my poor brother can't do anything very much. His speech is very slow and extremely poor. So I will speak for him.'

Rizwan Sheikh managed to nod.

His brother smiled. 'Mrs Hakim, your husband was a very bad man,' he said.

'You don't have to tell me that.' Mumtaz leant against the bedroom door, as if making sure of a swift exit. 'He left me in debt and he brutalised myself and his own daughter. Whatever he did to you, he did far worse to us.'

'You think so?'

'Well then, tell me otherwise,' she said. 'I know you want to shock me in some way. But you've already done that by bringing me here. Get on with it.'

'Your husband, Ahmet Hakim, made my niece, Rizwan-ji's favourite and youngest daughter, Aqsa, pregnant.'

Ahmet had been with other women. He'd boasted about it. But to have sex with the favoured daughter of a gangster was reckless, even by his standards. Was it true?

Mumtaz worked hard not to appear ill at ease. She said, 'How do I know you're telling the truth?'

The man on the bed made a noise. His brother put a hand on his arm. He turned his head towards Mumtaz.

'You don't,' he said. 'But I can show you the report written by the coroner.'

He passed her a double-sided document headed Eastern District of London Coroner's Court. It was dated 2011, the same year Ahmet had died.

'You should note that my niece was fourteen at the time.'

Fourteen, four months pregnant and she had died by ingesting disinfectant. Mumtaz put a hand to her mouth. The verdict had been suicide. But she knew that 'suicide' could have different meanings.

She threw the paper down onto the bed. 'Did you make her kill herself?'

'No.'

'Because I know what "honour" means,' she said. 'Not that such an abomination is anything to do with honour . . .'

'The poor child came home one afternoon and committed the sin of suicide all by herself.'

'So, how do I know that Ahmet was the father of this . . .'

'Because I tell you that he was,' Wahid Sheikh said. 'And because, as I think you have finally realised yourself, Mrs Hakim, why would we pursue your family so relentlessly if this were just about money?'

Now Mumtaz needed the door behind her for support. She said, 'And so you make me, who suffered at that man's hands, suffer . . .'

'Your husband is dead,' Wahid said. 'We cannot do anything more to him.'

'You killed him!'

'If my understanding is correct, then you believe that a man who is now dead, poor Aqsa's brother Naz, was the killer of your husband. Although you

356

said nothing of this to anyone, much less the police, at the time. And now that, as I say, Naz is sadly dead too, hence my brother's awful physical condition, we will never know.'

She felt herself slump, as if in defeat. Because at that moment she was defeated.

'And so all this is your revenge upon people who have done you no harm.'

'If the culprit is dead, then his family must pay . . .'

'And Shazia? She's a young girl, and contrary to what you say or believe, she had nothing to do with Naz's death . . .'

'Says you.'

'Says one who knows!' She shook her head. 'You are evil bastards! I take back my sympathy for Rizwan-ji. Rot in your bed of piss for all I care! Rot in hell!'

Oh God, she'd lost her nerve and her temper and this was doing no good because they were laughing at her.

'And so,' Wahid Sheikh said, when he'd finally finished laughing, 'as well as debt, we give you also the gift of guilt.'

They'd picked up bits of English, but they'd never really learnt it. Also sitting on the ground around a fire, it seemed more natural to speak Hungarian.

Szuszanna began. 'Will we go to prison?' she asked.

'I neither know nor care. But I might,' Eva said.

357

Her father stroked her hand. 'You won't. You were a child, an unhappy child.'

'Bela, I will keep my nails. I have decided.'

Tamas had been dementing for some years. Szuszanna too, probably.

'You do as you will,' the old man said. 'I have done what I can for each one of you. For right or wrong. I am finished.'

'You should have told me what I did . . .'

He looked at his daughter and shook his head.

'Maybe I would have settled, moved away from this life,' Eva said. 'Maybe if I had, Amber would still be alive . . .'

Szuszanna smiled. 'Amber . . .'

Eva wanted to slap the old freak, but she didn't. Only verbally.

'You all but killed her, you Nazi bitch.'

'It was an accident,' Bela said. 'You heard the policemen. No sign of foul play.'

'Doesn't stop those two being Nazis.'

'They've had their punishment,' Bela said. He closed his eyes. 'I made their lives a misery.'

'You let them live,' Eva said. 'Which is more than my poor Amber can do.'

'And I am sorry for that,' her father said. 'But you know, she so wanted to be like me . . .'

'And so it was your arrogance . . .'

'It was always my arrogance,' Bela said. 'When I flew, when I took the blonde-haired Adeline and made her image in Amber, when I rescued my brother and my sister and saved you, Eva, from

358

whatever they would have done to a child who kills, it was always and for ever about me.'

'Well then, you are evil,' Eva said. 'I always knew it. Although if you are to be believed, you killed no one. I still—'

'Sssh!' Tamas put a long, twisted fingernail up to his lips.

'Don't sssh me!' Eva said.

And then Szuszanna smiled and said, 'Don't speak too loudly. You will wake the dead.'

Which was when Eva saw that her father had stopped breathing.

CHAPTER 29

Berlin, One Month Later

'And so the fair moved on, as they do, leaving the old man lying in the same grave as his deceased wife.'

'This Eva, this sister you have, too?' Gunther Beltz asked.

Winter had deepened in Berlin and the two men sat around a much bigger fire than Irving Levy had experienced when he'd first visited this house.

'She wants nothing to do with me,' he said. 'Miriam.' He smiled. 'I am glad that I found her, even if she has deserted me. By the time the fair comes round again I may be dead.'

'Oh no . . .'

'It's possible. But no matter. At least I have a cousin on my mother's side.'

'I want nothing from you, Irving,' Gunther Beltz said. 'You know Frau Metzler, at the Jewish Centre, she is worried that I am only speaking to you because I want your money. I tell her, I have money of my own . . .'

'I will go and see her,' he said. 'There must be no more hatred, suspicion, revenge. We are all people, who do what we do to survive.'

'I fear Adeline did more than was necessary . . .'

'Maybe. But we weren't there and so we don't know,' Irving said. 'Life is complicated and messy. Which is why I prefer diamonds.'

They didn't speak for a while. Gunther Beltz sipped from a small glass of schnapps while Irving nursed what he considered to be only an 'adequate' cup of tea. Eventually, he said, 'For your information, Gunther, I have left my house and its contents to my Levy cousins.'

'It's not my concern.'

'No, but you are my cousin and I think you should know,' Irving said.

The German shrugged. 'This country is in a mess,' he said. 'I need to be here to help.'

Irving felt a small, cold breeze.

'But my business,' he said, 'is another matter. Including a considerable number of stones I have become fond of and kept, well that I have bequeathed outside my family.'

'To whom?'

And then Irving saw them outside the window, back from their shopping trip to Alexanderplatz. As he watched, he saw Lee bend down and kiss Mumtaz on the cheek. She pulled away, but she smiled. He had insisted they come with him on his trip back to see his cousin Gunther and it seemed they had become, at least in part, reconciled.

361

'To them,' he said. 'Because without them I would not be here today. And because I know they are in love.' Then he took something out of a bag he had brought with him and gave Gunther Beltz a small teddy bear.

'But this is for you,' he said. 'My sister Eva found it in the caravan that belonged to the Siamese twins. They had kept it hidden since 1962. It was your Aunt Adeline's, and now it is yours.'